PILGRIM'S PROGRESS
IN TODAY'S ENGLISH

PILGRIM'S PROGRESS

IN TODAY'S ENGLISH

JOHN BUNYAN

RETOLD BY JAMES H. THOMAS

MOODY PRESS

CHICAGO

Library of Congress Catalog Card Number: 64-25255

ISBN: 0-8024-6520-X

45 47 49 50 48 46

Printed in the United States of America

preface

WITH THE EXCEPTION of the Bible, *Pilgrim's Progress* has been read by more people than any other book in the English language. An accepted classic of English literature, it is a fascinating allegory—true to life as experienced by genuine Christians—and has a vital message for contemporary man.

Bunyan's narrative has been rewritten so as to appeal to present-day readers. The presentation is modern, though the pilgrims travel on foot and stay at lodges and inns, or in private homes, as old-time travelers used to do. To speed up the reader's progress with the pilgrims along their pathway to the Celestial City, some superfluous details have been omitted. The names of some characters have been changed, and two or three new characters have been added. In a few places there is amplification to clarify the author's meaning. Yet the message is unchanged.

May praise be given the Lord of Glory who used His faithful servant, John Bunyan, to write *Pilgrim's Progress* with its searching portrayal of human life and character and its marvelous revelations of God, eternal truth, and the way of salvation.

Appreciation is expressed to Mr. James H. Thomas for the care he exercised in preparing this new revision of Bunyan's classic work.

THE PUBLISHERS

contents

PART ONE

christian's journey

PART TWO

christiana's journey

PART ONE
christian's journey

CHAPTER

1

christian in trouble

As I WALKED through the wilderness of the world, I came to a place where there was a den. There I lay down to sleep; and as I slept, I dreamed a dream. In my dream I saw a man clothed with rags, standing by a path with a book in his hand and a great burden upon his back. His face was turned from his own house, which stood nearby. I saw him open his book and read, then begin to weep. No longer being able to control his feelings, he broke out with a mournful cry, saying, "What shall I do?"

In this condition he went into his house. Drying his tears, he restrained himself as best he could so that his wife and children might not know of his distress. But he could not be silent long, for his trouble increased. At length he began to tell his wife and children: "Oh, my dear wife and children, I, your father and companion, am undone by reason of an awful burden that lies heavily upon my heart. I am surely warned that this our city shall be burned with fire from heaven, in which terrible destruction all of us shall surely perish unless some way can be found whereby we may be delivered." His family were amazed—not that they believed what he was saying was true, but they thought he was losing his mind. Since night was falling, they hurriedly put him to bed, hoping that sleep would settle his nerves and relieve him of his dreadful fears. But he spent the night in sighing and tears.

When the morning came, they asked him how he felt. "Worse, and worse," he replied. When he began talking again of his condition, his family became impatient and rude. After hearing his mournful words for a while, they tried to drive away his pitiful mood by harsh, surly treatment—sometimes chiding, sometimes scolding, and sometimes ignoring him completely. Then he withdrew to his own room to lament his misery, and to pity and pray for his family. He would also walk alone in the field, occasionally reading from his book, and praying aloud.

One day, in deep meditation while walking in the field, he burst out, crying, "What shall I do to be saved?" He looked this way and that, as if he would run; yet he stood still, for he could not decide which way to go.

Meets Evangelist

Then I saw a man approach him, and heard him say, "My name is Evangelist. May I ask why are you so disturbed?"

He answered, "Sir, I understand from this book I hold in my hand that I am condemned to die, and after that to come to judgment. And I am not willing to do the first nor able to do the second."

"Why not willing to die," asked Evangelist, "seeing this life is attended with so many evils?" The man answered, "Because I am afraid this burden on my back will sink me lower than the grave, that I shall fall into Hell. And if I am not prepared to die, I am not ready for judgment, and to go from there to execution. The thoughts of these things make me weep."

"If that is your condition," said Evangelist, "then why do you stand here?"

"Because I do not know where to go."

Then Evangelist gave him a scroll which had these words written within: "Flee from the wrath to come."

Having read these words, the man looked earnestly at the Evangelist and asked, "But where must I go?"

Pointing with his finger over a very wide field, Evangelist said, "Do you see that little gate yonder on the far side of the field?"

"No," he said.

"Then do you see that tiny shining light?"

"I think I do," he answered.

"Now keep your eye on that light, and you will go straight to the little gate, at which, when you knock, you will be told what you must do."

Leaves City of Destruction

Now I saw in my dream that the man began to run. He had not gone far from his house when his wife and children came crying out after him to come back. But he put his fingers in his ears, and ran on, crying, "Life! Life! Eternal life!" He did not look back, but increased his speed toward the middle of the plain.

Pursued by Obstinate and Pliable

His neighbors came out to see him run and, as he ran, some mocked, others threatened, and some called after him to return. Among those who did so were two men who resolved to go after him and bring him back. The name of one was Obstinate, and the name of the other was Pliable.

Now by this time the man had gotten quite a distance away. But the two men were good runners, with strong resolution, and they soon overtook him.

Then said the man, "Neighbors, why have you come?"

"To persuade you to return with us," they answered.

He said, "That can never be. You dwell in the City of Destruction, the place where I also was born, and all those who die there will sink lower than the grave into a place that burns with fire and brimstone. Be convinced, good neighbors, and go along with me."

"What!" exclaimed Obstinate. "And leave all our friends and comforts behind?"

"Yes," said Christian (this was his name), "for all that you forsake is not worthy to be compared with a little of that which I seek to enjoy. If you will go along with me and keep in this way, you shall fare as well as I; because where I go, there is enough for all and to spare. Come with me and prove my words."

OBSTINATE: And what are the things you seek, since you leave all the world to find them?

CHRISTIAN: I seek an inheritance incorruptible and undefiled, that will never fade away, safely laid up in Heaven, to be bestowed at the appointed time on all who diligently seek it. Read it, if you will, right here in my book.[1]

OBSTINATE: Oh, bosh! Away with your book! Will you go back with us or not?

CHRISTIAN: No, because I have now put my hand to the plow.

OBSTINATE: Come then, Pliable, let us go back without him; there is getting to be a lot of these crazy fools, who, when they take a fancy to a thing, are wiser in their own eyes than seven men who can give a reason.

PLIABLE: Don't revile. If what the good man says is true, he is wiser than we are; the things he hopes to gain are much better than what we have. I am inclined to go with him.

OBSTINATE: What, more fools still? You had better listen

[1]I Peter 1:4.

and go back with me. Who knows where this unbalanced fellow may lead you? Be wise, and go back with me.

CHRISTIAN: No, come with me, Pliable. There are such things to be gained as I spoke of, and many more very wonderful things besides. If you do not believe me, read it here in my book; and the truth expressed in it is all confirmed by the blood of Him who wrote the book.

PLIABLE: Well, neighbor Obstinate, I am making my decision. I am going along with this good man; I cast in my lot with him. But now, good Christian, do you know the way to this delightful place?

CHRISTIAN: I was directed by a man whose name is Evangelist to hurry on to a little gate that is before us, where I shall receive instruction about the way.

PLIABLE: Then, let us be going.

OBSTINATE: And I will go back to my house. I will not be a companion of such deceived, fantastic fools.

Now, I saw in my dream that after Obstinate departed, Christian and Pliable went on together across the plain.

CHRISTIAN: Neighbor Pliable, tell me about yourself. I am glad that you have decided to go with me. If Obstinate had felt what I have felt of the power and terrors of that which is yet unseen, he would not have so lightly turned back.

PLIABLE: Now, since we are alone, tell me further, Christian, what these things are where we are going, and how they are to be obtained.

CHRISTIAN: I can conceive of them with my mind better than tell of them with my tongue; but, since you are desirous to know, I will read of them in my book.

PLIABLE: And do you think that the words of your book are certainly true?

CHRISTIAN: Yes, indeed; for it was written by Him who cannot lie.

Describes Heaven

PLIABLE: Well, then, what are they?

CHRISTIAN: There are crowns of glory to be given and bright garments that will make us shine like the sun in the firmament of heaven.

PLIABLE: That is marvelous. And what else?

CHRISTIAN: There shall be no more sorrow nor crying, for He who is owner of the kingdom will wipe away all tears.

PLIABLE: And what companions shall we have there?

CHRISTIAN: We shall be with seraphim and cherubim, dazzling beings to see. There also we shall meet with thousands and tens of thousands of the redeemed of this earth who have gone on before us to that happy land, all of them pure and good; every one walking in holiness, and enjoying the presence of the King forever. In a word, there we shall see the elders wearing their golden crowns; and the holy virgins with their golden harps; and there will be the transformed men who by the world were cut in pieces, or burned in flames, or fed to wild beasts, or drowned in the sea, because of their love for the Lord of the kingdom—all well and clothed with immortal bodies as with a spotless garment.

PLIABLE: The hearing of these things is enough to enrapture one's soul. But are they to be enjoyed by us? How shall we get to be sharers in them?

CHRISTIAN: The Lord, the Ruler of that country, has recorded it here in His book, the substance of which is this: If we really want Him and His kingdom and are willing to receive Him as our Lord and Saviour, He will grant our wish freely.

PLIABLE: Well now, my good companion, I am glad to hear of these things. Come, let us make better time.

CHRISTIAN: I cannot go as fast as I would, because of this load on my back.

Falls into Slough of Despond

Now, I saw in my dream that just as they ended this conversation they came near a miry slough that was in the middle of the plain. Being careless, they both fell into the bog, which was called the Slough of Despond. Here they floundered for a time in the mud. Soon Christian, because of his burden, began to sink.

Then said Pliable, "Ah, good Christian, where are you now?"

CHRISTIAN: Truly, I do not know.

At this Pliable became offended, and angrily criticized his fellow traveler: "Is this the happiness you have been telling me about? If we have such miserable misfortune as this at the beginning of our journey, what may we expect before we reach our journey's end? If I can but get out of this mess alive, you may have the heavenly country and all its glories, and enjoy it all alone, so far as I am concerned." With that, he gave a desperate lunge and got out of the mire on that side of the slough which was toward his own house. So away he went, and Christian saw him no more.

Christian, left to flounder in the slough alone, struggled on toward the far side—toward the wicket gate. But, though he struggled with all his strength and skill, he could not get out, because of his burden. Then I saw a man come to him whose name was Help, and he asked him, "What are you doing out there?"

CHRISTIAN: Sir, I was told to go this way by a man named Evangelist, who directed me to yonder gate that I might get rid of my burden and escape the wrath to come, and as I was going there, I fell in here.

HELP: But why did you not look for the steps?

CHRISTIAN: Fear took possession of my mind, and I took the nearest way.

Then said Help, "Give me your hand." So he pulled him out,

placed him on solid ground, and showed him the path that led to the little gate.

Then I went to the man who pulled him out and asked, "Sir, since this is the way from the City of Destruction to yonder gate, why has this place not been mended, that poor travelers might go to the gate of hope with more security?"

And he replied: "This miry slough is such a place that cannot be mended. It is the low ground where the scum and filth of a guilty conscience, caused by conviction of sin, continually gather, and for this reason it is called the Slough of Despond. As sinners are awakened by the Holy Spirit and see their vile condition, there arise in their souls many doubts and fears and many discouraging apprehensions, all of which merge and settle in this place; and that is the reason for this marshy slough.

"It is not the pleasure of the King that this place should remain so foul. His laborers, by the direction of His surveyors, have been employed for more than sixteen hundred years to improve this swamp, and it has swallowed up at least twenty thousand carloads of solid truth, and tons and tons of wholesome instructions, which have been brought at all seasons from every part of the kingdom—and those who know say that the best materials have been brought to make good ground of this place—but it is the Slough of Despond still, and it will so remain after they have done what they can.

"It is true," he continued, "that some good and substantial steps have been placed through this slough by order of the Lord of salvation, but at times this marsh spews out a lot of filth, and in times of changing weather the steps are hardly seen. Even if the steps are visible to a normal person, here a man's head often becomes so dizzy that he cannot see the steps; then he staggers to one side and mires down in the slime. Nevertheless, the steps are there. However, the ground is firm beyond the little gate."

Now, I saw in my dream that Pliable had gotten home with his family. His neighbors had come in to visit him. Some said he was a wise man for coming back; some called him a fool for hazarding his life with such a person as Christian; and others mocked at his cowardice, saying, "Surely, if I had begun to venture, I would not have been so weak and worthless as to give up and turn back because of a few difficulties."

Pliable sat sheepishly among them, but finally he gained courage enough to talk. Then they all turned on Christian and slandered him behind his back.

Joined by Worldly Wiseman

Now as Christian was walking alone, he saw one coming across the field toward him. This was Mr. Worldly Wiseman, who lived in the town of Carnal Policy, a town not far from Christian's home. He had heard of Christian's leaving home in search of an unseen country, and had an inkling of who he was. When they met, Mr. Worldly Wiseman began the conversation: "How are you, my good fellow? Whither bound in this burdened manner?"

CHRISTIAN: Burdened indeed, as much as any poor creature can be. And since you ask, I am going to that little gate yonder before me; for there, I am informed, I shall be directed in the way to be rid of my burden.

WORLDLY WISEMAN: Do you have a wife and children?

CHRISTIAN: Yes, but I am so troubled of late that I cannot enjoy them as I once did, and I feel as if I had none.

WORLDLY WISEMAN: Will you listen if I offer my counsel?

CHRISTIAN: If it is good, I will; for I need good counsel.

WORLDLY WISEMAN: Then I would advise you to assert yourself and throw off that burden at once, for you will never be settled in mind until you do; nor can you ever enjoy the blessings God has given you as long as you carry that burden.

CHRISTIAN: Well, that is what I am seeking—to be rid of this heavy burden—but I cannot get it off my mind. And there is no one in my country who can take it off for me. Therefore I am going this way, as I told you, that I may be rid of it, and be happy and free.

WORLDLY WISEMAN: Who told you to go this way to find deliverance from your burden?

CHRISTIAN: A man who appeared to be a wise and good person. His name is Evangelist.

WORLDLY WISEMAN: Evangelist! I hope he's punished for such advice! There is not a more dangerous and troublesome way in the world than this way into which he has directed you. Evidently you have met with misfortune already. I judge from your appearance that you have been in the Slough of Despond. And that slough is only the beginning of the sorrows that come to those who travel this road. Hear me, since I am older than you. You are likely to meet with pain, poverty, hunger, perils, dangers, lions, dragons, and even death, and you are sure to be weary and lonesome much of the time, trudging your way in darkness. This is most certainly true, having been confirmed by many who have gone this way. And why should a good and intelligent man so carelessly throw his life away, following the instructions of a crank?

CHRISTIAN: Sir, this burden on my back is more terrible than all these things which you have mentioned. I feel I do not care what happens to me, if I can only find relief from my burden.

WORLDLY WISEMAN: How did you come in possession of your burden in the first place?

CHRISTIAN: By reading this book in my hand.

WORLDLY WISEMAN: I thought so. It has happened to you as to other weak men. Some meddle with things too deep for them and suddenly find themselves in your condition, which not only unnerves men but also causes them to go on desperate ventures to obtain they know not what.

CHRISTIAN: I know what I want to obtain—to be free from this burden.

WORLDLY WISEMAN: But why do you seek for ease in this way, seeing it is filled with trouble and danger? Now, I can direct you (if you have the patience to hear me) into the way of obtaining what you desire, without your becoming exposed to these dangers and trials you will find in the road you are on. Yes, and relief is at hand. Besides, I will add, instead of perils and suffering, you shall find much safety, friendship, and contentment.

CHRISTIAN: Sir, that is what I want. Will you please give me the secret?

WORLDLY WISEMAN: Yes, in yonder village (the name of the village is Morality) there lives a man whose name is Legality, a very judicious man of good reputation, who has the skill to relieve one of such burdens as you carry. Yes, and to my knowledge, he has done a great deal of good in this way. Besides, he can cure those who have become somewhat unbalanced, carrying their burdens. To him you may go and be helped immediately.

His house is not quite a mile from this place; and if he should not be at home himself, he has a handsome young son, whose name is Civility, who can do quite as well as the old gentleman himself. There you may be eased of your burden; and if you do not wish to go back to your former dwelling place (which I would not advise), you may send for your wife and children and live in the village of Morality. There are vacant houses there now, one of which you might buy at a reasonable price; provisions there are plentiful, low-priced, yet good; and you certainly will have honest neighbors—everything to make your life pleasant.

For a moment Christian was somewhat undecided, but soon he concluded, "If what this gentleman has said is true, my wisest course is to take his advice." Having reached this conclusion, he said to Mr. Worldly Wiseman, "Sir, where does this man live, and how can I find his house?"

WORLDLY WISEMAN: Do you see that high hill yonder?

CHRISTIAN: Yes, I do.

WORLDLY WISEMAN: You go close by that hill, and the first house you come to is his.

Comes to Mount Sinai

So Christian turned out of the way to follow the road to Mr. Legality's house for help. But when he came near the hill, it seemed very high, and the cliff next to him appeared to extend out over the road. Christian was afraid to venture any closer lest the cliff should fall on him. There he stood, not knowing what to do. His burden seemed heavier now than before. Also, flashes of fire came out of the hill, which made him sweat and tremble. He was sorry that he had taken Mr. Worldly Wiseman's advice.

Rejoined by Evangelist

Then he saw Evangelist coming toward him, and he felt ashamed. Evangelist had a very stern look and began to reprove him.

"What are you doing here, Christian?" Christian did not know what to say. He was speechless. Then said Evangelist, "Are you not the man I found crying outside the wall of the City of Destruction?"

CHRISTIAN: Yes, sir, I must confess I am.

EVANGELIST: Did I not direct you to go to the wicket gate?

CHRISTIAN: Yes, brother, you did.

EVANGELIST: How is it then that you have so soon turned aside? For you are now far out of the way.

CHRISTIAN: Well, as soon as I had gotten out of the Slough of Despond, I met someone who led me to believe that I would find a gentleman in the village on the far side of the hill who could remove my burden.

EVANGELIST: Whom did you meet and what kind of person was he?

CHRISTIAN: He seemed like an honest man and he reasoned much with me, and at last persuaded me to take his advice. So I came here, but when I saw this threatening hill, jutting out over the road and sending forth fire and smoke, I stopped, for fear I should perish.

EVANGELIST: What did the man say to you?

CHRISTIAN: He asked me where I was going, and I told him.

EVANGELIST: And what did he say then?

CHRISTIAN: He said I should throw off my burden at once. I told him that it was relief I wanted. And, I said, I am going therefore to a certain little gate for further instruction on how to find the place of deliverance. Then he said he would show me a better way—a way not so full of difficulties as the way in which you had directed me. And, since I had fallen into the Slough of Despond, I was inclined to listen to his counsel, for he said, "This way will lead you to a gentleman's house who has skill in relieving people of their burdens." Since I realized I had gotten no relief in the way I was traveling, but rather more trouble, I believed him and turned out of the way into this way, thinking I might soon find deliverance. But when I came to this hill and saw how dangerous it would be to go on, I stopped for fear of losing my life. Now I do not know what to do.

Then said Evangelist, "Wait just a moment, that I may give you the Word of God." Christian stood trembling under his burden.

Then Evangelist said to him, "See that you refuse not Him

that speaks; for if they did not escape who refused him that spoke on earth, much less shall we escape, if we turn away from Him who speaks from Heaven."[2] He also said, "Now the just shall live by faith; but if any man draw back, my soul shall have no pleasure in him."[3] Evangelist then applied the words by saying, "You are a man running into trouble. You have begun to reject the counsel of the Most High, and to draw back your feet from the way of peace, almost to the hazarding of your soul."

Then Christian fell at his feet, crying, "Woe am I, for I am undone."

Evangelist took him by the right hand, saying, "All manner of sin and blasphemy shall be forgiven unto men. . . . Be not faithless, but believing." Then Christian revived and stood before Evangelist.

EVANGELIST: Now give more earnest heed to the things I tell you. I will show you who it was that misled you, and also who it was to whom he sent you. The man who met you on the plain is one Mr. Worldly Wiseman. He is rightly so named, because he is wise in the wisdom of this world but knows nothing about the life to come and because he loves the doctrine of this world best, for it shields him from the cross. Therefore he always goes to the town of Morality to church. Because he is carnally minded, he seeks to pervert the truth of your book. Now, there are three things in this man's counsel you must utterly abhor:

1. His turning you out of the right way.
2. His laboring to render the cross odious.
3. And his setting your feet in the way that leads to death.

First, you must abhor his turning you out of the way of truth—yes, and abhor your own consenting to it, for this was rejecting the counsel of God for the counsel of an unregenerate

[2]Heb. 12:25.
[3]Heb. 10:38.

man. Jesus, your Lord, says, "Strive to enter in at the narrow gate.[4] For narrow is the gate that leadeth unto life, and few there be that find it."[5] From this little gate, and from the way that leads to life, this wicked man turned you into the way that almost brought you to your destruction. Therefore hate his turning you out of the way, and despise yourself for being so easily led from the right way.

Second, you must detest his laboring to render the cross repulsive to you, for you are taught to prefer the cross before the treasures of Egypt. Besides, the King of Glory has told you that he who seeks to save his life shall lose it. Therefore, the teaching that the right way—without which we cannot have eternal life—is the way of death, is destructive indeed. You must therefore hate this doctrine.

Third, you must also consider him to whom he sent you, and how unable that person is to deliver you from your burden and eternal condemnation. This man Legality, to whom he sent you, is the son of the Bondwoman, who is in bondage with her children and, in a figure, is the same as this high hill, Mount Sinai, you were afraid would fall on you. Now, if she with all her children are in bondage, how can you expect any of them to set you free? This Legality, who was born on Mount Sinai, is unable to set you free from your burden. He has never freed anyone from his burden of sin, and never will.

You cannot be justified by the works of the law; for by the deeds of the law no man can be cleansed from his sin, or relieved of his burden. Therefore, Mr. Worldly Wiseman is an alien, and Mr. Legality is a cheat; and, as for his son Civility, notwithstanding his simpering looks, he is a sham, and cannot help anyone. Believe me, there is nothing in all this noise you have heard about these stupid men but a design to beguile souls and lead them away from salvation. This they have attempted to

[4]Luke 13:24.
[5]Matt. 7:13.

do to you by alluring you away from the way in which I sent you.

After this, Evangelist called aloud to the heavens for confirmation of what he had spoken. And with that there came fire and words out of the mountain under which they stood which made Christian's hair stand up. The words were loud and clear; "As many as are of the works of the law are under the curse; for it is written, Cursed is everyone that continueth not in all things which are written in the book of the law to do them."[6]

Now, Christian expected nothing but death, and he began to cry in a pitiful voice, even denouncing the time he met Mr. Worldly Wiseman, and calling himself a stupid fool for following his counsel. He also declared that he was deeply ashamed to think that this man's arguments had had enough influence with him—though they were only products of a carnal mind—as to cause him to forsake the right way and follow the way of the world. This done, he applied himself again to Evangelist's words of wisdom, spiritual instruction, and complete devotion to the King of Heaven.

CHRISTIAN: Sir, what do you think? Is there any hope for me? May I now go back, take up where I left off, and go on to the wicket gate? Or shall I be abandoned for this unfaithfulness, and sent away from the gate in shame? I am sincerely sorry that I heeded this worldly man's counsel and turned away from the right path, but may my sins be forgiven?

EVANGELIST: Your sin is very great. It involves two evils: you forsook the right way, and you walked in a forbidden path. Yet, the Man at the gate will receive you, for He has great mercy, and goodwill for all mankind. Only take heed that you do not turn aside again lest you "perish from the way, when his wrath is kindled but a little."[7]

[6]Gal. 3:10.
[7]Ps. 2:12.

CHAPTER
2
christian returns to the good way

THEN CHRISTIAN DETERMINED to go back to the good way; and Evangelist, smiling, gave him his hand, and said, "May God bless you." So he went back in haste, refusing to talk to anyone by the way. He walked like one treading on forbidden ground, for he did not feel at all safe until he was again in the way Evangelist had instructed him to go.

Back in the way, he finally came to the little gate. Over the gate was written, in bold letters: "KNOCK, AND IT SHALL BE OPENED UNTO YOU."

Enters the Wicket Gate

Christian knocked. There was no answer. He knocked again and again. No one came. He shouted, "May I now enter here? Will you please open to me? Though I have been an undeserving rebel, if I am forgiven and allowed to enter, I will never cease to sing God's praise."

At last one came to the gate whose name was Goodwill. He asked, in a deep voice, "Who's there, where did you come from, and what do you want?"

CHRISTIAN: I am a poor, burdened sinner. I come from the

City of Destruction, and I want to go to Mount Zion, that I may be safe from the coming wrath of God. I am informed that through this gate is the way to Zion. I would like to know, therefore, if you will let me in.

GOODWILL: Yes, I will, with all speed. Immediately Goodwill opened the gate and, just as Christian was stepping in, took hold of his arm and gave him a quick pull. "What does that mean?" asked Christian. Goodwill explained: "There on the outside, not far from this gate, is a strong castle, guarded by Beelzebub and his men; and from it, they shoot arrows at those entering here, that they might maim them, or prevent them from entering."

"I rejoice and tremble," said Christian. When he was safe inside, Goodwill asked him who had directed him there.

CHRISTIAN: Evangelist instructed me to come here and knock, and he said that you, sir, would tell me what I must do.

GOODWILL: An open door is set before you, and no man can shut it.

CHRISTIAN: Now, I begin to reap the benefits of my hazards.

GOODWILL: But how is it that you came alone?

CHRISTIAN: Because none of my neighbors saw their danger, as I saw mine.

GOODWILL: Did any of them know you were coming?

CHRISTIAN: Yes, my wife and children saw me leaving, and called after me to come back. Also, some of my neighbors stood calling me to return. But I put my fingers in my ears and came on my way.

GOODWILL: But did none of them follow you to persuade you to go back?

CHRISTIAN: Yes, two of my neighbors, Obstinate and Pliable. But when they saw that they could not prevail, Obstinate became abusive and turned back to his own house, and Pliable came with me a little way.

GOODWILL: But why did he not come on?

CHRISTIAN: We did indeed both come together to the Slough of Despond, into which we fell. Then Pliable was discouraged, and would not venture farther. Getting out again on the side toward his own house, he said, "You may have the good country for me," and went his way after Obstinate; and I came on without him.

GOODWILL: Alas, poor man! Was the Celestial City of so little value to him that he did not count it worth the hazards of a few difficulties to reach it?

CHRISTIAN: Surely, and when I tell you the truth about myself, it will appear that there is not much difference between him and me. 'Tis true he went back to his own house, but I also turned aside to walk in the way of death, being so persuaded by the false arguments of one Mr. Worldly Wiseman.

GOODWILL: Oh, did you meet him? He would have you vainly seeking fleshly ease at the hands of Mr. Legality! They are both nothing but miserable cheats. But did you take his counsel?

CHRISTIAN: Yes, as far as I dared. Following his instruction, I went to find Mr. Legality and came to the high mountain that stands by his house, which I feared would fall on me. There I was forced to stop.

GOODWILL: It is well you escaped being crushed to pieces. That mountain has been the death of many pilgrims, and will be the death of many more.

CHRISTIAN: I really do not know what would have become of me, if Evangelist had not come to me there. It was the mercy of God that he came just as I was brooding over my bewilderment; otherwise, I never would have come here. But now, such as I am, I am here—more worthy of death than to be here talking with you. Oh, what a favor this is to me, to be admitted inside the gate of pardon!

GOODWILL: We do not reject any who come. No matter what they have done before coming, they are in no wise cast out.[1] And now, my good pilgrim, come with me a little way, and I will show you the way to go. Now look yonder. Do you see that narrow way? That is the road you must take. It was traveled by the patriarchs in olden times, and by the prophets, and by Christ and His apostles; and it is as straight as a line can make it.

CHRISTIAN: But are there no turnings or windings by which a stranger may lose his way?

GOODWILL: Yes, there are many roads branching off from this one, but you can distinguish the right way from the wrong, for the right way is the only road that is straight and narrow.

Then Christian asked Mr. Goodwill if he would remove the burden from his back, for he was still carrying it and could by no means get it off without help. Goodwill counseled: "Be content to bear your burden a little longer, until you come to the place of deliverance. Then it will fall from your shoulders of itself."

Now Christian began to prepare for his journey. So Goodwill explained: "When you have gone a distance from this gate, you will come to the Interpreter's house. He will welcome you and give you a lot of valuable information." Then Christian bid his friend good-bye and went on his way.

Arrives at Interpreter's House

Walking for an hour or so, he came to a large house, which he thought must be the home of the Interpreter. After he had knocked several times, a voice from within asked, "Who's there?"

CHRISTIAN: "I am a pilgrim who was directed by a friend of the good man of this house to call here for instructions. I

[1]John 6:37.

wish to speak with the master of the house." Soon the Interpreter came and asked him what he would have.

CHRISTIAN: Sir, my name is Christian. I'm a man from the City of Destruction, and I'm on my way to Mount Zion. I was told by the good man at the little gate that if I would call here, you would show me excellent things, needful for my journey.

INTERPRETER: "Yes, indeed, come in. I will show you that which will be very profitable." He gave him a warm welcome; then directed his assistant to lead the way into the house. The assistant said, "Follow me," and led him into a private room, where he told a servant to open a door. When the door was opened, Christian saw a picture of a very grave person, whose eyes were looking toward heaven. He held the best of books in his hand. The expression of truth was upon his lips. The world was behind his back. He stood as if pleading with men, and a crown of gold hung over his head. The Interpreter was silent.

CHRISTIAN: What does this mean?

INTERPRETER: This man is one of a thousand. He can say in the words of the Apostle, "Though you have ten thousand instructors in Christ, yet you have not many fathers: for in Christ Jesus I have begotten you through the gospel"[2] and "My little children for whom I travail again in birth until Christ be formed in you."[3] And whereas you see him with his eyes lifted up to heaven, the best of books in his hand, and the law of truth written on his lips, it is to show that his work is to know and unfold dark things to sinners; and this is why he stands pleading with men. And whereas you see the world behind his back, and that a crown hangs over his head, that reveals to us that, slighting and despising the things of the present because of the love he has for his Master's service, he is sure to have glory for his reward in the world to come.

[2]I Cor. 4:15.
[3]Gal. 4:19.

"Now," said the Interpreter, "I have showed you this picture first, because it is the picture of the only one whom the Lord of the place where you are going has authorized to be your guide in all difficult places you may come to on your way. Therefore, take heed to what I have showed you, and remember what you have seen, lest you meet with some in your journey who pretend to lead you in the right way but whose course leads down to death."

Then he led him into a very large parlor that was full of dust. When they had observed it for a moment, the Interpreter called for a man to sweep it. When he began to sweep, the dust rose and filled the whole room so that Christian almost suffocated. Then the Interpreter said to a maid who stood by, "Bring water and sprinkle the room," which she did. Then the dust settled, and the maid swept the room clean.

CHRISTIAN: What does this signify?

INTERPRETER: This parlor is the heart of man that has never been sanctified and cleansed by the grace of God through the gospel. The dust is his original sin and corruption that have defiled the whole man. The man who began to sweep at first is the law. The maid who brought the water and finished the job is the gospel. The man, though working with all his might, could not clean the room; he only stirred up the dust and made it worse to live in. This shows you that the law, by its working, instead of cleansing the heart from sin, only revives sin, causes sin to show its strength, and increase its activity in the soul. Though it discovers and forbids sin, it does not give the life and power to subdue it. So man cannot of himself give up his sin, without first receiving divine life and help from above. This is why the maid came, sprinkled the room with water, and cleaned it with all ease, to show you that when the gospel of Christ comes to the heart, with all its sweet and gracious influence, new life comes in, sin is subdued and vanquished, and the soul is made clean by simple faith in Christ. Consequently, man is made fit for the habitation of the King of Glory.

Then the Interpreter took Christian into a little room where two children were seated, each in his own chair. The name of the older was Passion, and the name of the other Patience. Obviously, Passion was not at all content, while Patience was very quiet.

"Why is Passion so restless?" asked Christian.

"Their governess wants them to wait for their best things until next year," said the Interpreter, "but Passion wants all of his best things now; while Patience is willing to wait."

Then one came to Passion and poured out at his feet a bag of treasures which he quickly gathered into his arms with great joy. He laughed loudly and made fun of Patience. But soon he wasted everything he had received, and had nothing left but an empty bag.

"Explain this matter more fully," said Christian.

INTERPRETER: Passion represents men of this world; and Patience represents those who are of the next world. Men of this world must have all their rewards in this life; they cannot wait. "A bird in the hand is worth two in the bush" has more weight with them than all the promises of the Bible. But they soon go through what they have, and at the end of life they have nothing at all.

"Now I see," said Christian, "that Patience has the better wisdom, for many reasons. First, he waits for the best things. Second, he will enjoy the glory of his rewards when the other has nothing but rags."

INTERPRETER: Yes, and you may add this also: The glory of the next world will never pass away, or wear out, but the glories of this life are soon gone. Therefore, it is said of a certain rich man: "In thy lifetime thou receivedst thy good things, and likewise Lazarus evil things; but now he is comforted, and thou art tormented."[4]

CHRISTIAN: Then I judge it is best not to covet things of this world, but to wait for good things to come.

INTERPRETER: You speak the truth. "The things that are seen are temporal, but the things that are not seen are eternal."[5] Yet present things are so close to our fleshly appetites, and eternal things so far from our souls; we are apt to yield to our carnal desires rather than wait for the satisfaction of the eternal. Thus we become joined to the things of this world and so lose our future reward.

In another place there was a fire burning against a wall and one continually throwing water on it. But the fire still blazed higher and hotter.

"What is the purpose of that?" asked Christian.

INTEPRETER: This fire is the work of God's grace in the heart. The person throwing water on it is the devil. Still, you see, the fire burns brighter. Come around the wall here and you will see why. (On the other side of the wall was a person secretly pouring oil on the fire.) This shows you why it is hard for the tempted to understand how God's grace is maintained in the soul. This is the way Christ continues to supply grace in the soul of the believer through all the cold showers of the world and the temptations of the devil.

From there they went out into a beautiful park and came to a stately palace, on top of which walked radiant persons clothed in gold. The sight filled Christian with wonder. He said, "May we go in?"

Then the Interpreter led him up toward the door of the palace. At the door stood a great crowd of people. All were anxious to go in, but no one dared to enter. By this Christian

[4]Luke 16:25.
[5]II Cor. 4:18.

understood that a great many people who desire and intend to enter the kingdom of Heaven are kept back by fear.

The door of the palace was guarded by strong armed men. Between the crowd and the door sat a recorder at a table with book and pen, to write down the names of all who would enter. Out of the crowd came one called Courage, and gave his name to the man at the table. Then he put a helmet on his head, drew out a sword, and rushed toward the door. He was seized by the armed guards, but they could not hold him. He cut and slashed them with such fierceness that they fell back and let him go in. From the inside, and from the top of the building, came the words: "Come in, come in; eternal glory you shall win."

So Courage went in and was clothed with the beautiful garments of the palace. Christian smiled, saying, "I think I know the meaning of this."

Turning from this scene, they went into a very dark room. There Christian saw a man with a gloomy countenance in an iron cage, whose name was Hopeless. He sat with his hands folded, his eyes looking downward; and he sighed as if his heart would break.

"What happened to him?" asked Christian.

"I will let him tell you," said Interpreter.

HOPELESS: I certainly am not what I was.

CHRISTIAN: What were you?

HOPELESS: I was once a happy, professing Christian, both in my own way of thinking and in the eyes of others. I felt that I was fit for the Celestial City, and looked forward to entering that place with great joy.

CHRISTIAN: I see, but what are you now?

HOPELESS: I am now a man of despair, rejected, abandoned, shut up in this iron cage from which there is no escape.

CHRISTIAN: How did you get in that condition?

HOPELESS: I ceased to watch and be sober. I allowed myself

to doubt the Word of Life, and gave way to my passions. I sinned against the light of the Word and the goodness of God. I yielded to Satan's arguments and he took possession of my soul. I have provoked God to anger, and He has left me. I have grieved the Spirit, and He is gone. I have hardened my heart, and now I cannot repent.

Then Christian asked the Interpreter, "But is there no hope for him?"

INTERPRETER: Ask him.

CHRISTIAN: Is there no hope that you will ever escape from this iron cage of despair?

HOPELESS: No, none at all.

CHRISTIAN: Why not? The Son of the Blessed is very pitiful, and of tender mercy.

HOPELESS: Yes, but I have rejected His mercy; I have crucified Him to myself afresh and put Him to an open shame. I have despised His righteousness. I have hated His Lordship over me. I have offended the Spirit of grace. I have counted His blood, wherewith I was purchased, unholy. Therefore, I have shut myself out from all the promises; and now there remains nothing for me but threatenings, dreadful threatenings, fearful threatenings of certain judgment, and fiery indignation which shall devour me as an adversary.

CHRISTIAN: For what did you do all this and bring yourself into this state?

HOPELESS: For the lust of the flesh, for the pleasures and profits of this world: in the enjoyments of which, I did then promise myself much delight. But now every one of these bite and sting like a serpent. Oh, if I could but repent! But God has denied me repentance. I feel His Word gives me no encouragement to believe. He has shut me up in this iron cage of my own sin and unbelief, and will never, never, never set me free; nor can all the men in the world free me from this prison. Oh, eternity! eternity! How shall I cope with the miseries that shall be mine forever?

INTERPRETER TO CHRISTIAN: Let this man's words be remembered by you, and be to you a constant caution.

CHRISTIAN: Well, this is awful! God help me to watch and be sober, and to pray, that I may shun the evil and misery of those who go that way. Sir, is it not time for me to go on my way?

INTERPRETER: Wait till I show you one more thing; then you may go.

Then he took Christian into a chamber where he saw one rising out of bed who, as he dressed, trembled. "Why does this man tremble so?" asked Christian.

INTERPRETER: He can tell you. Then addressing Mr. Loveworld, Interpreter said, "Tell this man why you shake and tremble."

LOVEWORLD: I had an awful dream. The heavens turned exceedingly dark. Black clouds rolled across the sky. Vivid lightning flashed, and thunders roared, shaking the very earth. I heard a great sound of a trumpet. I saw a Man coming to earth on a cloud, followed by thousands of heavenly persons. They were all flaming like fire. Then I looked and the heavens were on fire; and I heard a mighty voice saying, "Arise, O dead, and come to judgment." Then the rocks began to roll and break apart, graves opened, and millions of the dead came forth. Some were exceedingly glad and looking upward; some were horrified and called for the rocks and the mountains to cover them.

Then I saw the One on the cloud open a book, and summon the world to come before Him. I heard Him also giving orders to those attending Him: "Gather up the tares, the chaff, and the stubble, and toss them into the fire." Then a bottomless pit opened right at my feet; and out of the pit came great clouds of smoke, and hideous noises. He also commanded: "Gather my wheat into the garner." Then many were caught up and carried away into the clouds, but I was left behind. I tried to find a place to hide but could not, for the Man who sat upon the cloud still kept His eye on me. My sins came before me, and my conscience condemned me severely. Then I awoke in terror.

CHRISTIAN: But why should you be afraid of this revelation?

LOVEWORLD: Why, I thought the day of judgment had come and I was not ready for it. What troubled me most was that the angels gathered up many for the heavenly kingdom, and left me behind. Also the pit of Hell opened before me and my conscience smote me dreadfully, and it seemed that the Judge always had His eye on me, and was observing me with indignation.

INTERPRETER (*to Christian*): Now, have you considered well all these things?

CHRISTIAN: Yes, and they give me hope and fear.

INTERPRETER: Well, keep them always in mind that they may warn you against the evil and goad you forward in the way you must go; and may the Comforter always be with you, to guide you in the way that leads to the Celestial City.

So Christian went on his way.

CHAPTER

3

journey toward the house beautiful

Loses His Burden at the Cross

NOW I SAW in my dream Christian walking briskly up a highway fenced on both sides with a high wall. He began to run, though he could not run fast because of the load on his back. On top of the hill, he came to a cross. Just as he got to the cross, his burden came loose, dropped from his shoulders, and went tumbling down the hill. It fell into an open grave, and I saw it no more.

Now Christian's heart was light. He had found relief from his burden. He said to himself, "He has given me rest by His sorrows, and life by His death." He stood gazing at the cross, wondering how the sight of the cross could so relieve one of guilt and shame. He no longer felt guilty of anything. His conscience told him that all his sins were forgiven. He now felt innocent, clean, happy, and free. He knew his sins had all been paid for by the death of the One who died on the cross. They were gone, buried in the Saviour's tomb, and God would remember them against him no more forever. He was so thankful and so full of joy that the tears began to flow.

As he stood looking at the cross, weeping for joy, three celestial beings stood near. They greeted him with, "Peace be unto thee." The first said, "Your sins are forgiven." The second stripped him of his rags and clothed him with garments white and clean. The third put a mark upon his forehead and gave him a book to read on the way and for identification at the celestial gate. Then Christian leaped for joy, and went on his way singing.

Meets False Christians

I saw him come to the bottom of a hill where, a little way from the road, lay three men fast asleep. All three had fetters of iron on their feet. The name of one was Simple; the second was named Sloth, and the third, Presumption.

Christian went near them to warn them of their danger. He shouted, "You are like them that sleep on top of a mast, or have lain down at the bottom of the sea. Wake up, and come with me. Permit me to take off your fetters. If the one who goes about as a roaring lion comes along, you will certainly be devoured."[1]

They sleepily looked up at him, each with a scowl. "I see no danger," said Simple. "Let me have a little sleep," said Sloth. And Presumption said, "Why should you worry? Every tub shall stand on its own bottom." Then they all lay down to sleep again. And Christian went on his way, disappointed at the thought of the danger these men were in. Yet they could not see it; and they had little appreciation for one who would try to help them.

Just then he saw two men come over the wall a little behind him. They walked fast and caught up with him. One was named Formality, the other Hypocrisy.

[1]I Peter 5:8.

Christian loses his burden at the cross.

CHRISTIAN: Gentlemen, where are you from and where are you going?

They said that they were from the town of Vainglory and were going to Mount Zion.

CHRISTIAN: Why did you not come in at the gate at the beginning of the way? You know it is written in the book by the Builder of the road: "He that cometh not in by the door, but climbeth up some other way, the same is a thief and a robber."[2]

They told him that to go to the gate from where they lived was considered too far by all and that the usual way was to take a shortcut and climb over the wall, as they had done.

CHRISTIAN: But will it not be counted a trespass and a violation of instructions by the Lord of the City where you are going?

They said he need not trouble his head about that, for they had a long-standing custom where they lived to guide them in their practice, and they could produce plenty of testimony of its practicality over a period of more than a thousand years.

CHRISTIAN: But will it stand the final test?

They thought so. They said that a custom of such long standing most certainly had been accepted and, without doubt, would be admitted by the impartial Judge at the end of the way. "And," they reasoned, "we are in the same way you are in. What does it matter how we got in? If we are in, we are in. In what way is your position better than ours?"

CHRISTIAN: I walk by the rule of the Lord of the way; you follow your own fancy: the crude invention of uninspired men. You are called thieves already by the Lord of the way. Therefore I doubt that you will be found true men at the end. You came in by yourselves without His direction, and you shall go out by yourselves without His mercy.

At this they told Christian to mind his own business; they

[2]John 10:1.

would take care of themselves. They said that they were quite sure of having kept the law and ordinances fully as well as he. "Therefore," said Formality, "we see no difference between you and ourselves except the coat on your back, which, no doubt, some neighbor gave you to hide your nakedness."

CHRISTIAN: By laws and ordinances you cannot be saved.[3] And as for this coat I am wearing, it was given to me by the Lord of the place where I am going. It was given, as you say, to cover my nakedness. And I wear it as a token of His kindness to me; for I had nothing but rags before. Now I feel sure that when I come to the gate of the Celestial City, the Lord will know me by this coat He gave me, by this mark in my forehead—which perhaps you had not noticed—placed there by one of His faithful servants, and by this book which I hold in my hand. All of these I doubt you have, because you did not come in through the gate.

They gave him no answer, but looked at each other and laughed. Then Christian walked on a little before them, often reading from his book, to refresh his spirit and overcome the disappointments of the day.

They were now nearing a long, steep hill called Difficulty, at the foot of which were two other roads, one leading to the right, and the other to the left of the straight and narrow way. Beyond these was a cool, refreshing spring, where Christian drank before attempting to climb the hill.

Formality and Hypocrisy also came to the foot of the hill. But when they saw that the hill was steep and difficult and that there were two other ways to go (they did not know that the name of one of the roads was Danger, and the name of the other, Destruction), supposing that the side roads would come again to the straight way on the other side of the hill, they took what seemed the easiest route. Formality took the road named

[3]Gal. 2:16.

Danger, which led him into a great forest where he was devoured by wild beasts; and Hypocrisy went down the road of Destruction, which led into a vast plain where there were many deep pits, into one of which he stumbled and fell, and rose no more.

When Christian began to climb the hill, he sang:

I must climb up to the mountain top;
  Never mind if the path is steep,
For I know that through strife lies the way to life,
  And the way-farer must not weep.
So courage! my heart, don't faint, don't fear
  Though the rough rock makes the way slow,
The easy track only leads me back,
  Up and on is the way I must go!

Soon his progress was slower, then he went on his hands and knees, because the way was very steep.

Loses Book at the Restful Arbor

Now, about halfway up the hill was a pleasant arbor, a place for rest for weary travelers, made by the Lord of the hill. Here Christian sat down to rest. He began to take pleasure in the good coat that was given him at the cross, and to enjoy reading from his book. So, pleasing himself for a while, he dozed, and the book dropped from his hand. Soon he fell sound asleep, which detained him until almost night. Then he heard a voice: "Go to the ant, thou sluggard; consider her ways, and be wise."[4] Startled, he awoke and hastened on his way.

At the top of the hill, two men came running to meet him. One was Timorous, and the other, Mistrust. Christian called out to them, "Sirs, what is your trouble? You run the wrong way."

Timorous answered that they were on their way to the City of Zion when they came to a most dangerous place. He said, "It

[4]Prov. 6:6.

seems that the farther we go the more dangerous it becomes, so we are going back."

"Yes," said Mistrust, "we saw, just ahead of us, a couple of lions. Whether they were asleep or awake, we do not know; but we felt sure that if we got near them they would tear us to pieces."

CHRISTIAN: You make me afraid; but where shall I go to be safe? If I go back to my own country, that is marked for fire and brimstone; I will certainly perish there. If I can get to the Celestial City, I know I will be safe there. So I must venture on. To go back is nothing but death; to go forward is fear of death, but life everlasting is beyond that. Therefore, I will still go forward.

So Mistrust and Timorous ran back down the hill, and Christian went on his way. As he thought of what he had heard, he felt in his bosom for his book, and found that he did not have it. Then he was in great distress. What had become of his priceless gift—a comfort and guide in time of trouble, and his pass for the Celestial Gate? How could he go on without it? He knew not what to do.

At last he remembered sleeping in the arbor, and he could not recall seeing the book since. Falling on his knees, he asked God to forgive him for his carelessness and his sinful act of sleeping on the way. With a heart full of regret and fear, he went back, looking for his book, sighing, weeping, doubting that he would ever find it and, if not, that there was any hope for him.

When he came in sight of the arbor, built by the good Lord to give lonely, weary, exhausted travelers a little rest so that they might continue their journey, he cried: "Oh, wretched man that I am, that I should sleep in the daytime in the midst of difficulty, indulging the flesh, using for my own selfish ease that which the Lord erected only to relieve the spirits of wayworn pilgrims!

How many extra steps have I taken in vain! This is what happened to Israel. For their sins they were sent back again by the way of the Red Sea to wander forty years in the wilderness. How far I might have been by now, journeying with delight, had it not been for my sinful sleep! And night is coming on and may overtake me on this difficult hill. Oh, that I had not slept!"

By this time he had come to the arbor and, not seeing his book, he sat down and wept. But at last (as Providence would have it), looking down, he saw there under the seat his lost book. Then his sadness turned to gladness, and he thanked God for leading him back and showing him where he had dropped his valuable book. Now he placed it in his bosom and hurried up the mountain.

Becomes Fearful

Before he reached the top, the sun went down. Seeing darkness approaching and perceiving the dangers he had brought on himself by his presumptuous sleep, he began to dread the road. "Now, I must walk in darkness," he said, "and hear the noises of the doleful creatures of night because of my careless sleep."

Then he remembered what Timorous and Mistrust had told him about seeing lions in the way. "These beasts," he thought, "prowl at night for their prey, and if they should attack me, I have nothing with which to defend myself. How could I ward them off, or escape being torn to pieces?"

While he was deploring his unhappy lot, he saw lights ahead, and a very stately building appeared in the gloom. It was the Lodge, the Palace Beautiful, standing a little way back from the road. With the thought that he might find lodging there, he quickened his steps. He entered the narrow trail leading to the house and saw two lions, one on each side of the path. Here were the dangers Timorous and Mistrust were talking about which caused them to turn back and depart from the heavenly way. He stopped to consider what he must do. He wondered if he too should not turn and run, as they had done; for he could see nothing but death before him.

But the Porter of the Lodge, whose name was Watchful, saw Christian hesitating as if he would go back, and called out to him: "Is your faith weak? Why be fearful? Don't be afraid of the lions, for they are both chained. They are placed there to try the faith of travelers and to discover those who have no faith. Keep in the middle of the path, and you will not be hurt." Then Christian ventured down the path between the lions, which roared and surged against their chains, but did him no harm. He praised the Lord of the hill and walked on to the gate where the Porter stood.

Arrives at the House Beautiful

"Sir, what house is this?" he asked. "May I stay here tonight?"

PORTER: "This house was built by the Lord of the hill to accommodate pilgrims."

The Porter also asked Christian his name, where he was from, and where he was going.

CHRISTIAN: My name is Christian now. However, at first it was Graceless. I am from the City of Destruction, and I'm going to Mount Zion. Since night has come and I do not know the way before me, I would like to spend the night here, if I may.

PORTER: But how does it happen that you come so late?

CHRISTIAN: I would have been here much earlier but, careless man that I am, when I sat down to rest in the cool arbor on the side of the hill, I went to sleep. I must have slept an hour or longer, and I was further delayed because in my sleep I dropped my sacred book and did not miss it until I got to the top of the hill. Then I had to go all the way back to the arbor to find it.

PORTER: Well, I will call one of the maids, and if she likes your story she will introduce you to the other occupants, according to the rules of the house.

So Watchful, the porter, rang a bell, and soon a beautiful, sedate lady appeared whose name was Discretion.

PORTER: This man is on a journey from the City of Destruction to Mount Zion. Night has overtaken him here and he would like to spend the night.

Discretion asked him his name, how he found the right way, and something of what he had seen on the way. Christian related a few of his experiences, and said: "I have a keen desire to stay here, for I am told that this place was built by the Lord of the hill for the relief and security of pilgrims."

She smiled, thought for a moment, with tears in her eyes, and then said, "I will call two or three of my helpers." Then she went to the door and called Prudence, Piety, and Charity, who, after brief conversation, invited him in to meet the others. He bowed courteously and followed them into a large front room. After he was seated, they brought him a cool refreshing drink, and entertained him while supper was preparing.

PIETY: Brother Christian, what caused you at first to come on this pilgrimage?

CHRISTIAN: I became troubled about my sins from reading the book which the pilgrims gave me, and I was warned by a voice that kept ringing in my ears. The voice said that my town and country were condemned and marked for destruction. This gave me a great burden. While seeking to be free from my burden, I was instructed by an Evangelist to come this way to find relief.

PIETY: Evangelist pointed you to the wicket gate, did he not, and you came by the house of the Interpreter?

CHRISTIAN: Yes, the Interpreter showed me many marvelous things. I could have stayed in his house a year, but I knew I had to go on. I still wore my old clothes from the City of Destruction and carried my burden, and he showed me the way to the cross.

PIETY: What did you find at the cross?

CHRISTIAN: I found peace. I had a vision of One bleeding, dying on the cross for my sins. Then my burden rolled away, and great joy came into my heart. I received this mark here in my forehead, and was given this coat I am wearing and this sacred roll I hold in my hand by three shining ones that appeared and vanished.

PIETY: But you saw other things on the way, I suppose?

CHRISTIAN: Yes, but these were the more important. I also saw Sloth, Simple, and Presumption sleeping by the way, and tried to wake them, but they were too sleepy. I also saw Formality and Hypocrisy come over the wall. They walked with me a little way until I came to this hill, where they left me and took easier roads.

"Do you think sometimes of the country you came from?" asked Prudence.

CHRISTIAN: Yes, but with shame and regret. But if I had preferred the country I came from, I would have returned to it, for I have had ample opportunity to do so. But now I desire a better country, a heavenly one.

PRUDENCE: Do you not still have some of the old country in you?

CHRISTIAN: Yes, to my humiliation. I still have my old inward carnal thoughts, such as my countrymen, as well as myself, once delighted in. But now they are my grief, and not my joy. If I could be rid of my fleshly nature, and do all I choose, I would never have another evil thought. But, I find even now, "When I would do good, evil is present with me."

PRUDENCE: Do you not find at times that those carnal things of which you speak seem to be purged?

CHRISTIAN: Yes, those times are the golden hours of my life. However, these experiences I do not have as often as I would, and they do not last as long as I wish they might.

PRUDENCE: Can you remember by what means you obtain those victorious, happy experiences?

CHRISTIAN: Yes. When I think on what I saw and what I received at the cross; or when I think of the country to which I am going; or read from the pilgrim's book and pray, all doubts and fears, anxieties and cares, and all evil seem to vanish away. Yet I feel that it is not I myself achieving this but the Spirit of Him who loved me and gave Himself for me.

PRUDENCE: What gives you such a strong desire to go to Mount Zion?

CHRISTIAN: Oh, I want to be with Him who gave Himself for my sins, and is giving me eternal life. I want to be with those who are like Him, and be free from pain and trouble and iniquity forever.

"Have you a family?" asked Charity.

CHRISTIAN: Yes, I have a wife and four children.

CHARITY: And why did you not bring them along with you?

CHRISTIAN (*weeping*): Oh, how gladly would I have done so, but they all were so utterly averse to my coming.

CHARITY: But did you talk to them and try to show them the sinfulness of the place and the danger of staying behind? And did you plead with them to come along with you?

CHRISTIAN: Yes, with all my power. I told them also what God had revealed to me of the destruction of the place, but I seemed to them as one who mocked and they would not believe me.

CHARITY: But did you pray to God that He would bless your message to them?

CHRISTIAN: Yes, with all the earnestness of my soul and all the love of my heart, for my wife and children are very dear to me.

CHARITY: But did you tell them of your own sorrow and fear of destruction?

CHRISTIAN: Yes, over and over again, often weeping.

CHARITY: But what did they say? Did they tell you why they would not come?

CHRISTIAN: My wife said it was foolish to give up the whole world for a fancy, and my children were completely wrapped up in their present joys—the trivial things of youth.

CHARITY: But did your own vain life nullify your earnest persuasion, and destroy your testimony?

CHRISTIAN: Well, indeed I cannot commend my life, for I am conscious of many failings; and I realize a person by his daily living may annul his good arguments and persuasion. Yet I was very careful not to give my family any occasion for offense at my unseemly conduct. I did not want them to be averse to going with me. But they often told me that I was too precise, that I denied myself of things (for their sake) in which they could see no evil. If they saw anything in me that hindered them from accepting the truth and coming with me, it was my extreme carefulness not to sin against God or do any wrong to anyone.

CHARITY: Indeed, Cain hated his brother because his own works were evil, and his brother's righteous.[5] If your wife and children were offended at you for that, they proved themselves impervious to true righteousness, and you have delivered your soul from responsibility for their condemnation.

In this way, they sat talking until dinner was ready, then they all went into the dining room and sat down to eat. The table was laden with good things. Their conversation at the table

[5]I John 3:12.

was about the Lord of the hill: what He had done; and how He had built that house; and from what they said Christian perceived that He had been a great hero in battle. He had fought and slain the one who had the power of death; that is, the power to bring death to the whole human race; yet He had accomplished this with great danger and suffering to Himself.[6]

They said (what Christian had already come to believe) that their Hero had achieved victory over the enemy of the race by the loss of His own blood and that He did it out of pure love for the country. Some of them at the table declared that they had seen Him and talked with Him since He died on the cross. And they implied that they had this story from His own lips: that He has such love for pilgrims in this wilderness journey as is not found in any other person in the universe. They said that He had given up all His wealth and power, stripped Himself of His glory, and made Himself of no reputation,[7] that He might help the poor and sinful, and provide for them a rich inheritance in a land of fadeless day. They recalled they had heard Him affirm that He would not dwell in the mountains of Zion alone. They said, moreover, that He had made princes of many pilgrims who had been beggars.

They sat and talked till late at night. Then, after they had prayed and committed themselves to their Keeper, they retired for the night. Christian slept in a large upper room with a window facing toward the sunrise. The name of the room was Peace. He slept till break of day.

In the morning, they all rose early; and after more enjoyable discourse, they told Christian that he should not leave until they had shown him some of the rare things of the place.

First, they took him into the study and showed him the records of antiquity: the genealogy of the Master of the hill, which revealed that the Master was the Son of the Ancient of Days

[6]Heb. 2:14-15.
[7]Phil. 2:7.

and had an eternal lineage. Here were the records of His accomplishments and the names of many hundreds He had placed in His service, giving them permanent, everlasting habitations.

Then they read to him some of the worthy deeds of His servants: how they had subdued kingdoms, wrought righteousness, obtained promises, stopped the mouths of lions, quenched the violence of fire, escaped the edge of the sword; how they were made strong in weakness, waxed valiant in fight, and turned to flight the armies of the aliens.[8]

In other records they read how willing the Lord was to receive into His favor anyone, even those who had offered strong affronts to His person and His proceedings. Here also were other records of noble deeds of righteous characters of the past, which Christian viewed along with attested prophecies and true predictions of things sure to take place to the confounding of unbelievers and the consolation of faithful pilgrims on their way to the better land.

The next day, they took him into the armory, where he saw all kinds of equipment for soldiers in the holy war: swords, shields, helmets, breastplates, effectual prayer, and shoes that would never wear out.[9] They told him that the Ruler of the hill had enough of this equipment to furnish every person who desired to resist evil in his progress to the promised land. No matter how great the number who needed such equipment, there was enough for all.

They also showed him some of the instruments with which old pilgrims had done valiant feats: Moses' rod; the hammer and nail with which Jael slew Sisera; the pitchers, trumpets, and lamps with which Gideon put to flight the armies of Midian; the ox's goad that Shamgar killed six hundred aliens with; a jawbone with which Samson destroyed a whole army of

[8]Heb. 11:33-34.
[9]Eph. 6:14-18.

Philistines; the sling and stone that brought down the mighty giant Goliath, used by young David; and many, many notable things in the armory of the Lord. This done, they went to their rest again.

Then I saw in my dream that on the morrow Christian got up to go on his way, but they persuaded him to stay until the next day. "Tomorrow, if the day is clear," they promised, "we will show you the Delectable Mountains, which, because they are beautiful and much nearer your desired haven, will lift your spirit, give you a stronger desire to go there, and courage for your journey." So Christian consented to stay.

Next day, when the sun was high, they took him to the top of the building and told him to look far away to the east. At a great distance, Christian could see a magnificent mountainous country. In this faraway land were great forests, green vineyards, sparkling fountains, broad fields, beautiful valleys, miles of fruit orchards, and marvelous landscapes of golden grain—very attractive indeed. He asked the name of the country. They said, "It is Immanuel's Land, and it is for all pilgrims, just as this hill is, and from there you will be able to see the gate of the Celestial City, as the shepherds there will show you."

He expressed his desire to go, and they were willing. "But first," they suggested, "let us go again to the armory." There they equipped him from head to foot with what he would need most in his journey. Being thus clothed, he walked out with his friends to the gate. He asked the Porter at the gate if he had seen any pilgrims pass.

"Yes," said the Porter, "one passed a little while ago."

"Did you know him?" asked Christian.

"No. I asked him his name, and he said it was Faithful."

CHRISTIAN: Oh, I know him. He is my close neighbor. He comes from my hometown. How far do you think he may be down the road by now?

PORTER: He must be to the foot of the hill by this time.

"Well, good Porter," said Christian, "may the Lord be with you and bless you abundantly for all the kindness you have shown to me." Then he resumed his journey.

Discretion, Piety, Charity, and Prudence accompanied him to the foot of the hill. They went on talking till they came to the brow of the hill. Then observed Christian: "I thought it was difficult coming up the hill, but it looks as if it is going to be more dangerous going down."

"Yes, it really is," agreed Prudence. "It is especially hard for one after being on this hill for a while to go down into the Valley of Humility without slipping at times. This is why we came along to go with you to the bottom of the hill." Now Christian walked very carefully; yet he did slip a time or two.

At the foot of the hill, Christian's good companions gave him a loaf of bread, a bottle of wine, and a large bunch of raisins. Bidding them good-bye, he went on alone.

CHAPTER
4
in the valleys of humility and death

Attacked by Apollyon

IN THE VALLEY OF HUMILITY, Christian had severe trials. He had not gone far when he saw the fiend Apollyon coming across the field toward him. The sight of him filled Christian with fear, and he began to wonder what he should do. Should he go back in haste, or stand his ground, going calmly on his way, as if he had no fears? Then it occurred to him that he had no armor for his back, and to turn his back to the enemy would give him the opportunity to pierce his back with darts. He decided to hold his ground and keep straight on his way; that would demonstrate his faith, uphold his principles, and be safer for his person than turning and running away.

Soon Apollyon came near. He was a hideous monster to behold: he was covered with scales like a fish, of which he was very proud; he had wings like a dragon, feet like a bear, and a mouth like a lion; and out of his belly came fire and smoke. He came up and stared at Christian with a most horrible look, and asked: "Stranger, where did you come from and where are you going?"

CHRISTIAN: I am from the City of Destruction, and I'm going to the City of Zion.

APOLLYON: Then you are one of my subjects, for all that country of Destruction belongs to me; I'm the prince and god of it. Why have you run away from your king? Were it not that I might get more service out of you, I would strike you down right here.

CHRISTIAN: I was indeed born in your dominion; but your service was too hard, and your wages were such that no one could live on them, for the wages of sin is death.[1] Therefore, when I had opportunity, I did like many others—I left that miserable country to find a better life.

APOLLYON: You must know that no prince in that dominion gives up his subjects willingly; neither will I give you up. But since you complain of the service and wages, we can fix that. You go back, and whatever the country can afford in the way of pay, I will see that you get it.

CHRISTIAN: But I have now given myself to another—to the King of all princes—and I cannot go back.

APOLLYON: You have done according to the proverb. You have gone from bad to worse. You have "jumped out of the frying pan into the fire." But it is common for those who have accepted your King's promise and given themselves to His service, after trying that way for a while, to give Him the slip and return to my dominion. You do the same, and all shall be well.

CHRISTIAN: My Lord has taken my burden and given me peace. I have given Him my faith, and sworn my allegiance to Him. If I go back now, I should be hanged as a traitor.

APOLLYON: You did the same to me, but I am willing to forget it, if you will go back and be loyal to your former master.

CHRISTIAN: What I promised you was in my youth, before I knew any better way. But now the Prince I serve is able to absolve me, and pardon all that I did while in your service. And

[1]Rom. 6:23.

besides, to tell you the truth, Mr. Apollyon, I like His service, His wages, His servants, His government, His company, and His country much better than yours and all you can promise—and you have never been one to keep your promise. I am His servant, and I will follow Him.

APOLLYON: That is pure sentiment. Consider again in cold blood, what you are likely to encounter in the way you have chosen. You know that, for the most part, His followers suffer reproaches, perils, weariness, stripes, stonings, imprisonment, pain and death, all because they oppose me and my kingdom. Think how many of them have been put to horrible death! And your Master never came from His mysterious, invisible, exalted dwelling place to deliver them. How can you count His service better than mine? Not many of my servants have ever been martyred. All the world knows very well that I deliver, either by power or by fraud, those who have followed me, from your Master and His power. And be sure I will deliver you.

CHRISTIAN: When He, for a time, does not deliver His servants from trouble, it is for their good;[2] it strengthens their faith and their love for the right, and affords an opportunity for them to show the sincerity of their love and add to their rewards.[3] And as for the death you speak of, it is only temporary. He delivers His servants out of death, and gives them a perfect life beyond. His servants do not expect immediate deliverance from the petty dangers and discomforts of this present perishing world, but are willing to wait on the Lord, knowing full well that they shall be more than well rewarded for all their sufferings, when He comes in His glory with all His holy angels.

APOLLYON: But you have already been unfaithful to Him.

CHRISTIAN: Wherein have I been unfaithful to Him?

APOLLYON: You stumbled and fell into the Slough of Despond; you turned aside out of the way to go to Legality's

[2]Rom. 8:28.
[3]Rom. 8:18.

house for help at the advice of one Worldly Wiseman; you slept and lost your book on the way; you were ready to turn back at the sight of the chained lions; and when you talk of what you have seen and heard in the way, and all your Lord has done for you, it is with a certain inward desire for vain glory.

CHRISTIAN: All this is true, and much more which you have left out. But the Prince I serve is merciful, and ready to forgive.

APOLLYON (*breaking into a terrific rage*): I am an enemy to this Prince. I hate His laws, His person, and His people. I have come for the purpose of arresting you.

CHRISTIAN: Be careful, Apollyon, what you do. I am in the King's highway, the way of holiness, and I am in His service. Therefore, take heed that you do not overstep your bounds.

Then Apollyon sprang across the highway in front of Christian, and said, " I am without fear in this matter. Prepare yourself to die, for I swear by all the infernal powers that you shall go no farther. I will take your soul right here." Then he hurled a flaming dart at Christian's heart. But Christian held out his shield and blocked it. Christian drew his sword and braced himself for battle. Apollyon came at him in fury, throwing darts as thick as hail. Some struck above and some below Christian's shield, wounding him painfully, in spite of all he could do to defend himself. Then he fell back a little. Seeing this, Apollyon came on with all his force. Here Christian remembered his effectual prayer and took courage. They fought up and down the highway for over half an hour, and Christian's strength was almost spent from loss of blood and sheer exhaustion. Apollyon perceived that Christian was gradually growing weaker. Taking advantage of this, he took hold of Christian and threw him to the ground. Then Christian's sword flew out of his hand. "Now," said Apollyon, "I am sure I have you," and he almost beat him to death.

But, as God would have it, as Apollyon gave his final blows to finish him off, Christian's hand touched his sword, which gave him fresh spirit. He gripped the sword with all his might and said, "Rejoice not against me, O my enemy: when I fall, I shall rise again,"[4] giving Apollyon a deadly thrust which caused him to fall back as if mortally wounded. Summoning all his strength, Christian rose to his feet and advanced toward him, crying, "In all these things we are more than conquerors through him that loved us."[5] This was too much for Apollyon; he spread his wings and flew away.

The battle over, Christian, breathing heavily, said, "I will give thanks to Him who delivered me out of the mouth of the lion and has helped me to defeat Apollyon."

Then there came to him a hand of mercy with healing leaves from the tree of life. Christian took the leaves and applied them to his wounds, which were soon healed. He sat down in that place to eat bread and drink from the bottle that was given him by Prudence. Now, being refreshed, he resumed his journey, with his sword in his hand, saying, "I do not know but that some other enemy may attack me."

Horrors of the Valley of Death

Beyond this valley was a deeper valley—the Valley of the Shadow of Death—where Christian suffered more than in the Valley of Humility. In my dream, I saw him come to the edge of this deep valley where he met two men, Self-love and Critic, coming back in a hurry. They were descendants of the spies who brought back an evil report of the good land of Canaan.

"Where are you going?" asked Christian.

They shouted, "Back! Back! We are going back, and you had better do the same, if you love your life."

[4]Micah 7:8.
[5]Rom. 8:37.

CHRISTIAN: Why, what is your trouble?

"Trouble! We were going down this same road you are traveling, and we went as far as we dared. In fact, we were almost past coming back; for had we gone but a little farther, we would not be here to tell the story and warn you."

CHRISTIAN: But what have you seen?

"Why, we were almost in the Valley of the Shadow of Death, when, as luck would have it, we saw the danger before we came to it."

CHRISTIAN: But what did you see?

"What did we see? Why, the valley itself! It was as dark as pitch. We saw the hobgoblins, satyrs, and dragons of the pit. We heard also hideous sounds—continual howlings and screamings, sounding like a great many miserable souls in iron chains of afflictions. And over the valley hung a dark cloud of confusion, and the Angel of Death hovered over it all. That valley is exceedingly dreadful and utterly without order."

CHRISTIAN: I fail to be convinced by what you say that this is not my way to the desired haven.

"You may have it your way," they said, "but as for us, we want none of it. We're going back."

So they went back and Christian went on his way, with his sword drawn ready for an attack.

Now he saw on one side of the road a very deep ditch—where the blind for centuries have led the blind—from which none have ever emerged; and on the other was a filthy quagmire where the lustful of all ages have fallen and have found no bottom for their feet. King David once fell in here and would have drowned had not the merciful Lord of all lifted him out.

The path between the ditch and the quagmire was exceedingly narrow and Christian had to be extremely cautious to stay on it. It was almost like walking a tight rope over the bottomless pit in the dark. To go on was very dangerous, but it was just as hazardous to attempt to turn and go back. He crept along, feeling his way, not knowing what minute he might come to the end of the path and plunge downward into death. In the middle of the valley, close by the path, was the mouth of Hell, from which came flames and smoke, rolling out toward the path. And there were hideous noises and doleful voices, against which Christian's sword was ineffective; yet he had another weapon that was always effective: "Effectual fervent prayer."[6] So he cried, "O Lord, I beseech Thee, deliver my soul." Then he had a little more faith.

He went on quite a distance, while flames occasionally leaped out toward him, and he continued to hear those dreadful noises. He heard sounds as of something rushing to and fro in front of him, making him feel as if he might be torn to pieces or crushed like a clod in the street. This continued to harass him for miles. Then he thought he heard a mob of fiends coming toward him. He stopped to decide what to do. He had half a notion to go back; yet he reasoned he might be halfway across the valley. Realizing that he had already passed many dangers and, thinking that the risks behind might be greater than those before him, he resolved to go on. Still the fiends seemed to come nearer and nearer. But when they came almost to him, he cried with a loud voice, "I will walk in the strength of the Lord God." Hearing those words, they drew back and came no farther.

I must not forget to record one thing: When Christian came near to the burning pit, he became so confused that he did not know his own voice. Just as he was passing by the pit a demon stole up behind him and whispered insulting blasphemies against God in his ears, which blasphemies Christian thought had proceeded from his own mind. This troubled him very much—more than any wrong he had done thus far on the

[6]James 5:16.

Christian advances through the Valley of the Shadow of Death.

way—because the wicked thoughts and words were so bitter and so utterly unjust against the One he loved the most, the One who had done the most for him. Yet it seemed that he could not help thinking these words and whispering them to himself. But he did not know where the evil words came from nor how to stop his ears from hearing them.

After he had traveled in this disconsolate state for some time, he thought he heard a voice up ahead of him saying, "Though I walk through the valley of the shadow of death, I will fear no evil; for thou art with me."[7] Now he was glad because: First, he believed that someone who feared God was in this dismal valley as well as himself. Second, he believed God was with that person, whoever he was, or he could never have spoken such words. And he said, "If God is with him, then He is also with me, or I never would have heard these good words in such a place, though here I did not realize it." Third, he was glad because he believed he could overtake this person and have good company the rest of the way. So he hurried on as fast as he could go, calling to the one before. But there was no reply. Whoever was in the path ahead of him must not have known the meaning of what he heard, or its source, thinking that he himself was alone on the road, and so he did not answer.

Emerges from Darkness of Valley

But now the day was dawning. Viewing the eastern hills, Christian said to himself, "He hath turned the shadows of death into the morning." Looking back over the way he had come, he wondered how the Lord had gotten him through. He remembered the verse: "He discovereth deep things out of darkness, and bringeth out to light the shadow of death."[8] He was deeply moved when he saw all the dangers from which he had been delivered.

[7]Ps. 23:4.
[8]Job 12:22.

Now the sun was shining, and this was indeed a great blessing because the worst part of the road was still ahead. Before him to the end of the valley were snares, traps, pitfalls, slippery places, large, gaping holes, and deep pits. No one could have ever avoided them all in the dark, and not to avoid them would have meant certain death. But now he could see his way, and he went on past them all, saying, "His candle shineth on my head, and by His light I go through darkness."

In this light from above he came to the end of the valley. Now, in my dream, I saw these at the end of the valley: blood, ashes, bones, and thousands of mangled bodies of faithful pilgrims who had gone this way. While I was wondering what had caused this wholesale murdering of human beings, I saw a little before me a cave where two giants, Pope and Pagan, dwelt in old times. By their power and tryranny the men and women whose bones and ashes lay before me were cruelly put to death.

When Christian went by this place without danger, I wondered why he was not molested. Then I learned that Pagan had been dead many a day and that Pope was very old. I also learned that because of Pope's many brushes with the government in his younger days he had grown so crazy and stiff in his joints that about all he could do now was sit in the mouth of his cave, grinning at pilgrims as they went by and biting his nails because he could not now get at them.

At the sight of the old giant, Christian didn't know what to think, until the giant said, "You will never mend your ways until more of you are burned." But Christian held his peace with an unperturbed face, and went by the Pope's slaughter ground unhurt.

CHAPTER

5

christian and faithful

Faithful Is Joined by Christian

NOW CHRISTIAN ASCENDED a little mound, which had been made that pilgrims might see the road ahead. Then he saw Faithful on the road. He shouted: "Ho, ho! Wait, and I'll go with you." He saw Faithful look back. "Wait," Christian cried, "till I catch up." But Faithful answered, "No, I have an enemy on my trail and I must not lose any time."

This put Christian on his mettle and, putting out all his energy, he soon caught up with Faithful and, being elated, ran past him. Then Christian turned and smiled with a little vainglory because he had gotten ahead of his brother. But, not watching his steps, he stumbled and fell and, being a little fatigued, he could not get up immediately. Then Faithful came and helped him to his feet.

CHRISTIAN: My honored and well beloved Faithful, I am so glad to see you, and glad that God has tempered our spirits that we can walk together in this wonderful way.

FAITHFUL: My dear friend, I wanted to have your company from the very first when I left our town, but you had gotten too much of a start on me, and I had to come all these miles alone.

CHRISTIAN: How long did you stay in the City of Destruction after I left?

Faithful Tells of Gossip Back Home

FAITHFUL: Till I could stay no longer, for soon after you left there was a lot of talk that our city would in a short time be burned to the ground by fire from heaven.

CHRISTIAN: What? Did your neighbors talk that way?

FAITHFUL: Yes, for a while it was all the talk of the neighborhood.

CHRISTIAN: If they talked that way, why did no one else but you leave the place to escape the dangers?

FAITHFUL: Well, there was much talk about the report. Yet I do not think they believed it was true, for in the heat of discussion I heard them adversely criticizing you for leaving the town at so inopportune time on such a risky journey. Yet I believed—and still believe—that the report is true, that the city will be destroyed by fire and brimstone from heaven.

CHRISTIAN: Did you hear any of them speak of neighbor Pliable?

FAITHFUL: Yes, Christian, I heard that he followed you to the Slough of Despond where, as some said, he fell in—though he did not want that known. Yet I am sure it happened, because he had that kind of dirt on him.

CHRISTIAN: And what did his neighbors say to him?

FAITHFUL: Oh, they all condemned him; some despised and mocked him; and scarcely any of them would have anything to do with him. He is now seven times worse off than if he had never left the city.

CHRISTIAN: But why should they be so hard on him, since they themselves despise the road he forsook?

FAITHFUL: Oh, they said, "Hang him; he is a turncoat; he was not true to his profession." This seems to be one of the evil quirks of human nature, to condemn others for things you do yourself.

CHRISTIAN: Did you have occasion to talk with him any before you left?

FAITHFUL: No, I met him on the street one day. But he crossed over to the other side, as if he were ashamed of what he had done; so I did not say anything.

CHRISTIAN: Well, at first I had hopes of that fellow, but now I fear he will perish with the city. For it has happened to him according to the true proverb which says, "The dog is turned to his vomit again, and the sow that was washed to her wallowing in the mire."[1]

FAITHFUL: Those are my fears for him, too, but who can hinder that which will be?

CHRISTIAN: Well, tell me, neighbor Faithful, what happened to you on the way.

Faithful Recounts His Temptations

FAITHFUL: Well, I escaped the big slough, which I heard you fell into, and I got up to the gate without much trouble. But I met with a pretty clever woman, whose name was Mrs. Wanton. She almost turned me from the right way into the way of destruction.

CHRISTIAN: It is well you escaped her net. You remember Joseph fell into the company of such a woman, and he escaped her; but it almost cost him his life.[2] King David was tempted in something of the same way, only he was "drawn away of his own lust and enticed,"[3] and he fell into the quagmire of corruption you saw back there in the valley. While it is true the merciful Lord lifted him out, yet he had trouble all the rest of his life.

[1]II Peter 2:22.
[2]Gen. 39:11-20.
[3]James 1:14.

FAITHFUL: You cannot imagine (unless you have had a similar experience) what a flattering tongue that woman had. She complimented my courage and good judgment in choosing the right way; she spoke of my seeming strength and healthy appearance, and said she thought I would be a lovely person to know. She asked questions about my book and manner of life, as if she might be interested in the way of salvation. She wondered if it were possible to attain to the original innocence of Adam and Eve. I suspected that she was trying to attract me to her trim figure by her behavior and sympathetic understanding of human nature. Yet she had a good personality, likable ways, and an agreeable attitude. She was so attractive, especially when she spoke of human freedom and natural love, that she almost persuaded me to turn aside with her. "Just a little way," she said, "just for a few moments of pleasure." She promised me all kinds of contentment, and said if there was anything wrong about it, the good Lord would forgive me, as He did David.

CHRISTIAN: I'm sure she did not promise you the contentment of a good conscience.

FAITHFUL: No, you know what I mean—all kinds of carnal contentment and fleshly satisfaction.

CHRISTIAN: Thank God you escaped her! "The mouth of strange women is a deep pit; and he that is abhorred of the Lord shall fall therein."[4]

FAITHFUL: But I do not know whether I wholly escaped her or not.

CHRISTIAN: Why, I trust you did not consent to her treachery.

FAITHFUL: Oh, no, she wanted to go the limit, but I did not defile my body. I remembered a sacred warning which says: "Her feet go down to death; her steps take hold on hell."[5] So

[4]Prov. 22:14.
[5]Prov. 5:5.

I closed my mind to her subtle, seductive suggestions, and my eyes to her shapely figure, and would not yield to her warm embraces. Then she cursed me, and went her way. Yet, I cannot say that I have acquired a wholly pure mind since. The Lord knows I wish I had never met her.

CHRISTIAN: But maybe you will be stronger and will be able to help others avoid this great danger. But did you meet with any other temptation on the way?

FAITHFUL: Yes, when I came to the foot of the Hill Difficulty, I met a very old man, who asked me who I was and where I was going. I told him I was a pilgrim going to the Celestial City. Then he said, "You look like an honest fellow. Would you like to dwell with me for the wages I will pay you?"

I asked him his name and where he lived. He said his name was Adam the First, and he lived in the town of Deceit. I asked him then what his work was and how much he paid his help. He said his work was hoarding and enjoying the things of the world, and my pay would be to inherit everything he had. I further asked him what kind of house he kept and what other servants he had. He told me that his house was provided with all the luxuries of life, and his servants were his three daughters: Lust-of-the-Flesh, Lust-of-the-Eyes, and Pride-of-Life.[6] They had charge of all his work, and they would be delighted to have me. Either one—or all three—would marry me if I would but gratify their wishes. I asked him how long he would want me to live with him. He said as long as he lived; then I might remain in the house as long as I lived, or do whatever I would with the property. I would not then need to go on self-denying pilgrimages. I could pay the traveling expenses of other pilgrims. Many would reach the Celestial City by means of my money.

[6]I John 2:16.

CHRISTIAN: Well, what conclusion did you and the old man come to?

FAITHFUL: Why, at first I was inclined to accept his offer. He seemed to be fair, and quite reasonable. But then I remembered the words of an old faithful pilgrim, the Apostle Paul: "Be not deceived; God is not mocked: . . . he that soweth to his flesh shall of the flesh reap corruption."[7] Then, looking at his face as he talked to me, I saw these words written across his forehead: "Put off the old man with his deeds."

CHRISTIAN: Then what?

FAITHFUL: Then the thought came to me that this old man wanted me for his slave, and once he got me into his house he would be ready to sell me to anyone who had the money. So I told him I could not give up my pilgrimage to live such a life with him; that I would not consider it, not for all he had. Then he denounced me as a fool and a bigot, and said he would send one after me who would make my way miserable. I turned to go, and just as I turned from him he threw his arms around my body, saying that I was his son in the first place, and he gave me such a pull backward that I thought I would be pulled in two before I could get loose from him. Then I cried, "O wretched man,"[8] and I felt an invisible One take hold of me on the other side, pulling me toward the top of the hill. So I went on my way up the hill. About halfway up the hill, I looked back and saw one coming after me, swift as an eagle. This one overtook me where the arbor stands.

CHRISTIAN: That is where I sat down to rest and went to sleep, and lost this precious book out of my bosom.

FAITHFUL: Well, isn't that strange? But hear the rest of my story: As soon as my pursuer overtook me, he blurted out something and struck me a terrific blow. When I recovered sufficiently, I asked him why he did it. He said that because of

[7]Gal. 6:7-8.
[8]Rom. 7:24.

my secret inclination to Adam the First, I rightly belonged to his house. Then he struck me again, completely knocking me out. When I came to, I begged for mercy. He said, "The law knows no mercy," and with that he knocked me down again. He doubtless would have killed me, but just then the One who freed me from old man Adam came by and ordered him to desist.

CHRISTIAN: Do you know who that person was?

FAITHFUL: I did not know at first, but as He went by I saw scars in His hands and feet, and I knew He was our Lord.

CHRISTIAN: That man who pursued you was Moses, or one of his men. Moses spares no one and knows no mercy. With him all must pay the penalty of a broken law. His absolute rule is: "The soul that sinneth, it shall die."[9]

FAITHFUL: I know it very well. It is not the first time I had met with him. One time, back home, he told me that he would burn my house over my head if I stayed there.

CHRISTIAN: Not changing the subject, but did you see the big house on the top of the hill a little above where Moses overtook you?

FAITHFUL: Yes, and the lions, too, in front of the house. But I think the lions were asleep, for it was about noon. I had so much of the day before me, I passed by the Porter and came on down the hill.

CHRISTIAN: Yes, the Porter told me he saw you go by. Those lions were chained. I wish you had stopped at that house, at least for a day. They would have gladly received you. Their hospitality and fellowship are wonderful. They would have shown you many things that you could never forget. But pray tell me, did you meet with anyone in the Valley of Humility?

[9]Ezek. 18:4.

Faithful Relates Meeting with Discontent

FAITHFUL: Yes, I met one Discontent, who tried to persuade me to go back with him. He said the valley was void of honor. He said in the valley was the place to lose all self-confidence, and the confidence and respect of your kindred and friends; that my Mr. Pride, Mr. Arrogancy, Egotist, Worldly-glory, and others would have nothing more to do with me after I had been in that valley. "They think," he said, "no wise, self-respecting person will go there."

CHRISTIAN: How did you answer him?

FAITHFUL: I admitted that those he named might in one sense claim to be my kin (in fact they were related to me in the flesh), but that since I had become a pilgrim they all disowned me, as I had rejected them. I told him that now they are no more to me than those who have never been of my lineage. I also told him that he had gotten the wrong impression concerning the valley; that the valley, while having many unpleasant things, provided necessary discipline for pilgrims. I said, "Before honor is humility, and a haughty spirit goes before a fall. Therefore, I had rather go through this valley to real honor—honor that is so recognized by the wisest of men—than choose that which is esteemed most worthy by you and the worldly minded."

CHRISTIAN: Did you encounter anything else in the valley?

Faithful Relates Meeting with Mr. Shame

FAITHFUL: Yes, I met one Mr. Shame—he said his name was Shame—yet after I got a little acquainted with him I thought he had the wrong name and might be going under an assumed name. He was ashamed all right, but not of himself (which he might well have been), nor of anything he said or did; he was ashamed of me and the pilgrim way.

CHRISTIAN: Why, what did he say to you?

FAITHFUL: He objected to my religion. He said it was a

pitiful, low, shameful business for a person to surrender his will and life to become a servant of religion; that a tender conscience was an unmanly weakness; and that for a person to watch over his own words, attitude, and conduct, tying himself down to rules that destroyed his liberty—which all brave people of these times have accustomed themselves to—would make him the ridicule and laughingstock of present-day society.

He pointed out that not many wise men, not many noble, not many great men of our times were out-and-out pilgrims. He said the pilgrims were mostly the unfortunate, the ignorant, and the low-income people; that those of the higher class who professed to favor the pilgrim way had an ax to grind; they did it for profit or selfish reasons.

He tried to make me ashamed of many things which pilgrims believe in and practice. He said it was a shame for a man to sit whining and mourning under a sermon and then come sighing and groaning home; that it was a shame to ask my neighbor for forgiveness for petty faults, or make restitution for wrongs done to others.

CHRISTIAN: And what did you say to him?

FAITHFUL: I hardly knew what to say at first. I felt the blood come up in my face; perhaps I was ashamed of myself for not having a good, ready answer. But, thank the Lord, at last I thought of the Master's words: "That which is highly esteemed among men is an abomination in the sight of God."[10] Then I said, "Shame, you tell me what men are and what they will do, but you tell me nothing about God. On the day of judgment, I will not be asked what men thought of me; nor will I be judged by what you and the world think. But I will be judged by God's Word. What God says is best, though all the world be against it. Seeing then that God has chosen this way for men and desires a tender conscience, and seeing that they who are willing to

[10]Luke 16:15.

become fools in the eyes of the world for His sake are wisest and that the poor man who loves Christ is richer than the greatest man in the world who rejects Him, you may go your way and leave me! You are an enemy to my salvation. My Lord says, 'Whosoever shall be ashamed of me and of my words, of him will I be ashamed when I come in the glory of my Father.' If I entertain you, an enemy of my soul and of Christ Jesus, against the sovereign will of my Lord, then how shall I face Him when He comes, and how shall I expect His blessings?"

But I found that Shame was a bold and persistent villain. He was not to be easily shaken off. He continued to follow me, whispering in my ear at times about my insincerity, my blunders, and all the imperfections of pilgrims. But at last I told him he might as well shut up, that he himself was a hypocrite, that I gloried in my infirmities, and that all his talk was in vain. And at last I got past him, then I began to sing:

> Temptations to a pilgrim given
> (If he's obeyed the call from Heaven)
> From ev'ry side attack his flesh.
> They come, and then come back afresh
> That they may overcome the man
> And quite destroy him, if they can!
> So, pilgrim, guard against the wrong,
> And in thy mighty God be strong!

CHRISTIAN: I am glad you withstood this villain so well. I quite agree with you that he has the wrong name; for he is so bold as to follow us in the streets and attempt to put us to shame before all men; that is, to make us ashamed of that which is good. He would not do this if he were not so brazen. But let us still resist him; for, notwithstanding all his seeming bravery, he is in reality the chief of fools: "For the wise shall inherit glory," said Solomon, "but shame shall be the promotion of fools."[11]

[11]Prov. 3:35.

FAITHFUL: Yes, I think we must cry to Him who would have us be valiant for truth to help us against this imposter, Shame, that we may rid ourselves of his presence and influence; though we must be very careful not to offend our good friend and helper, Humility.

CHRISTIAN: You speak the truth, my brother. But did you meet with any other trouble in the valley?

FAITHFUL: No, for I had sunshine all the rest of the way through that valley and also through the Valley of the Shadow of Death.

CHRISTIAN: Good! It is well for you that you did.

Now, as they went on their way, there was a man walking on the far side of the road from them, going in the same direction. His name was Talkative.

Faithful called out to him: "Friend, which way? Are you going to the heavenly country?"

TALKATIVE: Yes, that is where I am going.

FAITHFUL: Fine, then I hope we may have your good company.

Christian and Faithful Joined by Talkative

TALKATIVE (*coming across the road*): Sure, I will be delighted to go with you.

FAITHFUL: Come on then and let us walk together; we can talk of things that are helpful.

TALKATIVE: That suits me fine. To talk of things that are good, with you or anyone else, is very acceptable to me. I am glad to meet with those who are interested in the better things of life; for, to tell you the truth, there are very few these days who want to talk about things of value. Most of our generation are interested only in the trivial things of no profit; this has been a heartache to me.

FAITHFUL: That is indeed regrettable, for what in this world is more worthy of our conversation than the things of God?

TALKATIVE: I like you very much. Your words are full of conviction. And what else is so pleasant and profitable, as to talk of things eternal? That is, if a person has any interest in that which is marvelous and enduring. For instance, if a person likes to discuss history or the mysteries of life, or if he loves to think of miracles, where will he find records so trustworthy or so beautifully related as in the Holy Scriptures?

FAITHFUL: That's true, but to be benefited by these things should be our aim.

TALKATIVE: That's what I say. To talk of these things is most profitable, for by so doing a man may get knowledge of many things, such as the vanity of earthly things and the value of things above. That is general; but to be specific, by this a man may learn the necessity of the new birth; the insufficiency of our works; the need of Christ's righteousness, and so on. Besides, by this a man may learn what it is to repent, to believe, to pray, to suffer, and the like. Also, by this you may learn what are the great promises and consolations of the Gospel, to your own comfort, and learn to refute false doctrines and opinions, to vindicate the truth, and also to instruct the ignorant.

FAITHFUL: All this is true; and I am glad to hear you say these things.

TALKATIVE: Alas! the lack of them is the cause of so few understanding the need of faith and the necessity of a work of grace in the heart in order to have abundant life, and of so many ignorantly living in the works of the law, by which no one can gain the kingdom of Heaven.

FAITHFUL: Yes, but heavenly knowledge of these is the gift of God; no man attains to them by human effort or by only talking of them.

TALKATIVE: All that I know very well, for a man can receive

nothing except it be given him from above. All is of grace, not of works. I could give you a hundred scriptures to verify this.

FAITHFUL: Well, then, what is the one thing that we shall discuss at this time?

TALKATIVE: Whatever you wish. I will talk of things heavenly or things earthly, things moral or things spiritual, things sacred or things profane, things past or things to come, things foreign or things at home, things essential or things circumstantial, provided that all be done in a profitable way.

FAITHFUL (*wondering a little what kind of person Talkative was, as Talkative was slowing up, walked up beside Christian, who was a few steps ahead, and spoke to him*): What a brave, well-informed companion we have. Surely he will make an excellent pilgrim.

CHRISTIAN (*modestly smiling*): This fellow, with his tongue, will mislead those who do not know him.

FAITHFUL: Do you know him, then?

CHRISTIAN: Know him! Yes, better than he knows himself.

FAITHFUL: Pray, tell me what kind of person he is.

CHRISTIAN: His name is Talkative, and he is from our town. I am surprised that you do not know him, even though our town is quite large.

FAITHFUL: Whose son is he, and where does he live?

CHRISTIAN: He is the Son of one Saywell. He lives on Prating·Row, and he is known to all who are acquainted with him as Talkative of Prating Row. Notwithstanding his large vocabulary and his glib, smooth tongue, he is a sorry fellow.

FAITHFUL: Well, but he seems to be true.

CHRISTIAN: Yes, away from home, to those who are not well acquainted with him. Like some artists' pictures you have seen, he looks best at a distance.

FAITHFUL: But you smiled, which almost led me to think you were jesting.

CHRISTIAN: God forbid that I should jest about this man or anyone else. Maybe I should not have smiled, but I was only smiling at your high opinion of him. Far be it from me to falsely accuse anyone; yet I will tell you the type of fellow he is. He is for any kind of company and any kind of talk. He prides himself on being adaptable. Like a chameleon, he changes his color every time he changes his environment. He can talk just as easily in a tavern as he is talking to you; and the more he drinks, the more he talks. Pure religion has no place in his heart, in his house, or in his daily living. His religion is only in his tongue. He uses religion for pastime conversation to entertain.

FAITHFUL: Is that so? Then, I am greatly deceived in him.

CHRISTIAN: Deceived you are, if you think he is a sincere pilgrim. Remember the proverb: "They say and do not."[12] But "the Kingdom of God is not in word, but in power."[13] When he talks of prayer, repentance, faith, and the new birth, he is not speaking of his own personal experience but merely repeating what he has heard. I have been in his home, and I have observed him both at home and abroad, and I know whereof I speak. His house is as void of the religion of Christ as the white of an egg is of flavor. In his life there is no sign of prayer or repentance. He is the very stain and reproach of Christianity to all who know him. The name of Christ is scorned in all that end of town because of him. Many of his neighbors say of him: "A saint abroad, and a devil at home." His family find it so. He is a rude, uncouth boor, with a temper like a buzz-saw and a tongue like a scorpion. When he gets angry, he can curse a blue streak. Those who have dealings with him say it is better to deal with an outlaw. If possible, he will go beyond what an ordinary crook will do to deceive, cheat, and defraud; yet, for his own safety, he manages to stay within the bounds of the law.

Besides, he is bringing up his sons to follow in his steps. And

[12]Matt. 23:3.
[13]I Cor. 4:20.

if he finds any one of them yielding to a sensitive conscience, he calls him a stupid blockhead and a timid fool. For my part, I am of the opinion that he, by his wicked life, has caused many to stumble and fall and, unless God prevents, he will be the ruin of many more.

FAITHFUL: Well, Christian, I'm bound to believe you, not only because you say you know him, but also because I know you are a truthful man. I cannot think that you speak these things from ill will, but I believe they are true and you think fellow pilgrims should know them.

CHRISTIAN: If I had known him no longer than you have, I might have thought of him as you did at first. Or if the source of my information had been only those who reject the Christian religion, I would have thought it was slander, which often comes from malicious tongues against good men's names and professions. But, of all these things—yes, and many more just as bad—I can prove him guilty by my own knowledge. Besides, the best of men are ashamed of him; the mention of his name to those who know him makes them blush.

FAITHFUL: Well, I see that saying and doing are two different things, and hereafter I shall watch that distinction more closely.

CHRISTIAN: They are indeed two entirely different things, as different as the soul and the body. For, as the body without the soul is dead, so saying alone is nothing but a dead carcass. The proof of pure religion is its fruits. "Pure religion and undefiled before God and the Father is this, to visit the fatherless and the widows in their affliction, and to keep oneself unspotted from the world."[14] Of this, Talkative is wholly unaware. He thinks that hearing and talking the Christian religion constitutes a Christian. Hearing is only momentarily receiving the seed in the mind, and talking about it is not sufficient proof that fruit

[14]James 1:27.

is indeed in the heart and life. And let us assure ourselves that, at the day of judgment, men shall be judged according to their fruits.

Paul says that one may speak with the tongues of men and angels and have not the love of God or charity, being nothing more than sounding brass or a tinkling cymbal.[15] Words giving no life, though spoken by men or angels, shall never be heard in the kingdom of Heaven among the children of life.

FAITHFUL: Well, I was not too fond of his company at the very first, but I am sick of it now. What shall we do to be rid of him?

CHRISTIAN: Why, go to him and start a serious discussion about the power of true faith to transform one's life, and ask him plainly whether this divine power is in his heart and life, and how it affects his home, and his everyday living.

FAITHFUL (*dropping back in company with Talkative*): Now since you left it to me to choose the subject, let it be this: How does the saving grace of God manifest itself in the heart and life of men?

TALKATIVE: I see then that our conversation is to be about the power of things, and that is a very good subject and you have asked an important question. I shall be glad to answer briefly. First, the grace of God in the heart causes a strong outcry against sin. Second—

FAITHFUL: Just a minute. Let's take one thing at a time. I think the grace of God shows itself by causing the soul to abhor its sins.

TALKATIVE: Well, what is the difference between crying out against and abhorring sin?

FAITHFUL: Why, a great deal. It is considered a good policy by some to cry out against sin. But no one can abhor sin except by a godly distaste for it. I have heard preachers cry out against

[15]I Cor. 13:1.

sin in the pulpit, who nevertheless welcomed sin in their heart and home and private life. Joseph's mistress cried out with a loud voice against what she falsely accused Joseph of, as if she had been very chaste, yet she had tried—and failed—to seduce Joseph to commit fornication with her. Some cry out against sin like a mother who scolds the baby in her lap, calling it a brat, or pig, then hugs it to her bosom and kisses it fondly.

TALKATIVE: I see, you like to set traps.

FAITHFUL: Oh, no, I only want to set things straight. But what is the second way you would prove that a man has the grace of God in his heart?

TALKATIVE: When he has extensive knowledge of Gospel truth.

FAITHFUL: This sign should have been first. But first or last, it is also false; for great knowledge may be obtained from others about Gospel truth, including the work of grace in a man's heart, by one who does not have that grace in his own heart. Paul says a man may have all knowledge, and understand all mysteries, and yet be nothing.[16] Christ said, "If you know these things, happy are you if you do them."[17] He did not say happy are you if you know them. He does not place the blessing in the knowledge that produces no doing. It is not enough just to know the truth, one must obey it. Therefore, your sign is of no value. Extensive knowledge pleases talkers and boasters, but a faithful obedient heart pleases God. Not that the heart can be made right without true knowledge. For without that it is untrustworthy. But knowledge without experience and good works is vain. "Give me understanding," says the Psalmist, "and I shall keep thy law; yea, I shall observe it with my whole heart."[18]

TALKATIVE: I see, you have studied the Holy Scriptures for

[16]I Cor. 13:2.
[17]John 13:17.
[18]Ps. 119:34.

argumentation, and to catch people up in their speech. This is not edifying.

FAITHFUL: Well, perhaps you have another sign or proof of this work of saving grace in the heart.

TALKATIVE: No, not I. And I see we shall not agree.

FAITHFUL: Well, if you do not have proofs, I will give mine, with your permission.

TALKATIVE: Use your own judgment.

FAITHFUL: A work of grace in the soul manifests itself both to him who has it, and to all who know him.

The grace of God in a person's heart brings a conviction of sin, especially the sin of unbelief, and reveals the defilement of one's nature; for which one feels sure he will be eternally condemned unless he finds the mercy of God through faith in the Lord Jesus Christ. This conviction and outlook works in him a deep sorrow and shame for sin. Then, through the power of the Holy Spirit and the Word of God, is revealed to him the Lamb of God (the perfect sacrifice for sin, the Saviour of the world) and the necessity of accepting Him at once as the only way of salvation. This creates in him a hunger and thirst for righteousness, which leads him to repent and believe on Christ for forgiveness and salvation. Now, the depth of his joy and peace, his love and holiness, his increase in knowledge and service to Christ, are determined by the amount and strength of his faith. And one's faith will grow with use, overcoming doubt and fear, self-condemnation, confusion, misunderstanding of inner experiences, and one's selfish, carnal, distorted reason, judgment and imagination. All this is irrefutable evidence to oneself that he has the grace of God.

This grace manifests itself to others in two ways: First, by an open confession of faith in Christ and being baptized in His name and uniting with others who believe in Him. Second, by a life lived in harmony with His teaching; to wit, praying daily for guidance and strength, earnestly studying God's Word to learn and do His will, witnessing to others of His saving grace, and giving of his time and money for service to Christ and others. By this, his family and neighbors know that he loves God and humanity not in word only but in deed and in truth. A hypocrite can talk of these things, but to have them and do them one must be a child of God.

Now, this is but a brief description of the work of grace, and how it is manifested to men. If you have an objection, feel free to express it. If not, may I propound to you a second question?

TALKATIVE: No, my part now is not to object but to hear. Therefore, let me have your second question.

FAITHFUL: It is this: Have you experienced the first part of this manifestation in your heart, and do your life and daily conduct demonstrate it to others? Or does your religion consist only in talk and not in deed and in truth? Now, please, if you feel disposed at all to answer this, say no more than what you know to be the truth and what God will be pleased with, and no more than what your own conscience will approve; for "not he that commendeth himself is approved, but whom the Lord commendeth."[19] Besides, to say I am thus and so, when my daily living and all my neighbors tell me I lie, is downright wicked.

TALKATIVE (*beginning to blush but recovering a little from his embarrassment*): You have gone into this matter of experience, conscience, and God; and of appealing to God for justification of what is said or done. This kind of questioning I did not expect, because I think these are private matters. And I do not consider myself bound to answer such questions, nor am I at all disposed to answer them. You may consider yourself an examiner, yet I refuse to accept you as my judge. But, pray tell me why you ask me such questions.

[19]II Cor. 10:18.

Faithful: Yes. Because I saw your forwardness to talk, and I did not know whether you had anything but words. Besides, to tell you the truth, I have heard that you are a man whose religion consists only in words and that your everyday life contradicts what you say. I am told that you are a blemish among Christians and that you bring reproach on the religion of Christ; that some have already stumbled over your wicked ways and that many more are in danger of being destroyed by your ungodly example. Furthermore, I am told that your religion and taverns, and covetousness, and uncleanness, swearing, lying, and immoral company-keeping go together. As the proverb says of a whore that "she is a shame to all women," so you are a shame to all professing Christians.

Talkative: Since you are ready to take up reports, and to judge one so rashly and unjustly, I cannot but conclude that you are a peevish, fault-finding, melancholy person, unfit for wholesome conversation; therefore, I will bid you adieu.

Christian (*having stopped for a moment, just ahead of them, now walks beside Faithful*): I told you how it would be. Your words and his lusts could not mix. He would rather leave your company and turn away from the truth than to repent and let Christ change his life. But he is gone, and let him go; the loss is all his own. He has saved us the trouble of separating from him. And unless he would have changed (which is doubtful), he would have been a bane and a blot in our company. Besides, the Apostle says, "From such withdraw thyself."[20]

Faithful: But I am glad we had this little discussion with him; it may be that he will think on these things. However, I have dealt honestly and sincerely with him, and feel that I am clear of any responsibility if he is finally lost.

Christian: You did right to talk plainly to him. There is not enough of this faithful dealing with souls these days, and

[20] I Tim. 6:5.

lack of that causes the people to undervalue the Christian faith. Then when these talkative frauds, whose religion is only in word and who are debauched in their living and vain in their conversation, are admitted into the fellowship of Christians with the hope that they may be converted or contribute money, the people of the world are puzzled, the sincere are grieved, and Christianity is blemished. I wish that all Christians would deal with such as you have done. Then they would either be truly converted, or they would show their colors and leave the congregation of the saved.

Thus they went on their way, talking of what they had seen and learned, making their travel both profitable and enjoyable. Otherwise, no doubt, their journey would have been tedious, for now they trudged through a wilderness.

CHAPTER

6

vanity fair and the city of vanity

Evangelist Foretells Trouble

NOW WHEN CHRISTIAN AND FAITHFUL were almost out of the wilderness, their good friend, Evangelist, overtook them.

After greeting them, Evangelist asked: "How have you been since I last saw you? What have you seen in your journey? And how have you conducted yourselves?"

Then they told him their experiences in the way and how, and with what difficulty, they had gotten to where they were.

EVANGELIST: Well, thank the Lord. I am very glad, not that you had trials, of course, but that you have gained victories and, notwithstanding your imperfections and mistakes, have continued in the pilgrim way. I am glad for my sake as well as for yours. I have sown, and you have reaped; and the day is coming when both he that sowed and they that reaped shall rejoice together; that is, if we hold out, and do not faint. "For in due season," says Paul, "we shall reap if we faint not."[1]

[1]Gal. 6:9.

There is an incorruptible crown awaiting us: "So run that you may obtain."[2]

There are some, you know, who set out to obtain the crown, and they run well for a time—some continue a long way. Yet they allow themselves to grow negligent, and let another take their crown. Hold fast, therefore, to that which you have, and let no man take your crown.[3] You are not yet out of "gunshot" of the devil. "You have not yet resisted unto blood, striving against sin."[4] Let the kingdom of God be always uppermost in your mind, and believe steadfastly concerning the things invisible. Let nothing this side of Heaven possess your soul. Guard well your hearts against all lusts and vanity, for, "the heart is deceitful above all things, and desperately wicked"[5] when not kept by divine grace. Set your faces like a flint toward your destination, for you have all power in Heaven and earth on your side.

CHRISTIAN: Thank you very much, brother Evangelist, for your wise and helpful exhortation. Now since we know God reveals to you things to come, we would like you to tell us something of what is before us—things that may happen to us, and how to meet them.

EVANGELIST: You have read in the Word that "we must through much tribulation enter the kingdom of God."[6] You may find, as did the Apostle Paul, that in every city bonds and afflictions await you.[7] Therefore, you cannot expect to travel far in your pilgrimage without having trials in some form. You have had some of this come to you already, and more will soon follow.

For now, as you see, you are almost out of this wilderness. You will soon come into a town, where you will be sorely tried

[2]I Cor. 9:24.
[3]Rev. 3:11.
[4]Heb. 12:4.
[5]Jer. 17:9.
[6]Acts 14:22.
[7]Acts 20:23.

by enemies of the truth, who will strive hard to put you to death, and one of you may seal his testimony with his blood. But be faithful unto death, and Christ will give you a crown of life. If one of you shall die there, although his death will be cruel and his pain great, yet he will be more fortunate than the other, because he will arrive in the Celestial City much sooner, and he will escape the trials that the other must endure in the rest of the way. But when you have come to the town and shall see fulfilled what I have here related, then remember your friend, and the Lord Jesus, and deport yourselves like men, and commit the keeping of your souls to God in well doing, "as unto a faithful Creator."[8]

Then I saw in my dream that they had left the wilderness and entered a town where there was a fair that continued all year long. Evangelist was no longer with them. The name of the town was Vanity, and the fair was Vanity Fair. The people of the town were vain, caring for nothing but money, pleasure, and fame. The town was very old, and the fair had been going for many, many years.

Almost five thousand years ago, pilgrims, on their way to the Celestial City, went through this town. Finally Beelzebub, Apollyon, and Legion, with their laborers, set up this fair to provide every kind of entertainment for travelers and to sell all types of merchandise all year long. And still, at this fair is sold such merchandise as fine houses, lands, stocks and bonds, false security, gay clothing, jewelry, expensive cosmetics, gold and silver, antiques, pearls, precious stones, fame, fortunes, reputations, virtue, honor, popularity, positions, phoney titles, counterfeit degrees, contests, chances, games, votes, elections, government offices, personal influences, padded reports, propaganda, falsehoods, fictitious news, deceptions, artificial personalities,

[8]I Peter 4:19.

schemes, tricks, comics, beauty queens, sex appeal, prostitutes, human lives, and souls of men.

Moreover, at this fair at all times are gambling, juggling, cheating, defrauding, embezzling, lying, stealing, swindling, rogues, knaves, libertines, carnivals, festivities, drinking, revelries, connivings, fools, thugs, lewd women, murders, adulteries, and all kinds of immoralities. The broad road that leads to destruction which brings the fair much trade lies through the town.

And in this town of Vanity are taverns, night clubs, roadhouses, seductive shows, popular casinos, culture societies, fashionable churches, synthetic Christians, sectarian denominational segregation, professional pastors (using mass psychology, setting themselves up as lords over God's heritage, ruling their congregations for "filthy lucre," beating and fleecing their flocks instead of feeding them or setting them a good example). There are also famous pseudoscientists, charlatan physicians, dishonorable crafty lawyers, unscrupulous politicians, clandestine bookmakers, racketeers—impostors of all kinds.

But, if anyone going to the Celestial City would miss this town of Vanity, he must of necessity go out of the world. The Prince of Peace, when here on earth, went through this town to His own country; and this same Beelzebub was then—as now—lord of the fair. He tried to sell the Prince many of his vanities. He even offered to make him manager of the fair. Because the Prince was such an influential person, Beelzebub led Him from section to section and showed Him all the various nations of the world and promised to make Him ruler over all, if He would but cheapen himself and buy some of his vanities. But the Prince did not care for any of the merchandise, and He left the town without spending a penny for any of Beelzebub's goods.

Christian and Faithful at Vanity Fair

Now, as soon as Christian and Faithful entered the fair they created a sensation, not only in the fair but throughout the town.

First, their dress was so different from the people of the place that everyone gazed at them. Some said they were cranks; some called them outlandish; others said they were there to create trouble.

Second, their speech was different. Few could understand what they said, for naturally they spoke the language of Canaan, while those who kept the fair were men of this world. From one end of the fair to the other, they seemed like barbarians.

Third, these pilgrims showed no interest in their goods, and this worried the people of the fair most. Christian and Faithful did not even care to see them, and when they were asked to buy they would stop up their ears and say, "Turn away my eyes from beholding vanity,"[9] looking upward as if they belonged to another country.

Mocked and Mobbed

One who had already heard of the men, observing their peculiar behavior, mockingly said to them, "What will you buy?" Then they fastened their eyes upon him and said, "We buy the truth." At this an occasion was taken to persecute them. Finally the haters of the pilgrims created a mob and such commotion that all order was destroyed.

Word was brought to the ruler, who quickly came down and had these men taken into custody for a questioning. In the examination, the investigators asked them where they came from, where they were going, and what they were doing in Vanity Fair in such a garb. The men told them that they were pilgrims and strangers in the world, that they were going to their own country and their own city, New Jerusalem, and that they had given no

[9]Ps. 119:37.

occasion for this disturbance, and there was no reason why they should be abused and hindered in their journey. They told the examiners that the trouble started when a merchant asked them what they would buy and they replied that they would buy the truth; and that when they said this, they had no idea that it would cause such a commotion.

But the examiners did not believe them. They thought they were shrewd troublemakers who had come to the fair for the specific purpose of creating an uproar. So they took them and whipped them, smeared their faces with mud, put them into an iron cage, and placed them on exhibition before the people. There they were for a long time, without water or food. They were made objects of merriment and hatred. The manager of the place laughed with those who made fun of them.

Now the men were patient, controlling well their tempers, not rendering evil for evil, but showing kindness to those who abused them, speaking good words for harsh treatment, giving favors for injuries. Therefore, some individuals in the crowd, who were more observing and less prejudiced than the rest, began to speak against the wrong done to the men. This caused the ruffians to become furious. They flew into a rage at those who tried to defend the prisoners, calling them confederates of jailbirds, and saying they deserved to be in the cage with them, sharing their punishment. But they replied that as far as they could see, the prisoners were quiet and sober men, intending no harm, and were far less deserving of the treatment they were getting than many at the fair.

Then there was an exchange of angry words, and soon a fight broke out, in which some were seriously injured (the men themselves all the while acting very sensibly, showing no ill toward anyone). This angered the deputies even more. They took the pilgrims again before the examiners, this time charging them with causing the fight and all the confusion at the fair. The examiners beat them more severely, hung heavy irons around their necks, and marched them in chains up and down the streets as an example of terror to others lest any should join them or attempt to stir up a mob in their favor.

Christian and Faithful behaved themselves so well, taking their disgrace and shame with such meekness and patience, that several of the witnesses were won to their side. This made their persecutors more furious. They became so enraged that they decided to put them to death. They solemnly proclaimed that neither cage nor iron had conquered these insurrectionists, and now they would have to die for instigating rebellion and deluding customers at the fair. Then they were shut up in the iron cage again, awaiting further orders, and their feet were made fast in the stocks.

Here they recalled what their faithful friend Evangelist had told them, and praised the Prince of Peace, who suffered before them, for counting them worthy to suffer shame for His name. And they also remembered the comforting words of Evangelist: that the one who would be called on to give his life would be honored and blessed above the other, because he would escape the troubles of the road and come into the Celestial City much sooner. Therefore, each man secretly desired to have that preferment. Yet with calm contentment they committed themselves to the will of Him who does all things well. They accepted their lot as the will of God for them at this time and waited patiently until they should be otherwise rewarded.

Placed on Trial

At a convenient time the authorities brought them forth to trial in order to condemn them. The judge was Lord Hategood. Their indictment was one and the same in substance, though varying somewhat in form. The contents were: That they were antagonistic to the rules and trade of the fair, and disturbers of the peace; they had created a disturbance and division in the town; and they had persuaded some good honest persons to embrace their poisonous and most dangerous doctrine.

Then Faithful answered that he had only opposed that which set itself against the Word and will of his Lord and Director, the Creator and Ruler of the universe. He said, "As to disturbance, I have created none, being myself a man of peace; and the persons who were won to us made their own choice by seeing the truth and our innocence and the cruelty and injustice of those who condemned us; and they have only turned to the right way. And since you spoke of your king, who is none other than Beelzebub, the enemy of all good, I defy him and all his cohorts."

Then request was made that those who had anything to say for the king Beelzebub against the prisoner at the bar should come and give their testimony. There were three who came to the front: Mr. Envy, Mr. Superstition, and Mr. Deception. They were asked if they knew the prisoner at the bar and what they had to say for their lord, the king, against him.

Mr. Envy stood and said: "Your honor, I have known this man a long time, and I will swear before this court that—"

JUDGE: Hold a moment! Clerk, give him his oath.

ENVY: Your honor, this man, nothwithstanding his plausible name, is one of the most corrupt men in this country. He neither regards ruler nor people, law nor custom, but does all he can to force his disloyal ideas upon others. These ideas he calls principles of faith and holiness. I heard him say that Christianity and the customs of this town of Vanity had nothing in common and, in fact, were diametrically opposed to each other and could not be reconciled. By such a statement, he not only condemns all our laudable ways but condemns us also for following them. Now, I could say much more, but I don't want to be tedious to the court, and there are others to testify. But if necessary, when the other gentlemen have given their testimony, I will enlarge on my testimony against him, rather than leave anything out.

Then the judge called Superstition and said, "See this man at the bar? What can you say for the lord and king of this city against him?" Then they administered the oath to him.

SUPERSTITION: Your honor, I am not well acquainted with this man, nor do I desire to be. However, this I know, that he is a very troublesome fellow. The other day, while talking with me, he said that our religion was not from God, and that no one could possibly please God by following it, which means that he charges that we worship in vain, that we are still in our sins and shall finally be damned.

Then was Deception sworn in, and asked to tell what he knew.

DECEPTION: Your honor, and gentlemen of the jury, I have known this fellow a long time, and I have heard him speak things that ought not to be uttered. I have heard him use blasphemous language against our noble Prince Beelzebub, and condemn his honorable friends, Lord Oldman, Mr. Carnal Delight, Lord Luxurious, Lord Vainglory, Lord Lechery, Mr. Havegreed, and all the rest of our nobility. And I have heard him say that if everybody here were of his mind, not one of these great citizens would remain in this town. Besides, your honor, he has not been afraid to speak evil of you, his duly appointed judge, calling you an ungodly villain. With many such slanderous terms he has smeared the good name of most of the prominent men in this city.

When Deception had finished testifying, Judge Hategood spoke to the accused man at the bar: "You vagabond, renegade, traitor, heretic, have you heard what these reliable citizens have witnessed against you?"

FAITHFUL: Judge, may I speak a few words in my own defense?

JUDGE: You reprobate, you deserve to die, to be stoned to death right here. But that all men may see our gentleness and fairness toward you, you vile wretch, let us hear what you have to say for yourself.

FAITHFUL: In reply to what Mr. Envy said, I wish to state that what I said—and all I said—was that all rules, laws, customs and people that are against the Word of God are diametrically opposed to Christianity. If I am wrong in this statement, I am open to conviction. Show me wherein I am wrong, and I will retract my statement and apologize.

As to Mr. Superstition and his charge against me, I said only this: "In the worship of God there is required a divine faith. But there can be no divine faith without a revelation of the divine will of God. Therefore, whatever is incorporated in the worship of God that is not agreeable to divine revelation of the will of God is of human faith, and such faith cannot procure eternal life."

And as to what Mr. Deception has said, I say—I did not use the terms he accused me of using, but I did say, and I will abide by it—that the prince of this town and all his rabble-rousing friends are more fit to be in Hell than in this town and country. If that be disloyalty and blasphemy, make the most of it. I am at your mercy.

JUDGE HATEGOOD: Gentlemen of the jury, you see this man about whom this great uproar has been made in this town, and you have heard what these worthy gentlemen have testified against him. You have also heard his reply and confession. Now it is in your power to execute him or save his life, but I will instruct you as to the law.

There was a law made in the days of Pharaoh, the great servant of our prince, that lest those of a contrary religion should multiply and grow too strong for him, their males should be thrown into the river.[10] There was also a law passed in the days of Nebuchadnezzar, another of our prince's servants, that whoever would not fall down and worship his golden image should be thrown into a fiery furnace.[11] And there was an act passed in the days of Darius, that whoever made a practice of worshiping any other god but him should be thrown into the lions' den.[12] Now, the substance of these laws has been broken by this rebel not only in thought (which is not to be borne) but also in word and in deed, which cannot be tolerated.

Now the law of Pharaoh was made upon supposition, to prevent disaster, no crime yet being apparent; but here is an open crime, known to all. And for the second and third law, you see and hear his opposition to our religion. For the reason that he has confessed, he deserves to die.

Then the jury left the room, whose names were Mr. Blindman, Mr. Worthless, Mr. Malice, Mr. Lustful, Mr. Liveloose, Mr. Heady, Mr. Highbrow, Mr. Enmity, Mr. Humbug, Mr. Cruelty, Mr. Judas, and Mr. Obstinate. When they were alone in the jury room, they all expressed their opinions, and the jury reached a verdict of guilty, and recommended the death penalty.

Faithful Executed

The judge heard the verdict, accepted the recommendation, and set the day of execution. So Faithful died on the gallows, true to his convictions, sealing his testimony with his own blood.

Then I saw that there stood behind the crowd a golden chariot and a couple of fiery steeds, waiting for Faithful, who (as soon as his adversaries had done all they could against him) was taken up into it and whisked away up through the clouds, the nearest way to the Celestial City. I thought I heard the sound of a trumpet when he reached the pearly gate.

[10]Exod. 1:22.
[11]Dan. 3:6.
[12]Dan. 6:7.

Christian Imprisoned, Then Released

As for Christian, he had a little respite. He was remanded back to prison, where he remained for some time. Then, as the Lord of all would have it, he was finally released. And he went on his way singing:

> Faithful, you have fulfilled your worthy name.
> "Faithful" to Him with whom you now are blessed.
> While pleasure-seekers, men without your faith,
> Cry out in fear, and cannot hope for rest.
>
> Sing, Faithful, sing! Your name will now survive,
> For though they killed you, you are still alive!

CHAPTER
7

journey to the delectable mountains

Joined by Hopeful

CHRISTIAN HAD NOT GONE FAR from the town when he came upon Hopeful, who had just recently become a pilgrim. He told Christian that he was from the town of Vanity, that he had seen the unjust and cruel treatment of him and Faithful by the brutal people of the fair and had witnessed Faithful's execution. He had observed the good behavior of him and Faithful in their sufferings which, he said, "caused me to turn from the world and its ways to the belief and the life of a pilgrim."

The two men entered into a covenant with each other to be good companions to the end of the way. Hopeful told Christian that there were many others at the fair who would in time follow his example. Then Christian felt that his suffering and Faithful's cruel death had not been in vain.

Meeting with Hypocrites

They had not gone far when they overtook a man whose name was Crafty, who told them that he was from the town of Fairspeech and was going to the Celestial City. But he did not tell them his name.

CHRISTIAN: From Fairspeech! Do you have many good citizens in your town?

CRAFTY: Yes sir, it is a good town.

CHRISTIAN: My name is Christian, and this is my good friend, Mr. Hopeful. What is your name?

CRAFTY: I'm a stranger to you, and you to me; if you are going my way, I shall be glad to have your company.

CHRISTIAN: This town of Fairspeech, I have heard of it; and as I remember, they say it is a wealthy place.

CRAFTY: Yes, it is, and I have many wealthy kinfolk there.

CHRISTIAN: Who are some of your kindred there, if I may ask?

CRAFTY: Almost everyone in town. The most prominent ones are Lord Turnabout, Lord Timeserver, Lord Fairspeech, from whose ancestors the town first took its name, also Mr. Smooth, Mr. Dualface, Mr. Anything, and the Pastor of the largest church, the Rev. Mr. Doubletongue, my mother's own brother. And to tell you the truth, I am a gentleman of the nobility, though my great-grandfather was a boat-rower, and most of my estate was acquired by those of that occupation.

CHRISTIAN: Are you a married man?

CRAFTY: Yes, and my wife is a popular lady, the daughter of a refined, cultured woman, Lady Feigning. She comes from a very honorable family; and she has attained to such a quality of sociability that she knows how to be ingratiating and thoughtful to high and low, rich and poor, prince and peasant. It is true that our religion is a little different from that of the stricter sort in two points: First, we never strive against the current. We follow that verse of Scripture [?] which says, "When you are in Rome, do as Rome does"; second, we are always more zealous for religion when it is clothed in culture and popular demeanor. When religion walks in sunshine with silver slippers and the people applaud it, we are glad to be counted followers of it. But we know how to withdraw from religion when it appears in rags, without education or money, and is unacceptable to the better class.

Then Christian stepped aside to Hopeful, and said in a low voice, "It strikes me that this fellow is a Mr. Crafty of Fair-speech. If he is, we have as big a cheat as can be found in all this country."

"Ask him," said Hopeful. "He should not be ashamed of his name."

Then Christian went over to him and said, "Sir, is not your name Mr. Crafty? Are you not known as Crafty of Fairspeech?"

CRAFTY: That is not my real name. That is a nickname given to me by those who did not like me. It is a reproach, and I have to bear it everywhere I go. But other good men have borne theirs before me.

CHRISTIAN: But why did they call you by such a name?

CRAFTY: As I have said, they did not like me. All that I ever did that displeased my acquaintances was that I always looked ahead and had the good judgment or wisdom to choose the best for myself before they could see clearly what was best, and it has been my good luck to get the best things in life that way. But if good things come my way, let me count them a blessing, and let the jealous and malicious who brand me with a false name be condemned.

CHRISTIAN: I thought you must be the man I heard of, and now I fear that this name belongs to you more properly than you are willing to admit.

CRAFTY: Well, if you think so I cannot help it. However, you will find my company agreeable, if you still admit me as an associate.

CHRISTIAN: If you go with us, you will have to go against

the tide, which, according to what you have said, is against your policy. You must embrace our religion as well when it appears in rags against the frowns of the world as when it walks in silver slippers, parades in sunshine, and receives the applause of men. And you must be true to it when bound in iron, the same as when rejoicing in liberty.

CRAFTY: You must not impose your belief on me or lord it over my faith. Leave me to my own free will and choice, and let me journey with you.

CHRISTIAN: That is impossible, for how "can two walk together except they be agreed?"[1] "What fellowship hath righteousness with unrighteousness? And what communion hath light with darkness? And what concord hath Christ with Belial? Or what part hath a believer with an infidel?"[2]

CRAFTY: Well, I will never desert my old principles, since they are harmless and profitable. If I may not go with you, I must walk alone, as I did before you came along, until someone else overtakes me who will be glad to have my company without trying to mold me after his pattern.

Then Crafty dropped behind. Looking back, the pilgrims saw three men catch up with him. He bowed to them, and they responded with the same friendly gesture. They were old acquaintances. The three men were Mr. Earthy, Mr. Moneylove, and Mr. Save-all. They had been in school with Crafty in other days. They had all gone to Mr. Grasping's school in Lovegain, a town in the county of Coveting. This schoolmaster taught his students how to acquire, by flattery, lying, fraud, violence, or by putting on a guise of religion; and these four gentlemen had learned so well the art of their master that each one could have taught such a school himself. After they had saluted each other and exchanged greetings, Mr. Moneylove asked, "Who are those fellows up the road yonder?"

[1]Amos 3:3.
[2]II Cor. 6:14-15.

CRAFTY: They are a couple of far countrymen who, after their mode, are going on pilgrimage.

MONEYLOVE: Alas! why did they not wait, that we might have had their good company? For I hope we are all going on pilgrimage.

CRAFTY: So we are indeed. But these men are so narrow, so rigid, they love their ideas so much and think so little of the opinions of others, that they would not care to have our company. Let a man be ever so godly, yet if he does not agree with them in everything, they refuse to associate with him.

SAVE-ALL: That is bad; but we read of some who are too religious, too conscientious, and their strictness causes them to judge and condemn everybody but themselves, and those who agree with them. But tell us, what fault did they find with you?

CRAFTY: They did not like my waiting for wind and tide. They, after their headstrong manner, thought it was their duty to rush on their journey in all kinds of weather and against all opposition. They are for hazarding all for God without a moment's hesitation. I am for caution and for taking advantage of every favorable condition to secure my holdings, my life and safety, and gain my objective. They are for holding fast to their notions, though all men be against them. But I am for religion when the times and conditions and my own safety permit. They are for religion when it is in rags and contempt, but I demand of religion that it walk in silver slippers in the sunshine and receive applause.

MR. EARTHY: Right you are, Mr. Crafty. It seems to me that a person who has the liberty to keep what he has, and lets it go for some elusive promise of religion, is a religious fool. God expects us to use wisdom. Let us be wise as serpents. Wise people make hay while the sun shines, not in the rain. God makes both sunshine and rain, but He expects us to judge as to the best time to do our work. For my part, I like that religion best that secures for us God's blessings; for who that is ruled by reason can imagine that since God has bestowed upon us all the good things of this life He would not want us to keep them for His sake? Abraham and Solomon grew rich, and they were very religious. Job said that if one would "return to the Almighty," he would "lay up gold as dust"; but he was not like the two gentlemen ahead of us, who, as you say, value gold as dust.

SAVE-ALL: I think we are all agreed on this matter, and it needs no further discussion.

MONEYLOVE: No, there is no more need for words about this. We have both Scripture and reason to prove our viewpoint, and the person who follows neither Scripture nor reason knows nothing of true liberty, nor cares for his own safety.

CRAFTY: As you see, we are all on pilgrimage and, for better diversion, may I suggest this question:

Suppose a man—a tradesman or a minister—sees an opportunity to advance himself in the world by becoming more zealously religious about some things he had not before considered very worthy or important, may he not take advantage of his opportunity and use this means to attain his end without lowering his moral standard or cheapening his character? Can he not do this and still be an upright, honest man?

MONEYLOVE: I see what you mean, and with the permission of the rest, I will give you an answer. First, as it concerns a minister: Suppose a good worthy minister, with small income and but little of this world's goods, desires more for himself and family and sees an opportunity of getting it by altering his principles and methods a little, which pleases his congregation—by being more studious, advertising himself and his church more effectively, preaching more often and with greater zeal, selecting and shaping the Scriptures to serve his purpose, building stronger and better sermons on tithing and giving to increase the income of his church and put himself in position to get a better salary, and thereby enhance his reputation in his community and denomination. I see no reason why he should not take advantage of this opportunity. In fact, I think he should.

First, because his desire for gain is natural and lawful, and the opportunity to obtain is set before him by Providence. Then he may get more if he can, asking no questions for conscience' sake.

Second, his desire makes him more studious, a more zealous preacher, causes him to improve his talents, and so makes of him a better man, which must be the will of God.

Third, as to his complying with the wishes of his people by yielding some of his principles to serve them, I think that is commendable; for it shows that he is of a self-denying spirit and of a sweet and winning disposition, which demonstrates that he is better fitted for his profession.

I conclude, therefore, that a minister who changes from a small charge and salary to a larger and more remunerative one should not be judged as covetous for so doing. Rather, since he has improved the quality of his service he should be considered as one who is judiciously following the rules of his calling and making the most of an advantage placed before him to do good.

Now to the second part of your question concerning the tradesman: Suppose a tradesman or a workman, receiving little profit or small wages, can, by becoming religious, improve his situation—marry a rich woman, gain more or better customers, or get a better job—I do not see why this may not be legitimately done. My reasons are these: To become religious is a virtue, by whatsoever means. It is not unlawful to get a rich wife, or more trade or better wages. Besides, the man who gets these by becoming religious gets that which is good by becoming good himself. So the result is a good life, a good wife, more money, more customers, or better wages, or more business, all by becoming religious. Therefore, to become religious to obtain all these is a good motive.

This answer by Mr. Moneylove was enthusiastically received by all. And they all thought that no man could successfully refute it. So they decided to go to Christian and Hopeful with the question, since they both had rejected Mr. Crafty and his ideas. They called to Christian and Hopeful to wait. As they approached them, they agreed that Mr. Earthy should put the question, instead of Mr. Crafty, because of Christian's attitude toward Mr. Crafty in the previous discussion.

So after greetings, introductions, and a few brief remarks about the journey and the weather, Mr. Earthy presented the question to Christian.

CHRISTIAN: Why even a beginner can answer that question. Anyone should know that it is wrong to become religious for gain! For if it was wrong to follow Christ for the loaves and fishes, it is far worse to use Him and His religion as a decoy to gain and enjoy things of the world.

The hypocritical Pharisees were of that spirit: long prayers were their methods, but to get widows' houses was their aim. Jesus said they would receive greater damnation.

Judas, the traitor, was also of that belief. He was religious for the money bag he carried. And he is called a thief, a devil, and the son of perdition, and it is written of him that he went to his own place, which was Hell, where all devils go.

Simon, the deceiver, was of this belief, too. He tried to bribe the apostles into giving him the power of the Holy Spirit that he might use it for his own profit and glory. But Peter told him that his heart was wicked, that he was in the gall of bitterness and in the bond of iniquity.

Satan is the author of these ideas. He is the one who induced

Ananias and his wife Sapphira to keep back part of their possessions for a rainy day and live out of the common treasure of the church—off the labors of others—deceiving the Christians and using their religion for gain. But God struck them dead.

Therefore, the person who takes up religion to gain the world is a thief, a liar, a robber, a cheat, a Judas, a hypocrite who will throw religion away for the world—just as Judas sold his Lord for thirty pieces of silver. This doctrine may sound plausible, but it is of the Devil, and if you accept it as true, your reward will be according to your works.

Then the four stood staring at each other in silence. Hopeful said, "Amen." And Mr. Crafty and his companions fell behind as Christian and Hopeful went on their way. When they were some distance ahead of the others, Christian said to Hopeful, "If these men cannot stand before men, how can they hope to stand before God? And if they are mute when dealt with by vessels of clay, what will they do when rebuked by the flames of devouring fire?"

Traversing the Plain of Ease

Christian and Hopeful went on until they came to a delightful plain, called Ease, where they walked with freedom and contentment. The plain was narrow, and they were soon over it. Now at the farther side of the plain was a little hill, called Lucre, and in the hill a silver mine where some, because of the uniqueness of the place, had turned aside to look. But they went too near the brink of the pit and never came back. The ground beneath them gave way and they fell in. Some were killed, and others were maimed for life.

Meeting Demas

A little off the road and over against the pit stood a man named Demas, calling to the passers-by to come and see the mine. Demas said to Christian and Hopeful, "My friends, turn aside here and I will show you something."

CHRISTIAN: What can you show us that is important enough to turn us out of our way?

DEMAS: Here is a silver mine, and people digging in it for riches. If you will come, you will see that you can by a little effort provide yourselves with great wealth.

"Let us go and see," said Hopeful.

CHRISTIAN: Not I. I have heard of this place and of many who have lost their lives there. Besides, that treasure is a snare to those who get it; it tarnishes, and cankers, and poisons one's body and mind.

Then Christian called to Demas, "Is not the place dangerous? Has it not been the cause of the wrecking and ending of many pilgrimages?"

"No, not very dangerous," Demas said with tongue in cheek, "except to those who are careless."

Then said Christian to Hopeful, "Let us not take one step in that direction, but keep straight on our way."

HOPEFUL: I think that when Crafty comes along, provided he is given the same invitation that we have had, he will turn in there to see.

CHRISTIAN: No doubt, for his principles lead him that way; and he will probably die there.

Then Demas called out again, "But will you not come over and see?"

CHRISTIAN: Demas, you are an enemy to the cause of Christ, and you have already been condemned by one of God's good judges for turning aside from the right way. And now you want to bring us into the same condemnation. You know very well that if we turn aside, the Lord, our King, will know about it and put us to shame when we desire to stand before Him unafraid.

Soon Christian and Hopeful were beyond the sound of Demas' voice.

By this time Crafty and his friends arrived on the hill, and at the first invitation from Demas they went over to view the silver mine. But whether they went too close and fell in, or went down into the mine to dig silver and suffocated in the gas, I do not know; but this I observed, that they were never seen again on the road.

Viewing the Pillar of Salt

Again, I saw in my dream, that just on the far side of the plain stood an old monument close by the highway. It was very strange. It was shaped like a pillar, but had the face of a woman. Here Christian and Hopeful stood viewing it for a long time, trying to make out the meaning. At last Hopeful saw writing on it but, not being a scholar, he could not make out the words. He called Christian's attention to the writings, and Christian finally made out the Hebrew words: "Remember Lot's wife." They concluded that this was the pillar of salt that Lot's wife became when she looked back with covetous eyes to the burning city of Sodom, when fleeing for her life.

CHRISTIAN: Ah, brother Hopeful, this is a good reminder to us at this time, after the invitation of Demas to come and see Lucre Hill. If we had gone over, as he wanted us to, and as you were inclined to do, who knows but that we, like this woman, might have been made a public spectacle for future generations?

HOPEFUL: I am sorry I was so foolish. And I am made to wonder why it did not happen to me as it did to this curious woman, for I wonder how my sin differs from hers. She only looked back, and I had a desire to go and see. Let grace be adored, and let me be ashamed that such a thing should have ever entered my mind.

CHRISTIAN: Let us take notice of what we see here for our

profit for time to come. This woman escaped one judgment by obeying the angel of the Lord, but was overtaken by another when she disobeyed by looking back.

HOPEFUL: True, and she may be to us both caution and example: caution, that we should shun her sin, and an example of the judgment that will come to those who are not checked by caution.

Walking Beside the Happy River

They soon came to a crystal river which the Apostle John called "the river of the water of life."[3] Now their road was along the bank of this river, where they walked with delight. They stopped to drink of the river water, which was refreshing to their spirits. And on both banks of the river were green trees that bore all kinds of delicious fruit, and the leaves of the trees were good for medicine. With the fruit of the trees they satisfied their hunger, and they ate of the leaves to prevent diseases that are incident to those who travel in that country. On either side of the river was also a beautiful meadow, green all the year long and adorned with lovely flowers. In this meadow they lay down and slept in perfect safety. When they awoke they ate again of the fruit and drank the river water and lay down again to sleep. This they did several days and nights. They sang and rejoiced in the goodness of God.

When they were disposed to go on (for they were not yet at their journey's end), they ate and drank, and departed.

Going Aside Into Bypath Meadow

They had not journeyed far when the river and the highway parted, at which they were displeased, because the road by the river had been smooth. Now the way was rough, and their feet were sore from travel. A little before them, on the left hand of

[3]Rev. 22:1-2.

Christian and Hopeful are refreshed at the River of the Water of Life.

the road was a meadow and a stile leading to a path on the other side of the fence. On the stile were the words, "Bypath Meadow." When they came to the stile, Christian said, "If this meadow lies along by our road, let us go over." And he went to the stile to see. He saw a smooth path along by the way on the other side of the fence. "It is as I wished," said Christian: "here is easier going. Come, good Hopeful, and let us go over."

HOPEFUL: But what if this path should lead us away from the road?

CHRISTIAN: That is not likely. Look, does it not go along by the highway?

So Hopeful, being persuaded by his fellow companion, followed Christian over the fence. They found the path in the meadow easier on their feet. Before them walked a vain man whose name was Self-Confidence. Christian called to him and asked where this path led.

"To the Celestial Gate," he cried.

"Now," said Christian, "did I not tell you? By this we know we are right," and they followed Self-Confidence. But soon the night came on, and in the darkness they lost sight of Self-Confidence, who, not seeing the way, fell into a deep pit which was made by the owner of the grounds to catch wayward travelers. Christian and Hopeful heard him fall and called to know what had happened, but there was no answer. They heard only a groan.

Then said Hopeful, "Where are we now?" Christian was silent, regretting that he had led his fellow out of the way. It began to thunder and rain, and water rose over the low grounds. Then Hopeful groaned, saying, "Oh, that we had kept on our way!"

CHRISTIAN: Who would have thought that this path would lead us away from the road?

HOPEFUL: I was afraid of it at the very first, and therefore gave you the gentle warning. I would have spoken plainer, but you are older than I.

CHRISTIAN: Good brother, do not be offended. I am sorry I led you astray and have put you to such imminent danger. Please forgive me; I did it with no evil intent.

HOPEFUL: Don't worry, my brother, I forgive you, and I believe that in some way this must be for our good.

CHRISTIAN: I am truly glad I have with me a merciful brother. But we must not stand still. Let us try to go back again to the road.

HOPEFUL: All right, good brother, but let me go before.

CHRISTIAN: No, if you please, let me go first, so that if there is any danger I will be the first to take the risk and to suffer, because I am to blame for our present plight.

HOPEFUL: No, no, brother, you shall not go first. Since your mind is troubled, you might lead us the wrong way again.

Then they heard a voice, saying, "Stand ye in the ways, and see, and ask for the old paths, where is the good way, and walk therein, and ye shall find rest for your souls."[4] But by this time the waters were so high that it was exceedingly dangerous to go either way. Then they remembered the saying, "It is much easier to get out of the right way, than to get back in once you are out." Yet they still went back toward the stile, but the night was so dark and the water so high that they almost drowned.

And they did not make it back to the stile that night. At last, coming to a little shelter on higher ground, they sat down to wait for the dawn. But, being weary, they fell asleep.

Not far from where they lay there was an old castle called Doubting Castle, owned by one Giant Despair; and it was on his grounds they were sleeping. And, as his habit was, the giant rose early and was inspecting his grounds and fences after the rain when he came upon Christian and Hopeful sleeping on

[4]Jer. 6:16.

his premises. With a gruff voice he told them to wake up, and commanded them to tell where they were from and what they were doing on his grounds. They told him that they were pilgrims and had lost their way.

Captured By Giant Despair

Then said the giant, "You have trespassed on my property this night; therefore, you must come along with me." They were compelled to go, because he was much stronger than they. They had but little to say in their defense, for they knew they were at fault. The giant drove them before him into his castle and put them in a very dark dungeon—a nasty, stinking place. There they lay from Wednesday until Saturday night without food or water and without a ray of light or anyone to console them. They were in a pitiful plight, far from friends and acquaintances. Now Christian had double sorrow, because it was his ill-advised, hasty decision that had brought them into all this trouble.

Giant Despair had a wife whose name was Gloom. So when he had gone to bed, he told his wife he had taken two prisoners and locked them in the dungeon for trespassing on his property, and asked her what he ought to do with them. After he had told her what they were, where they were from and where they were going, she advised that when he arose next morning he should beat them unmercifully. When he got up next day he took his knotted, crabtree club and went down to the dungeon. First, he berated them shamefully as if they had been sheep-killing dogs (they never returned an unkind word), then he fell upon them and beat them severely. They were helpless to resist or to ward off his blows. Then he left them in the dark to pity themselves and mourn in agony. They spent the whole day sighing and groaning.

The next night Gloom advised her husband to induce the men to do away with themselves. So when morning came, he went down in a very ugly mood and said to the pilgrims: "Since you will never get out of here alive (I will never give you anything to eat or drink, and the only possible way of escape from your miseries is to end your own life—either with knife, or rope, or poison), then would it not be smart to take the quick way out of your suffering? For why should you choose to live, seeing life holds nothing for you now but extreme bitterness?" Yet they pleaded with him to let them go.

At that he rushed upon them and would have beaten them to death, but he had one of his fits and lost the use of his arm for the moment. So he withdrew and left them to consider what he had told them. Then the prisoners consulted each other as to whether it was best to take his advice or not.

CHRISTIAN: Brother Hopeful, what shall we do? The life we now have is extremely wretched. For my part I know not whether it is best to live like this for a time, then starve to death, or be beaten to death by this brutal man, or to die now and get out of it. Surely the grave is to be desired rather than this dungeon.

HOPEFUL: Well, of course, our present condition is intolerable, and death would be far better to me than to spend the rest of my days in this place—whether they be many or few. But let us consider that the Lord of the country to which we are going has said, "Thou shalt do no murder." Not only are we forbidden to kill another person; much more are we forbidden to kill ourselves. For he that kills another kills only his body, but he who kills himself kills body and soul. And you talk of ease in the grave, but have you forgotten the Hell to which all murderers go? For you know that "no murderer hath eternal life." And let us consider again that all the law is not in the hands of Giant Despair. Others, I understand, have escaped out of his hands. Who knows but that God, who made the world, may cause the Giant to die, or that at some time or other the

Giant may forget to lock us in, or in a short time he may have another of his fits and lose the use of his limbs? And if that should ever happen again, I am determined to act the part of a man and do my utmost to break loose from him. I was a coward when I did not do it before. However, my brother, let us be patient, and endure hardness as good soldiers of Jesus Christ,[5] at least for a while. The time may come when we will receive a happy release. Anyway, let us not be our own murderers.

With those words, Hopeful succeeded in stabilizing the mind of his friend. So they waited in the darkness another day in their pitiful state.

Toward evening the giant came down again to see if they had submitted to his counsel. He found them alive, but only barely alive, for they were perishing for food and water, and suffering miserably from their wounds. Seeing them still alive, the giant flew into a terrific rage, storming out at them: "You have disobeyed my counsel! Now it shall be worse with you than if you had never been born."

At his terrible words, they shook with fear, and Christian went into a swoon. When he had come to himself again, they remembered their discussion about taking their own lives. Christian was now inclined to favor the idea. But Hopeful made a second plea: "My brother, remember how valiant you were with Apollyon. He could not defeat you, nor were you defeated by all you saw and heard in the Valley of the Shadow of Death. What hardships, terror, and amazement you have already come through! And, you see, I'm in the dungeon too, a far weaker person by nature and experience than you, receiving the same punishment and suffering the same agony. This giant has wounded me and has also cut off bread and water from my mouth. And along with you, I mourn without the light. But let us exercise a little more patience. Remember how brave

[5]II Tim. 2:3.

and strong you were at Vanity Fair. You did not shrink from chains, or iron cage, or bloody death. Then, let us (at least to avoid the shame of conduct unbecoming to Christians) bear up with patience as best we can. Deliverance will come by and by."

That night the giant's wife asked him about the prisoners. She wanted to know if they had taken his counsel. "No," he said, "they are sturdy rogues. They choose to bear all hardships rather than do away with themselves."

She replied: "Tomorrow, take them into the castle yard and show them the bones and skulls of those you have disposed of and make them believe that before the week ends you will tear them in pieces, as you have done with all others."

So when morning came, he took them into the castle yard and showed them the skeletons of those he had murdered. "Those," he said, "were once pilgrims like you. They trespassed on my property, and when I saw fit I tore them to pieces, just as I will do to you within ten days if you remain alive on my premises. Now go down to your dungeon and think it over." With that he beat them all the way into the dungeon. There they lay all day Saturday in a deplorable condition.

That night the giant remarked to his wife that he could not understand how his prisoners remained alive. He had not been able by blows or threats or counseling to bring them to their end.

Then Gloom said, "I am afraid that they live in hopes that someone will come to their rescue; or they may have tools for picking a lock, thus hoping to get out."

"That is true," he said. "In the morning I will search them."

Escape from Doubting Castle

About midnight Saturday night, Christian and Hopeful began to pray, and continued until almost break of day. Then Christian suddenly broke out in amazement, "What a fool! What a fool I am to lie here in this stinking dungeon when I might walk free on the highway to glory! I have a key in my bosom called Promise which I am sure will open any door in Doubting Castle."

HOPEFUL: That is certainly good news, my brother. Get out your key and try it.

Then Christian took the key of Promise and pushed it into the lock of the dungeon door. The bolt fell back and the door came open. They walked out into the castle. Then they went to the door leading to the castle yard. The key opened that door also. Now they came to the great iron gate leading outside. The lock to the gate was exceedingly difficult, yet they unlocked it and pushed the gate open to make their escape. But the gate made such a creaking sound that it woke the giant, who jumped out of bed to pursue his prisoners. Then he was seized by one of his fits and lost the use of his limbs. The prisoners ran to the King's highway, where they were safely beyond Despair's jurisdiction.

CHAPTER
8

at the delectable mountains

CHRISTIAN AND HOPEFUL finally came to the Delectable Mountains, and went up to view that wonderful land. There were orchards and vineyards and gardens everywhere, and such breathtaking scenery as their eyes had never beheld.

Getting Acquainted with the Shepherds

They drank and washed themselves at one of the fountains, and ate freely of the fruit along the way. On the mountains were shepherds feeding their flocks near the highway. They went to one of the shepherds and asked, "Who owns these mountains, and whose sheep are these?"

SHEPHERD: These mountains are in Immanuel's Land; they are within sight of His City; and the sheep are also His.

CHRISTIAN: Is this the way to the Celestial City?

SHEPHERD: Yes, sir, you are on the right road.

CHRISTIAN: How far is it to the city gate?

SHEPHERD: Too far for any except the faithful.

CHRISTIAN: Is the way safe, or fraught with dangers?

SHEPHERD: It is safe for those who are true. "But the transgressors shall fall therein."[1]

CHRISTIAN: Is there shelter in this place for pilgrims?

[1]Hosea 14:9.

SHEPHERD: Yes, plenty, for our Lord has given us the charge: "Be not forgetful to entertain strangers."[2] Therefore, you will be welcomed everywhere.

Then the shepherds asked them these questions: "Where are you from? How did you come into the way? By what means have you persevered so far?" And they added, "Very few who set out for the Celestial City are ever seen on these mountains."

When they heard the answers of these disciples, the shepherds were convinced that they were true pilgrims and gave them a warm reception, asking them to stay a while and get acquainted with the mountain people. The shepherds said, "Do it for our pleasure and your strength," which the pilgrims agreed to do.

The names of the shepherds were Knowledge, Experience, Watchful, and Sincerity. They invited the pilgrims into their tents and gave them the best they had. Christian and Hopeful enjoyed the fellowship with the shepherds' families and the good things they had to eat. They took supper with the Watchfuls. After supper, neighbors came in to meet them and hear of their travels. They sat talking until a late hour, then went to bed. Christian dreamed of his wife and boys—thought he saw them on a pilgrimage with a strong guide.

They awoke next morning feeling good. The sun was shining across the mountains. Breakfast was waiting. After breakfast, the other shepherds came to take them on a tour.

Warning of the Shepherds

As they were walking along a path, enjoying the magnificent scenery, they came to the brink of Error Hill, and Knowledge told them to look down. At the bottom of the precipice were broken bodies and bones of those who had ventured too close to the edge and had fallen over.

"What does this mean?" asked Christian.

[2]Heb. 13:2.

KNOWLEDGE: You have heard of the people who lost their faith by listening to the false teaching of Hymeneus and Philetus on the resurrection?[3] Well, there they are. They have remained unburied as an object lesson to others who would climb too high and fail to heed warnings of danger.

Then they led them to the top of another mountain, named Caution Peak, gave them field glasses and told them to look far away in the direction whence they had come. They saw what appeared to be a number of blind men stumbling among tombs, unable to find their way out. "What does that indicate?" asked Christian.

"Before you came to the foothills of these mountains, did you see a stile that lead into a meadow on the left-hand side of the road?"

"Yes," they both answered.

KNOWLEDGE: From that stile there is a path that leads directly to Doubting Castle, which is kept by Giant Despair. These men you saw among the tombs came on pilgrimage until they got to that stile. And because the road was rough at that point, they decided to go out of the road into the meadow. There they were taken by Giant Despair and thrown into Doubting Castle, where they were kept for a time shut up in a dungeon. Then the giant put out their eyes and led them out among the tombs, where he left them to wander, that the saying of the Wise Man might be fulfilled, "The man that wandereth out of the way of understanding shall remain in the congregation of the dead."[4] Christian and Hopeful looked at each other with tearful eyes but said nothing.

Then they went down into a canyon to a door in the side of a hill. When the shepherd opened the door, they saw that the cave was very dark inside and filled with smoke, and they

[3]II Tim. 2:17-18.
[4]Prov. 21:16.

smelled an odor like burning sulfur. They also heard a roaring sound like fire, and cries of persons in torment.

"What is this?" asked Christian.

KNOWLEDGE: This is a byway to Hell, a route taken by hypocrites like Esau, who sold his birthright; Judas, who sold his Master; Alexander, who blasphemed the gospel; and Ananias and Sapphira, who lied and dissembled.

HOPEFUL: I suppose all of these were clothed as pilgrims?

KNOWLEDGE: Yes, and they continued in the way a long time too.

HOPEFUL: How far do these pretenders get on the way to glory?

KNOWLEDGE: Some farther, and some not so far as these mountains.

Then said Christian, and Hopeful agreed, "We need to pray for great strength."

KNOWLEDGE: Yes, and you will need all you can get.

By this time, the pilgrims had a desire to resume their journey. So they all walked together to the end of the mountains. Here they came to the top of a high peak called Clear.

KNOWLEDGE: Let us show you now the gate of the Celestial City. You may be able to see it through this glass. (The name of the glass was Eye-of-Faith.) Look far away yonder to the east, the way your road leads!

The pilgrims, looking through the glass, saw something like a gleaming gate on the distant horizon. But they were still trembling slightly from what they had seen in the cave, and they could not hold the glass steady enough to get a good view.

As Christian and Hopeful were leaving, one of the shepherds gave them a sketch of the way. Another said, "Beware of the Deceiver." A third said, "Be sure you do not sleep on the enchanted ground." And the fourth bid them Godspeed. Then they went on their way rejoicing.

CHAPTER 9

in the low country of conceit

Meeting the Young Man Ignorance

NOW I SAW THE PILGRIMS going down the mountainside toward the City. A little below these mountains, on the left of the road, was the backward country of Conceit, from which a little crooked lane led to the highway. At this intersection they met a brash young man named Ignorance, coming out of the country of Conceit. Christian asked him where he was from, and where he was going.

IGNORANCE: Sir, I was born back there in the country a little to the left, and I am going to the Celestial City.

CHRISTIAN: But how do you plan to get in at the gate? For you may have some difficulty there.

IGNORANCE: Sir, I know the Lord's will. I have lived a good life. I pay every man his own. I pray, fast, pay tithes to my church, and give to charity. And I have left my country for the one to which I am going.

CHRISTIAN: But you did not come through the gate at the beginning of the way. You came in through this crooked lane, and I am afraid, however well you may think of yourself, that when the reckoning time comes you will be counted a thief and a robber instead of being admitted to the City.

IGNORANCE: Gentlemen, you are utter strangers to me; you just be content to follow your religion, and I will follow mine. As for the gate you speak of, that is a long way from my country. I do not suppose that there is a person in our parts who knows the way to it. And it does not matter whether they do or not, since we have, as you see, a nice, pleasant, green lane leading down from our country, the shortest way into this road.

When Christian saw that the young man was wise in his own conceit, he caught up with Hopeful and whispered: "There is more hope for a fool than for him.[1] Even when the fool walks along the road, he shows a lack of sense; he reveals to everyone else that he is a fool.[2] What do you think? Shall we talk further to him, or outwalk him, leaving him to think of what we have said?"

HOPEFUL: It is not good to say all to him at once, I think. Let us go on and talk to him again later, as he is able to receive it.

Observing the Man Bound By Demons

So they went on ahead of Ignorance. After they passed him a little way, they entered a very dark lane where they met a man from whom an evil spirit had once departed, "seeking rest but finding none," but now the spirit had gone back into the man, taking with him seven other spirits more wicked than himself. These eight spirits had the man bound with all kinds of vices, and were taking him back toward the dark door on the side of the hill. The pilgrims trembled when they saw him. As the devils led the man away, Christian looked to see if he knew him. Since the man kept his face down, Christian could

[1]Prov. 26:12.
[2]Eccles. 10:3.

not be sure, but he thought the man was one Mr. Turnaway, from the town of Apostasy.

Passing Mr. Little-Faith

They passed a Mr. Little-Faith, whose enemies, Guilt, Mistrust, and Faintheart, had overcome him completely, leaving him destitute, not only of sufficient comfort but also of courage, so that instead of being glad that they did not get his passport to the City, he went all the rest of the way grieving and talking of his loss.

CHRISTIAN: When we hear of those who have been foiled, let us never desire to encounter an enemy, nor brag as if we could do better than others, nor exult in the thoughts of our manhood. Persons with such attitudes usually come to the worst when they are tried. Remember how Peter boasted, when his vain mind prompted him to say to Jesus: "Lord, I am ready to go with thee, both into prison and to death. . . . If I should die with thee, I will not deny thee in any wise."[3] Yet, he did not fully know himself; for he did deny the Lord three times—at a time when it must have hurt Jesus most—rather than run any risk of having to suffer with Him.

It is best not to trust in one's own strength but to "put on the whole armor of God," for the Apostle, who had great skill, said, "Above all, take the shield of faith, wherewith you shall be able to quench all the fiery darts of the wicked."[4] It is good also that we desire of the King a convoy; yes, that He will go with us Himself. His presence made David rejoice in the Valley of the Shadow of Death. If He will but go along with us we need not fear ten thousand opponents. But without Him we can do nothing.[5]

I have been in the conflict a long time, and through the good-

[3]Luke 22:33; Mark 14:31.
[4]Eph. 6:10-16.
[5]John 15:5.

ness of God I am still alive. But I cannot boast of my accomplishments or my faith. I shall be glad if I meet with no more such attacks from the enemy as I have felt, though I fear we are not yet beyond all danger.

Following a Deceiver

So Christian and Hopeful went on, and Ignorance followed. They came to a dividing of ways. Both ways seemed straight, and they did not know which way to go. They were standing at the forks of the road, trying to decide which road to take, when a man in a white robe came to them and asked why they stood there. They answered that they were going to the Celestial City but did not know which was the right road. "Follow me," said the man, "I'm going there too."

So they followed the man in white. After a while the road began to turn, gradually at first, but it kept turning until they were going directly away from the City of Zion, yet they kept following the man. By and by they were caught in a net, in which both were so entangled that they could not free themselves. Then the white robe fell from their guide's back and they saw he was a black imp.

Then Christian said, "Now I see my mistake. The shepherds told us to beware of a Deceiver. Now we have found it just as the Wise Man said: 'A man that flattereth his neighbor spreadeth a net for his feet.' "[6]

HOPEFUL: The shepherds also gave us a note of directions about the way which we forgot to read; consequently, we have not kept ourselves from the path of the destroyer.[7]

Led Back to the Right Way

They lay in the net, weeping. At last they saw a Shining One coming toward them. He came with a whip of small cords in

[6]Prov. 29:5.
[7]Ps. 17:4.

his hand. He asked them where they were from and what they were doing there.

They replied that they were pilgrims going to Zion but had been led out of the way by a black man clothed in white who said he was going to Zion too.

Then said the Shining One, "He was Deceiver, the false prophet, who has transformed himself into an angel of light."[8] So he tore the net and let them out. "Follow me," He said, "that I may put you in the way again." He led them back to the way they had left to follow Deceiver. Then He asked them, "Where did you stay last night?"

They replied, "With the shepherds on the Delectable Mountains."

Then He asked them if the shepherds had not given them a note of direction for the road. They answered, "Yes."

"But," He asked, "did you not read your note when you stopped at the forks of the road?"

"No, we forgot."

"Did not the shepherds tell you to beware of the Deceiver?"

"Yes," they said, "but we did not imagine that this smooth-spoken man dressed in white was the Deceiver."

He gave them such a look that it seemed that His whip was raised to strike, which caused them to burn with shame and weep with remorse. Then He said, "As many as I love, I rebuke and chasten: be zealous therefore, and repent."[9] Then He bade them go their way and heed carefully the other instructions given them by the shepherds. They thanked Him for His kindness, and went softly along the right way singing.

After a while they saw someone coming to meet them. Then said Christian, "Yonder is a man with his back toward Zion, and he's coming this way."

[8]II Cor. 11:13-15.
[9]Rev. 3:19.

HOPEFUL: Let us watch ourselves. He may be a deceiver also.

Meeting Mr. Atheist

So the man drew nearer, and at last came up to them. His name was Atheist, and he asked them where they were going.

CHRISTIAN: We are going to Mount Zion.

Atheist shook with laughter.

CHRISTIAN: What do you mean by laughing?

ATHEIST: I laugh to see what ignorant persons you are, to take upon yourselves such a tedious journey and receive nothing for your toil and pains but travel and troubles.

CHRISTIAN: Do you think we shall not be received?

ATHEIST: Received where? There is no such place as you dream of in all this world.

CHRISTIAN: But there is in the world to come.

ATHEIST: When I was at home in my own country, I heard of this city you talk about, and I went to see. I have been seeking this city these twenty years, yet I have found nothing except a lot of fools on the road.

CHRISTIAN: We have not only heard but also believed the Word, and now we have the witness within ourselves,[10] we have seen the gate—with the Eye-of-Faith—as shown to us by the shepherds.

ATHEIST: I believed so too, when at home. Had I not believed the story, I certainly would not have come this far. I have been farther than you, and I am sure that if there had been such a place I would have seen something of it. But after going so far and finding nothing, I'm going back where I came from and enjoy once again the things I left for the hope of finding this shimmering mirage a reality.

CHRISTIAN (*to Hopeful*): Is this that he is saying true?

[10]I John 5:10; Rom. 8:16.

HOPEFUL: Take heed, my brother, he is one of the deceivers. Remember what it has cost us already for listening to impostors on the road. What? No Mount Zion? Do we not have the words of Evangelist? Of the Interpreter? Of the maids at the Palace Beautiful and of the shepherds? Did we not have peace within when we believed the Word? Let us go on lest the man with the keen whip overtake us again. We must now walk by faith.[11] You should have taught me these words which I will now sound in your ears: "Cease, my son, to hear the instruction that causeth to err from the words of knowledge."[12] Let us refuse to hear him, and let us believe to the preserving of the soul.

CHRISTIAN: My brother, I did not put the question to you because I doubted the foundation of our faith myself, but to hear your answer to his arguments. As for this man, I know he is blinded by the god of this world. While our faith is incomplete, we believe the truth, "and no lie is of the truth."[13]

HOPEFUL: Now I rejoice in hope of the glory of God.

So they turned away from Atheist who went his way, laughing at them.

Hopeful's Temptation to Sleep

Christian and Hopeful journeyed till they came to a region where the air seemed to induce sleep. Hopeful became very drowsy and said to Christian, "I am so sleepy I can hardly hold my eyes open; let us lie down here and take one good nap."

CHRISTIAN: Oh no, by no means! We might never wake up.

HOPEFUL: Why not? Sleep is good for the laborer.

CHRISTIAN: Don't you remember what the shepherd said: "Be sure you do not sleep on the enchanted ground"? Then, "let us not sleep as do others; but let us watch and be sober."[14]

[11]II Cor. 5:7.
[12]Prov. 19:27.
[13]I John 2:21.
[14]I Thess. 5:6.

HOPEFUL: I acknowledge my weakness, and I thank you for reminding me. If I had been alone, I would have slept and endangered my life. I see now that what the Wise Man said is true: "Two are better than one."[15] All along the way your company has been a blessing to me. You shall have a rich reward.

Hopeful Tells of His Experiences

CHRISTIAN: To prevent drowsiness in this place, let us engage in lively conversation.

HOPEFUL: Very well, that is a good idea.

CHRISTIAN: To begin, let me ask you this question: What first caused you to think of becoming a pilgrim?

HOPEFUL: For a long time I continued to be interested in the things at Vanity Fair—which I now see, had I not changed, would have drowned my soul in torment.

CHRISTIAN: What, for instance, do you refer to?

HOPEFUL: All the treasures and riches of the world. I also took pleasure in rioting, drinking, revelling, swearing, lying, free-love, sensuality—those things that destroy the soul. But, thank God, at last I learned the truth. By listening to you and Brother Faithful at the fair I learned that the end of those things is death,[16] and that the wrath of God will come on the children of disobedience.[17]

CHRISTIAN: And did you immediately submit to the power of this new conviction?

HOPEFUL: No, I was not willing at first to acknowledge the sinfulness of my life nor to see the ruin that follows as the result of such a life. But instead, when my mind began to be troubled by the truth, I endeavored to close my eyes against the light.

CHRISTIAN: But what finally caused you to realize that God's

[15]Eccles. 4:9.
[16]Rom. 6:21-23.
[17]Eph. 5:6.

Spirit was dealing with you, revealing to you the truth and requiring you to face it?

HOPEFUL: At first, of course, I was ignorant of the fact that God's Spirit was dealing with me. I did not know that God begins His work of converting a sinner by pricking his conscience with divine truth, illuminating his mind with divine light, enabling him to see his sins, and making him feel guilty of sin. Next, though I was now awake to my wrong-doing, still, sin was precious to me because of the evil bent of my mind and the carnality of my body, and I was unwilling to give it up. I did not want to part with my old associates; their company and friendship were dear to me. Yet the long hours in which I suffered under conviction, and self-condemnation, were very trying, and sometimes heartbreaking.

CHRISTIAN: But did it not seem at times that you were free of these troubles?

HOPEFUL: Yes, but they would soon return, more burdensome than ever.

CHRISTIAN: Just what was it that brought your sins to mind again?

HOPEFUL: Many things; such as meeting a good man on the streets, hearing someone read or quote the Bible, feeling pain, or becoming sick in body, hearing that some friend or neighbor was sick, hearing the church bell toll for a funeral service, hearing of an accidental or sudden death, thinking about dying, but especially when I thought of coming before God in the judgment.

CHRISTIAN: And could you, at any time, easily throw off the feeling of guilt?

HOPEFUL: No, indeed, for when I tried to do that, sin seemed to take a stronger hold on me. Still, when I considered going back to my old sins, that brought on additional distress, for my mind had been changed, and the idea was repulsive.

CHRISTIAN: And what did you do then?

HOPEFUL: I tried to mend my ways, for I thought that was the only way to escape condemnation and find peace.

CHRISTIAN: In what way did you improve?

HOPEFUL: I quit not only my sins—what I considered sins—but also my sinful company and I took up good works, such as praying regularly, reading the Bible, going to church, giving to charity, being prompt in all my obligations, and speaking the truth. These things and many others I was careful to observe.

CHRISTIAN: Then did you imagine that you were all right?

HOPEFUL: Yes, for a while—until my conscience troubled me again.

CHRISTIAN: How did it happen that your troubles came back, since you were living a good moral life?

HOPEFUL: Several things caused me to doubt and to feel that all was not well. For instance, such sayings as these: "Not by works of righteousness which we have done";[18] "All our righteousnesses are as filthy rags";[19] "By the works of the law no flesh shall be justified";[20] "Whatsoever is not of faith is sin";[21] "Being justified by faith, we have peace with God";[22] "Except a man be born again he cannot see the kingdom of God."[23] From those plain, emphatic statements of truth I would reason like this: If it is not by works of righteousness or works of the law that a man is justified and saved, then I am not saved. All my righteousnesses are as filthy rags. And if whatsoever is not of faith is sin, all my works are sinful, because I do not have true faith. If I had real faith, I would be justified and have peace in my heart. Therefore, it must be that I am not born of God. And if I am not born of God, I can never see the kingdom of God. Furthermore, if my works were all righteous and ac-

[18]Titus 3:5.
[19]Isa. 64:6.
[20]Gal. 2:16.
[21]Rom. 14:23.
[22]Rom. 5:1.
[23]John 3:3.

cepted of God, they could never pay for the sins I committed before I resolved to live a better life. Then the old account is not settled, and I am going deeper and deeper in debt to God. I will have an awful lot to pay for when I stand before the Judge.

CHRISTIAN: A very good application, but please go on.

HOPEFUL: Another thing that troubled me after my reformation was when I examined closely my best deeds. I could see evil mixed with the good—wrong motives, selfishness, and pride. So I was forced to conclude that in spite of all my efforts and good opinions of myself, I was still committing enough sin to send me to Hell, even if all my former life had been faultless.

CHRISTIAN: And what did you do about that?

HOPEFUL: Do? I did not know what to do until I went to Faithful with my problem (he and I were close friends). He told me that unless I could obtain the righteousness of a man who was perfect and who had never sinned, neither my own righteousness nor all the righteousness of the world could save me.

CHRISTIAN: And did you believe he was telling you the truth?

HOPEFUL: Yes, but if he had told me that when I was pleased with myself, I would have thought he was a crank. But after I saw my own corruption and the sin that clung to my best performance, I had to admit that he was right.

CHRISTIAN: But when he first suggested it to you, did you believe that such a man could be found?

HOPEFUL: Well, I must confess that at first the idea seemed fantastic. But after further discussion with him, and feeling something of his faith and buoyant spirit, I believed him definitely.

CHRISTIAN: And did you ask him who this man was and where he could be found?

HOPEFUL: Yes, and he told me that the man was Jesus the Christ, who was now seated at the right hand of God,[24] and he said that I must be justified by Him by trusting in Him and what He did for me when He died upon the cross. I asked him how that man's righteousness could be effectual in justifying another before God. And he told me that He died not for Himself but for me, to atone for my sins, to pay off all my debt to God, and that God had accepted what He did for me, and that when I believed in Him and what He did, His righteousness would be imputed to me.

CHRISTIAN: What did you think of that?

HOPEFUL: I believed that Jesus was righteous and that He died for the sins of the world; yet I doubted that He would impute His righteousness to one so sinful as myself, and I imagined that He would condemn such before God—and rightly so.

CHRISTIAN: And what did Faithful say to that?

HOPEFUL: He said, "Why not go to Him and see?" I said that would be presumption. But he said, "No, for you are invited to come."[25] Then he gave me a book of the very words of Jesus, encouraging me to come; and he said that every dot and iota of that book stood firmer than heaven and earth.[26] I asked him what I must do when I came to Christ. He said I must plead with all my heart and soul to the Father to reveal Him to me. Then I asked him what I must say in my pleading. He said, "You will find Him on a mercy seat, where He sits all the year long, granting pardons and forgiveness to them that come. You simply say (and mean it with all your heart): 'God be merciful to me a sinner. I acknowledge and confess my sinfulness and all my sins. Help me to know and believe in Jesus Christ, for I see that without His righteousness and mercy, and unless I

[24]Heb. 10:12.
[25]Matt. 11:28.
[26]Matt. 24:35.

believe in that righteousness and accept His offered mercy, I shall be lost forever. Lord, I have heard that you are a merciful God, and that You have ordained your Son Jesus Christ to be the Saviour of the world, and that You are willing to bestow His goodness and mercy upon a poor lost sinner like me—and I am a wretched, helpless sinner indeed. Lord, now take my sins and give me Your righteousness: magnify Your grace in the salvation of my soul. In Jesus' name, amen.' "

CHRISTIAN: And did you do as you were instructed?

HOPEFUL: Yes, over and over again.

CHRISTIAN: Then were you not tempted to give up?

HOPEFUL: Yes, a hundred times, but I continued to believe that what Faithful had told me was true. I thought if I gave up I would surely die, and if I kept on praying I might die, but if so, I would die at the throne of grace. Then the words of the Book came to me: "Though it [the vision] tarry, wait for it; because it will surely come";[27] "They that wait upon the Lord shall renew their strength";[28] "Whosoever shall call on the name of the Lord shall be saved."[29] So I kept on praying till the Father revealed His Son to me.

CHRISTIAN: And how was He revealed to you?

HOPEFUL: I did not see Him with my physical eyes but with the eyes of my understanding. One day I was very sad, sadder than I had ever been, because of the vileness of my nature, the magnitude of my sins, and the helplessness of my condition. I was expecting nothing but condemnation in everlasting darkness when suddenly I thought I saw the Lord looking down upon me and saying, "Believe on the Lord Jesus Christ, and thou shalt be saved."[30]

I replied, "But, Lord, I am a very great sinner." He answered,

[27]Hab. 2:3.
[28]Isa. 40:31.
[29]Acts 2:21.
[30]Acts 16:31.

"My grace is sufficient for thee."[31] Then I asked, "But, Lord what is believing?" He said, "He that cometh to me shall never hunger; and he that believeth on me shall never thirst."[32] Then I concluded that coming and believing were the same. I knew that to some extent I had come. This proved to me that I had some faith, or I never would have come. Yet I was still hungering and thirsting—for something. How could I understand this?

Now, I heard the Apostle Paul saying, "They . . . have not submitted themselves unto the righteousness of God."[33] I knew that Christ was the righteousness of God and, like the Jews, I had not submitted myself to Christ. "If I had," I reasoned, "God would have accepted me before now, for His Word says, 'Him that cometh to me, I will in no wise cast out.' "[34] Then these marvelous Scriptures awoke in my mind: "To him that worketh not, but believeth on Him that justifieth the ungodly, his faith is counted for righteousness";[35] "Christ Jesus came into the world to save sinners";[36] "Christ is the end of the law for righteousness to every one that believeth";[37] "He was delivered for our offenses, and was raised again for our justification";[38] He "loved us, and washed us from our sins in his own blood."[39]

It was now clear to me that Christ was the "one mediator between God and men,"[40] and that "he is able . . . to save them to the uttermost that come unto God by him, seeing he ever liveth to make intercession for them."[41] Then I believed in the infinite goodness and boundless mercy of the Lord Jesus Christ and His great power to save, and His love and peace, like a river, flowed into my soul. I saw that He was not only righteous Himself, but He was able to make the worst of sinners righteous be-

[31] II Cor. 12:9.
[32] John 6:35.
[33] Rom. 10:3.
[34] John 6:37.
[35] Rom. 4:5.
[36] I Tim. 1:15.
[37] Rom. 10:4.
[38] Rom. 4:25.
[39] Rev. 1:5.
[40] I Tim. 2:5.
[41] Heb. 7:25.

fore God. Then I ceased from my own efforts and trusted wholly in Him, and He washed me white and clean, accepted me in the Beloved, and gave me a peace that "passeth all understanding," "sweet peace, the gift of God's love."

CHRISTIAN: That was a revelation of Christ to your soul, indeed. What particular effect did this have on your spirit and life?

HOPEFUL: My heart overflowed with joy and peace, also with love for Jesus Christ—His words, His ways, and His people. He let me see that all the world, notwithstanding all the righteousness in it, is in a state of condemnation and that God the Father, though He is absolutely just, can justly justify the ungodly sinner who believes. I was now extremely ashamed of my past life and perfectly amazed at my profound ignorance, for I had never before seen the unsurpassed beauty of the love of God revealed in the person of the Lord Jesus Christ. I now felt that if I had a thousand lives to give, I would gladly give them all in the service of the Lord Jesus Christ and for His sake.

CHAPTER
10
the talk with ignorance

BY THIS TIME the young man Ignorance had caught up with Christian and Hopeful on the way to the Celestial City. Christian said to him, "Come on, young man, why have you stayed so far behind?"

IGNORANCE: I like to walk alone most of the time, unless I am with those who think as I do.

Asking Probing Questions

CHRISTIAN: How is it, dear Ignorance, with your soul and God?

IGNORANCE: Very well, I hope, for I am always full of good thoughts that come into my mind and console me on the way.

CHRISTIAN: Will you share some of them with us? What have you been thinking?

IGNORANCE: Why, I think often of God and Heaven.

CHRISTIAN: So do all men.

HOPEFUL: But in my thoughts, I desire God and Heaven.

CHRISTIAN: So do many who may never see them. There is a sacred proverb that says, "The soul of the sluggard desireth, and hath nothing."[1]

[1]Prov. 13:4.

IGNORANCE: But I have given up all for them.

CHRISTIAN: One can think so and be mistaken. Giving up everything is much harder than many people imagine. What leads you to believe that you have given up all for God and Heaven?

IGNORANCE: My heart tells me that I have.

CHRISTIAN: But is your heart reliable? The Bible says, "He that trusteth in his own heart is a fool."[2]

IGNORANCE: That is spoken of a fool. I'm no fool. My heart is wise and good.

CHRISTIAN: But how do you know that? What means have you of testing your own heart?

IGNORANCE: My heart comforts me in the hope of Heaven.

CHRISTIAN: That may be through its deceitfulness. Jeremiah the prophet said, "The heart is deceitful above all things, and desperately wicked: who can know it?"[3] A man's heart may give him hope when there are no grounds for his hope.

IGNORANCE: But my heart and life agree, so my hope is well grounded.

CHRISTIAN: What proof have you that your heart and life agree?

IGNORANCE: My heart tells me so.

CHRISTIAN: Your heart tells you so! Except the Word of God bears witness, other testimony is of no value.

IGNORANCE: But is it not a good heart that has good thoughts, and is that not a good life that is according to God's commandments?

CHRISTIAN: Yes, indeed, but it is one thing to have these, and another thing only to think so.

IGNORANCE: Pray tell me, what are good thoughts, and what is a good life, according to the Bible?

CHRISTIAN: There are good thoughts of various kinds—

[2]Prov. 28:26.
[3]Jer. 17:9.

thoughts respecting ourselves, thoughts concerning God, and good thoughts toward humanity.

IGNORANCE: What are good thoughts respecting ourselves?

CHRISTIAN: Such thoughts as agree with the Word of God.

IGNORANCE: When do thoughts of ourselves agree with the Word of God?

CHRISTIAN: When we pass the same judgment on ourselves that the Word of God passes on us. For instance, the Word of God says of those in the natural state: "There is none righteous, no, not one; there is none that doeth good."[4]

IGNORANCE: I will never believe that my heart is bad. What are good thoughts concerning God?

CHRISTIAN: Even as I have said concerning ourselves: when our thoughts of God agree with what His Word says about Him. We have right thoughts of God when we think that He knows us better than we know ourselves, and can see sin in us when we can see none in ourselves.

IGNORANCE: Do you think that I am such a fool as to think that God can see no further than I, or that I would dare come to God trusting in my best performance?

CHRISTIAN: Well, how do you think in this matter?

IGNORANCE: Why, I think I must believe in Christ for justification.

CHRISTIAN: How can you imagine that you believe in Christ when you do not see that you have any need of Him? You neither see your innate nor your actual sins, but you have an opinion of yourself that plainly puts you beyond the need of the Redeemer. How then do you believe in Christ?

IGNORANCE: I believe well enough, for all that. I believe that Christ died for sinners and that I shall be justified before God from the curse through His gracious acceptance of my obedience to His law. Christ makes my religious duties accept-

[4]Rom. 3:10-12.

able to His Father by virtue of His merits, and the Father justifies me because of my obedience to His Son.

Difference between False and True Faith

CHRISTIAN: Let me answer your confession of faith in this way: First, you believe with a fantastic faith, for such faith is nowhere recorded in God's Word. Next, your faith is false, because it claims justification by the righteousness of Christ without accepting that righteousness. As long as you cling to your own imaginary righteousness, you reject His righteousness. Furthermore, your faith does not receive the death of Christ as necessary in your justification. Instead, you receive Him as an example and justifier of your action in believing, which is an invention of the carnal mind without Scripture foundation. Therefore your faith is deceitful and will leave you under the wrath of God in the day of judgment. True justifying faith makes the soul sensible of its lost condition and sends it fleeing for refuge to Christ—to His cross and righteousness—for salvation. His righteousness does not consist merely of an example and gracious action in accepting persons on the basis of their obedience to His law. Christ's righteousness includes His perfect obedience to the law of God and His becoming responsible for all mankind in their disobedience, to the extent of dying for their sins. This death, which was required of sinners, was borne by Him that the guilty who believe in Him might be acquitted, have His righteousness, and be justified. This is the righteousness that true faith accepts. Without this righteousness, every soul will be condemned.

IGNORANCE: What! Would you have us trust in what Christ in His own person, without us, has done? This presumptuous conceit would give license to all our lusts and encourage us to ignore God's commandments and live as we please. For what would it matter how we lived, so long as we are permanently justified by what Christ did for us, independent of anything we do?

CHRISTIAN: I think you have the right name. At least your answer indicates that such is the case, for you are evidently ignorant of what justifying righteousness is and also of soul security through faith in it. Yes, and you are ignorant also of the effects of soul-saving faith, which changes and wins the heart to God in Christ, so that one loves God's Word, His name, His ways, His service, and His people. Thus faith and love are the strongest, the most enduring virtues in the world. They are in reality the nature of God in human life.

HOPEFUL: Ask him if he ever had Christ revealed to him.

IGNORANCE: What! You believe in special revelations? I think that what you and all your kind say on that subject is nothing but the fruit of disorderly brains.

HOPEFUL: Why, son, Christ is so hidden in God from the comprehension of the natural man that He cannot by any be savingly known, unless God, the Father, reveals Him to them.

IGNORANCE: That is your faith, but not mine. Yet I am sure that mine is as good as yours, even though I do not have so many fantasies in my head.

CHRISTIAN: You ought not to speak so disrespectfully of so serious a matter. I, too, will emphatically affirm that no man can know Jesus Christ except by the revelation of the Father.[5] And I am just as emphatic about the faith by which the soul lays hold on Christ. The right kind of faith must be wrought by the mighty power of God, of which faith I perceive, dear man, you are totally destitute. Be awakened, dear Ignorance, and see your own wretchedness and condemnation, and flee for salvation to the Lord Jesus Christ, by whose righteousness alone you shall be delivered from the wrath to come.

[5]Matt. 11:27.

Ignorance Falls Behind Pilgrims

IGNORANCE: You fellows walk too fast for me. I can't keep up with you. Go ahead, if you like, and I will come on later.

Then Christian and Hopeful went on, talking to each other, and left Ignorance behind.

HOPEFUL: Alas, there are many persons in our town in his condition—whole families; yes, whole streets, many of whom call themselves pilgrims! And if there be so many in our town, through which the pilgrims pass every day, how many do you suppose there are in the town and country from which he comes?

CHRISTIAN: Well, the Word says, "He hath blinded their eyes, lest they should see." But what do you think of such persons? Have they at no time any conviction of sin, and no fear or dread of the future? Do you suppose that they ever imagine that their state and position is dangerous?

HOPEFUL: You are older than I. I would rather have you answer that question.

CHRISTIAN: I think that perhaps at times they do have some conviction of sin and some dread or fear of the future, but they do not know that such fear tends to their good. Therefore, they strive desperately to stifle their fear and, having put it out of their minds, they flatter themselves on being able to master their feelings.

HOPEFUL: I do believe that fear tends to conform men to the plan of God for the beginning of a pilgrimage.

CHRISTIAN: Without doubt, if it is the right kind of fear, for the Word says: "The fear of the Lord is the beginning of wisdom."[6]

HOPEFUL: How do you distinguish the right kind of fear?

CHRISTIAN: True or righteous fear is recognized by three things: it brings deep conviction of sin; it leads to repentance

[6]Prov. 9:10.

and saving faith in Christ; it creates in the soul a holy reverence for God, for His Word and His way, keeping the heart tender and causing one to shrink from anything that would turn one's life from Christ, grieve the Holy Spirit, encourage the enemy to speak reproachfully, or bring dishonor to the name of Christ.

HOPEFUL: Well said. I believe you have spoken the truth. Are we not now almost past the enchanted ground?

CHRISTIAN: Why, are you tiring of this discussion?

HOPEFUL: Oh no, by no means! But I'm wondering where we are.

CHRISTIAN: We have about two miles farther to go. But let us continue with our discussion. Now the ignorant do not know that such convictions of sin that put them in dread and fear are for their good; that is the reason they seek to erase them.

HOPEFUL: How do they remove them?

CHRISTIAN: They think that these fears are prompted by the devil (though in reality they are wrought of God) and, thinking so, they resist them as something evil that would unbalance the mind. They also think that such fears will undermine faith (what they have is only fancy, not faith), and they harden their hearts against them. They presume that fear is a weakness, and that it is wrong to be afraid. Therefore, in spite of their sincere convictions, they become unduly self-confident. They see that fear tends to destroy their happiness and their pitiful self-righteousness; therefore, they resist it with all their willpower.

HOPEFUL: I know something about that myself, for before I knew the meaning of conviction, I thought that way too.

Backsliding Discussed

CHRISTIAN: Did you, about ten years ago, know one Mr. Temporary in your country?

HOPEFUL: Know him? Yes, he lived in the town of Graceless about four miles from Honesty—next door, I believe, to one Turnback.

CHRISTIAN: Right! Once he lived under the same roof with Mr. Turnback. Well, Temporary was once very much concerned about right relationship to God, and I believe then he had some knowledge of his sins and the wages of sin.[7]

HOPEFUL: I agree with you. He lived only about three miles from me, and he would often come to me in tears for my advice. Really, I pitied the man and had hopes that he would find real faith and become a Christian, but now we see that it is not everyone who cries, "Lord! Lord!" that enters the kingdom.

CHRISTIAN: He told me once that he had resolved to go on pilgrimage. But all of a sudden he got acquainted with one Save-self, and then he became a stranger to me.

HOPEFUL: What was the reason of his sudden change, and why do others backslide in this way?

CHRISTIAN: That is a good question. What do you think is the reason?

HOPEFUL: In my judgment there are four reasons for it:

First, though the conscience of such men is awakened, yet their minds are not changed. So when the feeling of guilt wears off, they naturally turn to their old carnal ways again. Their guilty conscience causes them to fear Hell, and the fear of Hell begets their interest in Heaven. But when the feeling of guilt is gone, the fear of Hell vanishes and they lose their interest in Heaven. So they go back to the old life for the fleeting pleasures of the world.

Second, they have fears of men that enslave them, and "the fear of man bringeth a snare."[8] They seem to be anxious for Heaven so long as the flames of Hell roar in their ears. But with that terror gone, they have second thoughts; namely, that it is good to be wise and not to run the risk of losing all, or of bring-

[7]Rom. 6:23.
[8]Prov. 29:25.

ing themselves into unavoidable trouble. Therefore, to shun these they retreat to the ways of the world.

Third, they are proud, and the proud people of the world make them feel that the Christian religion is for the low and contemptible. Consequently, when they lose their sense of guilt and their apprehensions of torment, they return to their former course.

Then, because the thought of guilt and punishment is unbearable to them, they prefer to remain oblivious to their misery until they come into it. Though perhaps an honest facing of their guilt and future suffering would send them to Christ for forgiveness and joyous deliverance, yet they shun the thoughts of guilt and punishment, and thus get rid of their feeling about the wrath of God, and harden their hearts more and more against the truth.

CHRISTIAN: That is pretty near the truth of the matter. However, at the bottom of all their behavior is a stubborn will. At first they seem to be penitent, but they are like the criminal who weeps before the judge not because of his crime but because he was apprehended and must face punishment. Give him his liberty, and he will be a thief or a murderer still. Whereas, if his mind is changed, he will be a good citizen.

HOPEFUL: I have shown you the reason for their going back. Now you show me the manner of their backsliding.

CHRISTIAN: Well, I think it is like this: First they withdraw their thoughts as much as possible from the remembrance of God, death, and judgment to come. Then by degrees they give up their self-discipline, such as private prayer, curbing their lusts, watching their conduct, regretting sin, and the like. Then they shun the company of lively, warmhearted Christians. After that they grow negligent of public duty, such as hearing and reading the Word of God, attending meetings, and the like. Then they begin to find fault with Christians, picking holes in the coats of the godly (because of some weakness which they fancy they have seen in them), and casting aspersions on the good name of disciples behind their back. Then they begin to associate with worldly, loose, and evil-minded people. They also give way to carnal, lustful, and immoral practice in secret; and seek to find such practice in those who are counted true, that they may say they are their example. After this they play with sin openly. Then, being hardened, they show themselves as they are: downright wicked. Now, being bogged down again in the gulf of misery, they perish forever in their own deceivings unless a miracle of grace prevents it.

Christian and Hopeful journey through Beulah Land.

CHAPTER
11
near to the city of God

Enjoying a Stay in Beulah Land

NOW I SAW that the pilgrims had gotten past the enchanted ground, and were entering the country of Beulah. The air was very sweet and invigorating. They rested and enjoyed themselves in this land for some time. Here they heard the continual singing of birds, and flowers were blooming everywhere. They heard also the voice of the turtle in the land. In this peaceful country, the sun shone all year long. This was far from the Valley of the Shadow of Death, and beyond the reach of Giant Despair. In this sunny land no one could get even a faint conception of Doubting Castle. Here the pilgrims were within sight of the Holy City. Here also they met some of the inhabitants of that eternal metropolis, for here in the land of Beulah the heavenly ones often walked with the lowly, for it was on the border of Heaven. In this land also the vow of the bride and the bridegroom was renewed. Here they had no lack of good things, for there was an abundance of all the things the pilgrims had desired in their journey. They even heard voices from the City, saying, "Say ye to the daughters of Zion, 'Behold, thy King cometh! Behold His reward is with Him!' " and all the inhabitants of the land called the pilgrims "the holy people and the redeemed of the Lord."

As they walked through this country, they had more joy than they had known in the places more remote from the kingdom to which they were going. Drawing nearer, they had a more perfect view of the City and could see it was built of pearls and precious stones and the streets were paved with gold. By reason of the natural glory of the City and the reflection of the sunbeams upon it, Christian, with deep desire, fell sick. Hopeful, also, had a siege of discontent. So here they lay for days, crying out because of the pangs of their heart, "If you see my Beloved, tell Him that I am sick with love."

But they received more grace and were able to go on their way. As they came nearer and nearer to the gates of light, they saw orchards, vineyards, and beautiful gardens, whose gates opened into the highway. They asked one gardener, who stood in his gate, "Whose fruitful vineyards and gardens are these?" He answered, "They are the King's, and are planted here for His own delight and the enjoyment of pilgrims." Then the gardener invited them into the vineyard and told them to help themselves to the delicious grapes. He also showed them the King's walks and His restful arbors. There they tarried and slept.

They talked much in their sleep. I wondered why, and the gardener said to me, "Do you wonder at the pilgrims talking so much in their sleep? They are happy. It is the nature of these grapes to be so sweet and satisfying as to cause the lips of them that sleep to speak."

I saw when they awoke that they prepared to go up to the City. However, the reflection of the sun upon the City, which was pure gold,[1] was so extremely bright that they could not with the natural eye look directly upon it. They had to look

[1]Rev. 21:18.

through a glass made for that purpose. As they went on, they were met by two men in golden raiment whose faces shone like the light.

They asked the pilgrims where they were from, where they had lodged, what blessings and pleasures they had experienced, and what difficulties they had come through on the way. Christian and Hopeful related their experiences. Then the shining ones said, "You have but two more difficulties to overcome; then you will be in the City."

Christian asked the men to go along with them. They said they would, but added, "You must go on your own faith." So I saw in my dream that they all went on together till they came in sight of the gate.

Passing Through the River of Death

Between them and the gate was a deep river, dark and cold, and there was no bridge. At the sight of the river the pilgrims turned pale, and were silent. The two men said, "You must go through, or you will never get to the gate."

"Is there no other way?" they asked.

"Yes," said the men, "but since the foundation of the world only two, Enoch and Elijah, have been permitted to go that way, nor shall any others ever be so permitted until Christ comes again."

Then they accepted the inevitable. Entering the water, Christian began to sink. He cried to his good friend Hopeful, "I sink in deep water; the billows go over my head; all His waves go over me."

"Be of good cheer," said Hopeful, "I feel the bottom, and it is good."

Then said Christian, "Ah! my friend, sorrows of death have surrounded me; and I shall never see that happy land." Then an awful horror and darkness came over Christian so that he could not see what was before him, and to a great degree he lost his sense of what was transpiring around him. He could not quite remember or speak coherently of the good things he had enjoyed in the way of his pilgrimage. But what words he spoke indicated that he had great fears of dying in that river before reaching the beautiful gate. They that stood by perceived that he was troubled over sins he had committed, both before and after he became a pilgrim. They assumed also that he was seeing visions of hobgoblins and evil spirits, since he mumbled about such in his coma.

Hopeful, therefore, had all he could do to keep his brother's head above water. Sometimes he would go under for a second; then he would rise up again, though half dead. Hopeful would try to console him, saying, "Brother, I see the gate, and I see the saints standing by to receive us."

But Christian would say, "It is you, it is you they wait for; you have been a hopeful person ever since I came to know you."

"And so have you," Hopeful would reply.

"Ah, brother, surely if I were right, Christ Jesus would now come to my rescue! But because of my sins He has brought me into this snare and left me," was Christian's reply.

Then Hopeful said, "My brother, you have quite forgotten the text which says of the wicked, 'There are no bands in their death: but their strength is firm. They are not in trouble as other men; neither are they plagued like other men.'[2] These troubles and distresses that you go through in these waters are no sign that God has forsaken you. They are sent to call to your mind that which you have received of His goodness, that you may trust Him in your distress."

Then Christian seriously reflected for a moment as Hopeful

[2]Ps. 73:4-5.

added these words, "Be of good cheer, Jesus Christ maketh thee whole."

Then Christian broke out in a strong voice: "Oh, I see Him again, and He is saying, 'When thou passeth through the . . . rivers, they shall not overflow thee.' "[3] Then they both took courage. After that, the enemy was as still as a stone. Soon Christian found ground to stand on, and the rest of the river was shallow.

Reaching the other side, on the bank of the river they saw the two shining ones waiting for them. When the pilgrims came out of the water, the two angels saluted them, saying, "We are ministering spirits, sent forth to minister for them who shall be heirs of salvation."[4]

Now they went along together toward the gate. Though the City stood on a great high hill, the pilgrims went up the hill with perfect ease because of the two heavenly ones leading them by the arms and because their mortal garments had been left in the river. Therefore they went up the great hill swiftly, even though the foundation upon which the City was built was higher than earthly clouds. They ascended through the regions of the air, joyously conversing as they went—exceedingly happy that they were safely over the river and had such wonderful companions.

Their conversation was about the glory of the place, which the shining ones termed inexpressible. "There," they said, "is Mount Zion, the heavenly Jerusalem, the innumerable company of angels, and the spirits of just men made perfect.[5] You are going now to the Paradise of God, where you shall see the tree of life and eat of its never-failing fruit. And when you come there, you shall have white robes and will walk and talk every day with the King, through all eternity. There you will never

[3]Isa. 43:2.
[4]Heb. 1:14.
[5]Heb. 12:22-23.

again see the sorrows, sickness, affliction, and death you saw when you were on the earth, 'For the former things are passed away.' "[6]

The pilgrims asked, "What shall we do in the Holy City?"

They were told, "You must there receive the rewards of all your toil, and you shall have joys for all your sorrows. You must reap what you have sown—the fruits of all your prayers, and tears, and your sufferings for the King in the way.[7] There also you shall serve continually with praise and thanksgiving Him whom you desired to serve faithfully in the world, though you had many problems because of the sinfulness of your flesh. You will wear crowns of glory, and enjoy the presence and beauty of the Lord, for there you shall see Him as He is.[8] You shall also enjoy your friends—those who preceded you to that happy clime, who believed your words and followed your example in the world, and came to the glory world because of your influence. There you shall be clothed in splendor, and ride with the King of Glory in a chariot of gold.

"When Jesus the Christ shall come back to earth, with trumpet sound, you shall come with Him in the clouds of heaven, riding upon the wings of the wind. And when He shall sit upon the throne of His glory, judging the nations, and shall pass sentence upon all the workers of iniquity,[9] whether they be angels or men, you will also sit with Him and have a voice in the judgment, because they were your enemies too. Also, when He shall return to the City, you too shall go with Him with sound of trumpet and shall ever be with the Lord."

When they drew near the gate, they were met by a company of the heavenly host, of whom, in introduction, the shining ones said, "These are the men who loved our Lord when in the world,

[6]Rev. 21:1-4.
[7]Matt. 5:12; I Cor. 3:8; Rev. 22:12.
[8]I John 3:2.
[9]Matt. 25:31-41; Jude 14-15.

and left all for His service. He sent us to guide them home, and we have brought them thus far, that they may go in and see the King." The heavenly host gave a joyous hallelujah, saying, "Blessed are they which are called to the marriage supper of the Lamb."[10] There also came out several of the King's trumpeters to welcome the pilgrims with heavenly music. Then they walked on together to the gate.

When they came to the gate leading to the City they saw written over it in letters of gold: "BLESSED ARE THEY THAT DO HIS COMMANDMENTS, THAT THEY MAY HAVE RIGHT TO THE TREE OF LIFE, AND MAY ENTER IN THROUGH THE GATES INTO THE CITY."[11]

Entering the Celestial City

The pilgrims gave their certificates to the gatekeeper and were admitted into the eternal City. They were given new costumes, which shone like white gold, and crowns and harps with which to praise and glorify the Lord. Then all the bells of Heaven rang out with joy, and one said, "Enter ye into the joys of thy Lord." Then all the multitude sang out with loud voices: "Blessing, and honor, and glory, and power be unto him that sitteth upon the throne, and unto the Lamb for ever and ever."[12]

Just as the gate opened to let them in, I got a glimpse of the inner glory of Heaven. The whole City shone like the sun. The streets were paved with gold, and the garments of those who walked the golden streets shone with a luster I had not seen before. Some wore crowns as kings. Some carried harps or palms in their hands. There were also those who had beautiful wings which could not be seen except when they wished to fly. Just as they began to praise God, saying, "Holy, holy, holy, Lord God Almighty," the gate closed.

[10]Rev. 19:9.
[11]Rev. 22:14.
[12]Rev. 5:13.

Ignorance Denied Admittance

While I was gazing on these things, I turned and saw Ignorance in my dream come to the river. He soon got across, without half the difficulty the other two men had, for it happened that there was one Vain Hope, a ferryman, who took him across in his boat. Then I saw him ascend the hill, but he was alone and no one met him at the gate. He read the sign above the gate and began to knock. Then I heard a voice from within, asking, "Who are you? Where are you from, and what do you want?" He answered, "Lord, I have eaten and drunk in Your presence, and You have taught in our streets." When the gatekeeper within asked for his certificate, he was silent. The gatekeeper said, "Have you no certificate?" Ignorance had no answer.

Then, being commanded by the King, the two shining ones came out and bound Ignorance hand and foot, and carried him away through the air, to the dark door I saw in the side of the hill in the Delectable Mountains, put him in, and shut the door. I asked the angels why he was not admitted to the Celestial City, and they said, "His name was not found written in the book of life,[13] and he had no certificate in his bosom."[14] Then I knew that there was a way to Hell from the gates of Heaven, as well as from the City of Destruction.

Then I awoke, and I knew that all I had seen was a dream.

[13]Rev. 20:15.
[14]I John 5:10.

PART TWO

christiana's journey

CHAPTER
12
christiana follows christian

SOME TIME after telling you my story about Christian, the pilgrim, and his hazardous journey through the wilderness of the world to the Celestial City, I had a dream about his family—Christiana, his wife, and her four sons. I remembered how she strongly opposed Christian's call to a pilgrimage life, and how rude she was to him before he left home because she regarded his troubled spirit as an affliction of the mind.

A Strange Visitor Brings a Letter

I dreamed now that after Christian passed on Christiana became troubled over her sinful state and the way she had treated her husband. One morning with her family after she had prayed and was sweeping the floor (in deep meditation) one knocked at her door. She called out, "If you come in God's name, come in!"

"Amen," said a resonant voice, and a strange man stepped into the room. "Peace be to this house! My name is Secret," he said. "I dwell in the City where Christian has gone. It is thought by the people where I live that you desire to go there. It is reported that you are sorry for the way you treated your husband in setting yourself against his good life, and in keeping your children in ignorance of the way everlasting. Christ, the Merciful One, has sent me to tell you that He is a God ready to forgive, that He takes great delight in pardoning offenses. He invites you to come to His mansion and to His table, and He promises to give you, your family, and friends the good things of His kingdom. Christiana, your husband is there with legions of his companions, and they will be glad with joy unspeakable when you arrive."

Christiana was greatly moved at this.

This strange visitor also said, "Here is a letter from your husband's King." She was amazed. Could this be real? When she opened the letter, she saw that it was written in gold, and she scented a fragrance of fine perfume. Reading the letter, she learned that the King would have her come to His City to live, as her husband had done.

The good woman was completely overcome, and she cried, "Sir, will you take me and my children to this wonderful King, that we may serve Him with Christian, my good husband, through eternity?"

Then said the visitor: "Christiana, the bitter is before the sweet. You must go through much tribulation,[1] as did your husband, to come to the Celestial City. Therefore, I advise you to go, as Christian did, to the wicket gate yonder over the plain, for that opens into the way you must take to reach the City of God; and I bid you Godspeed. I also charge you to keep this letter to read to yourself and your children on the way until you come to the City Gate, for it is one of the songs you will sing while here in the body of clay, the house of your pilgrimage, and you must present it as your passport at the City Gate."

So Christiana called her sons and spoke these words: "My dear children, as you know, I have of late been under a great burden about the death of your father. Not that I doubt in the

[1]Acts 14:22.

least that he is happy, but I have been much concerned about our own condition which, as you see, is miserable. Also, my attitude toward your father in his distress is now a great load on my conscience, for I set my mind—and yours too—against him and utterly refused to go with him in his quest for a better life.

"The thoughts of these things would now kill me but for a dream which I had last night, and the encouraging words of this man this morning. Come, children, get ready. Let us pack up and go to the gate that lets us into the way that leads to the City where your father dwells, that we may see him again and live with him and his companions in peace, according to the laws of that land."

The boys burst into tears of joy. So their visitor told them good-bye, and they began to prepare for their journey.

Commencement of the Journey

Christiana's neighbors came in and tried to dissuade her from going. They thought it was very foolish—too perilous for a woman, especially one with children. They reminded her of the trouble her husband had in his pilgrimage. They also reminded her that her husband was a strong man, while she was only a frail woman with four children to defend. But she had one neighbor, a young woman, a Miss Mercy, who thought she was doing the right thing. Not only did she think Christiana's course was right, she so loved and admired her that she decided to go with her and share her lot.

Now, I saw that Christiana and her four boys—Matthew, Samuel, Joseph and James—were on their way, and Mercy was with them. Christiana was glad not only that she had a good companion but that she had prevailed on this young woman to seek the Lord and follow the pilgrim way. So they went on together, and Mercy began to weep.

CHRISTIANA: Why do you weep, my dear?

MERCY: Alas, who can but grieve that rightly considers the state and condition of my poor relatives who still remain in our sinful town? And that which gives me most concern is the fact that they have no instructor, nor anyone to warn them of the coming destruction.

CHRISTIANA: Great love and deep emotions become pilgrims; and you are doing for your friends and loved ones as my husband did for me. He cried because I would not heed his plea nor regard him as being sound of judgment. But his Lord and ours gathered up his tears for us, and now both you and I and my dear children are reaping the benefits of his tears. I hope, Mercy, that these tears of yours will not be lost, but will result in the salvation of many of your people. The Word says: "They that sow in tears shall reap in joy. He that goeth forth and weepeth, bearing precious seed, shall doubtless come again with rejoicing, bringing his sheaves with him."[2]

Then Mercy recited this poem:

Let the Most Blessed be my guide,
If it be His blessed will,
Unto His gate, into His fold
Up to His holy hill.

And let Him never suffer me
To swerve, or turn aside
From His free-grace and holy ways,
Whate'er shall me betide.

And let Him gather them of mine
That I have left behind:
Lord, make them pray they may be Thine,
With all their heart and mind.

[2]Ps. 126:5.

Through the Slough of Despond

By being careful and prayerful, they finally struggled through the Slough of Despond, and were on their way to the wicket gate.

These words came to Christiana and she repeated them to the others: "Blessed is she that believed, for there shall be a performance of those things which were told her from the Lord."[3]

Then Mercy said to Christiana, "If I had as good ground to hope for a loving reception at the entrance as you have, no Slough of Despond would ever discourage me."

"Well," said Christiana, "you know your weakness, and I know mine."

Reception at the Gate of Hope

At the gate, Christiana began to knock. There was no response. She knocked again and again; yet they heard nothing but the sinister barking of a dog. There they stood, confused, not knowing what to do. They felt like giving up and withdrawing from the gate, but they thought that this might be known by the gatekeeper, and He would never let them in. On the other hand, another knock might stir the dog to action. However, at last Christiana mustered enough courage to knock very loudly. Then the voice of the Keeper asked, "Who's there?" Now the dog stopped barking, and the Keeper opened the gate.

Christiana made a low bow and said, "Let not our Lord be offended with us, that we have knocked at His holy gate."

"Where are you from, and what do you wish?" asked the Keeper.

CHRISTIANA: We are from Christian's former City of Destruction, and we want to go to his present city, New Jerusalem. I am his wife, and these are his sons.

[3]Luke 1:45.

The Keeper asked, "What? Has Christian's wife now become a pilgrim? She who but a while back abhorred that life?"

CHRISTIANA: Yes, and so have these my dear children.

Then He led them through the gate, saying, "Suffer little children to come unto me." He shut the gate, and called to a trumpeter in an upper room to play some loud and joyful music. And the trumpeter filled the air with melodious notes.[4]

During this time poor Mercy stood outside crying, thinking that she had been rejected. But when Christiana had gotten admittance for herself and her boys, she made a plea for Mercy.

CHRISTIANA: My Lord, I have a good friend and companion standing outside who came with me. She feels quite dejected because she has doubts that she will be accepted, since she came without invitation, except from me; whereas I have an invitation from the King.

Mercy began to be very impatient, for each minute to her seemed an hour, so she unknowingly interrupted Christiana's intercession for her by banging on the gate, so loudly that it frightened Christiana. Then the Keeper called out, "Who's there?"

"It is my friend," replied Christiana.

By the time the Keeper opened the gate, Mercy had fainted and fallen on her face. He took hold of her hand and said, "Damsel, I say unto thee, arise."

"Oh, sir," she murmured, "I am so weak there is scarcely any life left in me."

Then He said, "One once declared, 'When my soul fainted within me I remembered the Lord.'[5] Don't be afraid, young lady, you have come to the right place; stand up and tell Me why you have come."

MERCY: I have come without an invitation, except from my

[4]Luke 15:7.
[5]Jonah 2:7.

friend. Her invitation is from the King, while mine was only from her, and I have been afraid I would not be accepted.

KEEPER: Did she sincerely desire you to come with her to this place, and did you sincerely desire to come?

MERCY: Yes. And, as You see, I have come. If there's any grace and forgivenes of sin to spare, I beg You to let me share it.

Then He gently led her in, saying, "I pray for all who believe on the Lord, by whatsoever means they come."

When she saw that she was admitted, her spirit rose.

Now Christiana, Mercy, and all the boys were received with kindness, and they all confessed that they were sorry for their sins. They asked the Lord for pardon and for further instructions, and pardon was graciously granted. The Keeper spoke kindly to them, which made them glad. He also took them up to the top of the gatehouse, pointed out the cross farther up the road, and showed them by what deed they were saved, saying that they would see it more clearly farther on. Then He left them a while in the summer parlor below, where they talked among themselves.

CHRISTIANA: How glad I am that we got in here.

MERCY: And well you may be. But I, of all creatures, have reason to leap for joy.

CHRISTIANA: I thought one time, as we stood there before the gate, when there was no response to my knocking except the horrible barking of that dog, that all our trouble had been in vain.

MERCY: Yes, and so did I. But my worst fear came when you and the boys were taken in, and I was shut out. I thought it had happened to me according to the prophecy: "Two women shall be grinding at the mill; the one shall be taken, and the other left."[6] I had a hard struggle with myself to keep

[6]Matt. 24:41.

from crying out, "Undone! undone!" For a while I was afraid to knock any more; then I saw what was written over the door, and said to myself, "I must either knock or die." So I summoned all the strength I had and knocked again as hard as I could. Then I fainted.

CHRISTIANA: Your knocking was so loud it made me jump. I thought you would take the kingdom by force.[7]

MERCY: Well, who in my situation wouldn't have done something similar? There was a cruel dog out there somewhere, and the door was closed in my face. Who, I ask, so fearful as I, would not have knocked with all his might? Tell me, what did the Lord say about my rudeness? Was He not angry with me?

CHRISTIANA: No, when He heard your pounding, it seemed to amuse Him. His eyes brightened, and He smiled so pleasantly. I really believe what you did pleased Him. He showed no sign to the contrary. But I don't understand why He keeps such a dog. I think that if I had known about the dog before, I would have hesitated to come to the gate at all. But now we are all in, and I am glad.

MERCY: I think I shall ask, if you don't mind, why He keeps that wicked dog in His yard. I hope He will not take me wrong.

"Yes, do," said one of the boys, "and tell Him to chain the brute, for we are afraid he will bite us when we go out."

At last the Keeper came down, and Mercy fell on her knees before Him, saying, "Let my Lord accept my thanks for all His favors."

He said, "Peace be to thee; please stand." But she continued to kneel before Him, as she said, "Righteous You are, Lord, when I plead with You; yet let me talk with You about Your judgments.[8] Why do You keep such a vicious dog in Your yard? He frightens timid women and children from the gate."

[7]Matt. 11:12.
[8]Jer. 12:1-2.

KEEPER: That dog has another owner. He's over the fence on another man's ground. He belongs to the castle you see there at a distance, but he can come up to the wall of this place. He has frightened many an honest pilgrim into a stronger resolution by his big menacing bark. It is not out of any good will to Me or Mine that his owner keeps him. It is his intent to frighten pilgrims from this gate. The dog has broken out a few times, and worried some of My followers, but at present I take it patiently. However, I give My pilgrims timely help, and those who come to the gate usually have faith enough to believe that I do. And as a rule they are willing to face some dangers to escape from the torments of a life out of harmony with God. Even beggars that go from door to door are hungry enough to brave the dangers of vicious dogs to find a kind and gracious hand and a satisfying meal. And should a dog behind a wall in another man's yard keep any true seeker of salvation from coming to Me through this little gate?

MERCY: Lord, I confess my ignorance. I spoke without understanding. I acknowledge that You do all things well.

Then Christiana began to talk of their journey, and to inquire concerning the road ahead.

The Keeper served them a warm, wholesome meal, gave them a map of the road, and bade them Godspeed. Once more they were on their way, and the weather was fine.

The road, you remember from the story of Christian's journey, was walled in for a way. On the other side of the wall was an orchard belonging to the man who owned the barking dog; and some of the trees of the orchard extended their fruit-bearing branches over the wall. When Christiana's boys discovered that the fruit was ripe, that it was pleasant to the eyes and very desirable to a hungry boy, they partook of it. Next day at the lodge where they stopped, they were sick. Matthew, the oldest boy, had to have a doctor. Their mother had scolded them when they were getting the fruit, but still they went on picking and eating. She had said to them, "My boys, you transgress, for that fruit does not belong to us, and you are taking that which belongs to another." However, she did not know that the orchard belonged to the enemy, and that the tree had been planted there by the wall purposely to attract pilgrims.

Deliverance from Attack

They had not gone far from the Keeper's house when two evil-minded men attacked the women, and they might have been overpowered had not their screams been heard by the gatekeeper. Then a man, sent by the Keeper, came running. Seeing the terrific struggle and the children standing by crying, he shouted to the ruffians, "What are you doing there, you scoundrels? Would you force my Lord's people into sin?" He ran fast to get hold of them, but they escaped over the wall. He asked the women if they were hurt.

CHRISTIANA: No, not physically. We are shocked and nervous. We did not expect such a thing to happen on the King's highway.

RELIEVER: I marveled when you were at the gatehouse that you did not ask the Lord for a guide, thinking that you must be aware of the fact that you were frail women, and that there were dangers on the way. If you had asked the Lord, He would have gladly granted you a guide. Then you might have avoided this trouble.

CHRISTIANA: Alas, kind Reliever, we were so taken up with our present blessings that dangers to come were forgotten! Besides, who would have imagined that such characters would be lurking so near the King's palace? Yes, it would have been better if we had asked for a guide, but since the Lord knew our needs and knew all about the dangers of the way, I wonder that He did not send someone along with us.

RELIEVER: It is not always best to grant things not asked for. Some do not appreciate such gifts as they should, nor see their true value. But when the need of a thing is felt and that thing is asked for and received without charge, then it is rightly appreciated, and the giver is endeared to the receiver. If your Lord had granted you a conductor without your asking for one, you would not have discovered your thoughtlessness, your utter dependence, and your lack of faith. Now you have more foresight and more caution, and you have learned to ask more freely for what you need.

CHRISTIANA: Then should we go back and confess our folly to the Keeper and ask for a guide?

RELIEVER: No, you will have opportunity all along the way to confess and pray. But remember this: the King has sufficient to supply pilgrims with everything they will need; still, He would be enquired of to do things for them,[9] and it is a very poor thing indeed that is not worth asking for.

When he had said this, he went back to his place, and the pilgrims went on their way.

MERCY: What a jolt! I thought surely we were past all danger, and that we would never see any more trouble.

CHRISTIANA: Your innocence may excuse you, but I should have known better. My husband's report of the way should have made me more thoughtful.

MERCY: Well, by this neglect we have discovered our imperfections, and the Lord has revealed to us the riches of His grace; for in spite of our carelessness, He has followed us with His unmerited and unasked-for favors, out of the goodness of His heart, protecting us and delivering us from dangers.

[9]Ezek. 36:37.

CHAPTER

13

at the interpreter's house

WHEN THEY HAD CONVERSED a little longer, they drew near to the Interpreter's house. They recognized the place from the description Christian had given of it. When they came to the door, they heard conversation inside, and someone spoke Christiana's name. Those dwelling there had heard that Christiana and her children had left the City of Destruction to follow her husband on pilgrimage to the Celestial City and that she had already passed the gatehouse, but they had no idea that she was then standing at the door.

Now Christiana knocked. A young girl named Innocent came to the door. She said, "With whom do you wish to speak?"

CHRISTIANA: We understand that this is a special place for pilgrims and, as you see, the day is almost gone. We would like to stay here for the night, if we may.

INNOCENT: What is your name?

CHRISTIANA: My name is Christiana. I am the wife of Christian, the pilgrim who came this way some years ago. And these are his four boys. This girl is my friend and companion, our neighbor, who is traveling with us to the better country.

Then Innocent ran into the house, and said, "Guess who's at the door! Christiana, her children, and her girl companion!"

They were all surprised, but very happy and went and told their master. He came to the door. After making himself acquainted with the visitors, he asked Christiana, "Are you the Christiana whom Christian left behind when he took up the life of a pilgrim?"

CHRISTIANA: I am the same woman who was so hardhearted as to slight her husband's troubles and to let him go on pilgrimage alone, and these are his four children. But now I also have taken up the pilgrim's life, convinced this is the right way.

INTERPRETER: Then is fulfilled that which was written of the man who said to his son, "Go work today in my vineyard." The son said to his father, "I will not," but afterwards he repented and went.[1]

CHRISTIANA: Right! May I be a true demonstration of what that parable means, and may God grant that I may stand before Him at last in peace, without spot and blameless.

INTERPRETER: But why stand outside? Come in! We were just now speaking of you, for we had just heard that you had become pilgrims. Come in, all of you. So he led them into the living room and asked them to be seated.

Then all those living and serving in the Interpreter's house came in, and expressed their delight in having them. They seemed especially fond of the boys.

Object Lessons Seen

After a while, as supper was not yet ready, the Interpreter took them into his significant rooms and showed them what Christian had seen some years before. They saw the man in the cage, the man and his bad dream, the man who cut his way through his enemies, and all those things which were so revealing and profitable to Christian.

Then, after they had had time to think of what they had seen,

[1]Matt. 21:29.

the Interpreter took them into a room where there was a man raking up dirt and trash with a muckrake. He had no time for anything else. There was revealed a celestial being standing over him, offering him an everlasting crown for his muckrake, but he could not see it. The only way he could look was downward, and he kept exceedingly busy, raking up the trash of the floor.

CHRISTIANA: I think I see the meaning of this. Is he not a man of this world who has no time for eternal things?

INTERPRETER: You are right, and his muckrake shows his carnal mind. He is bent on gathering as much trash of the world as possible before he dies. He has no time to think of eternal things. To many, Heaven is but a fable, and the material things of this perishing world are the only substantial values. As you see, he can look no way but downward. This reveals the power of earthly things to capture men's minds and close their hearts to the love of God and the realities of the world to come. "The god of this world hath blinded the minds of them which believe not, lest the light of the glorious gospel of Christ, who is the image of God, should shine unto them."[2]

CHRISTIANA: Oh, deliver me from this muckrake.

INTERPRETER: That prayer has been unused so long that it is almost rusty. "Give me neither poverty nor riches" is hardly the prayer of one in ten thousand.[3] "Give me not poverty, but riches" is the prayer most often prayed today.

"Alas," said Christiana, "that is too true."

Now the Interpreter took them into the finest room in the building and said, "Now look around and see if you can see anything that has a good lesson in it."

They looked and looked, yet found nothing. There was nothing to be seen of significance except a big spider on the wall, and they overlooked that.

"I see nothing," said Mercy. But Christiana was silent.

[2]II Cor. 4:4. [3]Prov. 30:8.

"Look closely," suggested the Interpreter.

Mercy looked again and said, "I see nothing unusual but an ugly spider who hangs by his hands to the wall, but what that means I do not know."

INTERPRETER: "The spider takes hold with her hands, and is in kings' palaces."[4] The spider—an ugly, poisonous creature—may lay hold of the beautiful things of the King with the hand of faith, so that he is no longer a spider but may be likened to a butterfly. Also, this large beautiful room, containing a poisonous spider, shows that a large, clean, beautiful heart may unwittingly let in an ugly, poisonous spider and harbor it for quite a while. This demonstrates the stealthiness and forwardness of sin.

They were all glad to have these valuable truths impressed upon their minds in such a clear, unforgettable manner by this wonderful person. They looked at each other with tears in their eyes, and bowed to the Interpreter.

Then he showed them another room, where there was a hen with her chickens. One little chick went to the trough to drink.

"See," said the Interpreter, "what this little chicken does? He lifts his eyes toward Heaven—as we should do with thankful hearts for everything we receive—because God is the source of all things, both spiritual and material."

Then he called their attention to the voice of the hen. They observed that she had four different calls: a common clucking call continuously, a special call occasionally, a brooding note of love, and an outcry of danger.

INTERPRETER: Now compare this hen to your Lord, and these chickens to His obedient followers. By His common call of the gospel, He gives nothing but a promise. By His special call of the Holy Spirit, He always gives something of permanent value. He also has a soothing, brooding voice of love for those

[4]Prov. 30:28.

who have surrendered to Him. And He has an outcry of alarm, to warn His followers of danger.

CHRISTIANA: Many thanks, Interpreter! Let us see more.

So he led them into the slaughterhouse, where men were killing a sheep. They observed that the sheep was not excited, but submissive, taking his suffering quietly in patience.

Then explained the Interpreter: "You must learn from this sheep to suffer patiently, to put up with wrong treatment without murmuring or complaining. Christ is the Good Shepherd, and He calls you His sheep."

After this he showed them his garden of flowers. He said, "You see here many flowers. They differ in size, shape, color, and beauty. Some are more valuable than others; yet they all stay and grow in the same garden, where the gardener has placed them, each giving off his own fragrance without strife or quarreling with others."

Then he had them out in his wheat field. But the wheat had been headed, and only the straw remained. He asked, "What shall I do with this crop now? This ground was fertilized and plowed well before planting."

"This straw is good for nothing," replied Christiana, "but to be plowed under, or burned."

INTERPRETER: You see, fruit is what you look for, and without that you condemn the plant to the fire, or to be trodden under foot of men. Take heed that in this you do not condemn yourself, for it is said that "he will . . . gather his wheat into the garner; but he will burn up the chaff with unquenchable fire."[5]

Now, as they were coming in from the field, they saw a little robin on the yard fence with a big spider in his mouth. "Look!" he exclaimed, pointing to the robin.

"What a pity," remarked Christiana, "to see such a beautiful

[5]Matt. 3:12.

bird, who has a sweet voice and is loved and admired by all, relish such a heinous thing. I thought he lived on crumbs of bread or tiny seeds. I did not imagine that he could enjoy such a diet. I think less of him than I did."

INTERPRETER: This robin is a symbol of some professing Christians. You will meet some who in appearance are as proud and pretty as a robin. They associate with the best class of people and outwardly have all the earmarks of culture. They like to be seen in the house of the Lord on Sunday, and they can sing like a lark. But when they are alone, or in evil company, they can swallow spiders of sin and drink iniquity like water.

Proverbs Heard

When they had come into the house and were waiting for supper, Christiana desired more instruction, so Interpreter spoke to them in proverbs:

"The fatter the sow, the more she loves to wallow in the mire; the bigger the ox, the more bravely he goes to the slaughter; and the more successful and prosperous the person, the more prone he is to evil. One leak will sink a ship, and one sin will destroy a life. He who forgets his friend is ungrateful to him; but he who forgets his Saviour is unmerciful to himself. He who lives in sin and looks for happiness is like the man who sows his field with thistle seed and expects to fill his barn with wheat. If this trouble-filled life is valued so highly by us, what about a perfect eternal life in a perfect world! We are so accustomed, as we should be, to praise the goodness of men; but how many of us always see and praise the goodness of God? We seldom dine without leaving something on the table; so there is more merit and righteousness in Christ than the whole world will ever use or need."

When the Interpreter had finished his proverbs, he again took his guests into the garden, and showed them a tree that was nothing but a hollow shell; yet it was alive and covered with green leaves.

"What does this mean?" asked Mercy.

INTERPRETER: This tree, whose outside is fair, represents those in the garden of God who make an outward show of the Christian life but have no heart for anything divine. Jesus said of them: "This people draweth nigh unto me with their mouth, and honoreth me with their lips; but their heart is far from me."[6]

Then there came a call to supper, so they all went in and sat down. The Interpreter gave thanks, and they all began to eat. A minstrel played, and someone sang a beautiful song.

Testimonies Given

When the music ended, the Interpreter asked Christiana what had moved her to become a pilgrim.

CHRISTIANA: At first, I was grieved over the loss of my husband. I could not keep from thinking about the trials and troubles my husband had gone through, and of the way I had treated him at home every day and, finally, in refusing to go with him. Then I felt guilty not only of mistreating him but also guilty before God of rejecting Jesus Christ who died for me. Then I had a dream of my husband—of seeing him in his happy state, and I thought one came to me with a letter from his King, inviting me to come to that beautiful country. I decided that the call was from God, and I sold out all my earthly possessions and came. But I did not leave my children behind. They were more than glad to come with me.

"Your beginning is good," said the Interpreter. Then he turned to Mercy, and asked, "What moved you to come this way?"

Mercy blushed, and for a moment said nothing. "Don't be afraid," he said, "only believe and speak your mind."

[6]Matt. 15:8.

MERCY: Honestly, sir, my lack of experience makes me want to keep silent, and I am filled with fear of falling short of what a pilgrim should be. I cannot tell of visions and dreams, as my friend Christiana can; nor do I know what it is to mourn the loss of a loved one, or to regret refusing the counsel of close relations.

INTERPRETER: Then, what was it, dear heart, that prevailed on you to do as you have done?

MERCY: Well, when my friend here was packing up to leave, another lady and myself happened to call on her. Seeing what she was doing, we asked her what was the meaning of her packing. She said that she was sent for to go to her husband. Then she told us how she had seen him in a dream, dwelling in a marvelous place, among wonderful people, wearing a crown, playing a harp, eating at the King's table, and singing praises to the King in sweet heavenly tones. And while she was telling this story, my heart burned within me and I said to myself, "If this be true, I will leave father and mother and the land of my nativity. If Christiana will accept me as a companion, I will go along with her." So I inquired further of the truth of these things and whether she would let me go with her, for I gathered from her story that there was no longer any safety in our town. But I came away with a heavy heart, not because I was unwilling to come—for I was more than willing—but because I was leaving my closest friends and relatives behind. But now I have come with all the desire of my heart, and I will go—if I may—with Christiana to her husband and his King.

INTERPRETER: Your beginning is commendable. You have believed and given credit to the truth. You are like Ruth, who, for the love she had for Naomi and her Lord, left father and mother and her native land to go into a strange country and live with people she had not known.[7] The Lord will reward you and

[7]Ruth 1:16-17; 2:12.

richly bless you in the way, since you have come under His protecting care.

Now supper was ended, and preparation was made for bed. The women slept in separate beds in the same room; and the boys slept two and two in another.

But Mercy could not sleep for hours. She was so happy. All her doubts and fears were gone. For a long time she lay blessing and praising God in her heart for showing her such wonderful kindness.

Departure

In the morning, they rose with the sun and began to prepare to go on their journey. But the Interpreter asked them to stay a little longer, that they might be fully equipped for the road.

Now, Innocent, following instructions, had them bathe in the pool of the garden, and put on new, white, linen uniforms. Thus clothed, the women looked so beautiful that they looked on each other with awe. For each could see the glory only in the other, and each esteemed the other better than herself.[8] "You are fairer than I," said one. "And you are more beautiful than I am," said the other. The children also stood amazed to see their new appearance.

Then the Interpreter called for the seal,[9] with which all are sealed who have been washed in the water of regeneration.[10] So he sealed them and set his mark upon them that they might be recognized in the places where they were to go. The mark placed on their foreheads added much to their appearance.

Then the Interpreter called a man servant, one Mr. Greatheart, and told him to take a sword, a helmet, and a shield and conduct these new pilgrims to the house called Beautiful, where they would make their next stop. Then he bade them Godspeed, and all his family of servants wished them well on their journey.

[8]Phil. 2:3. [9]Eph. 1:13. [10]Titus 3:5.

CHAPTER
14

the guidance of greatheart

Explaining Free Pardon

WITH GREATHEART going before them, the pilgrims soon came to the place where Christian's burden fell from his back and tumbled into the grave. Here they paused and worshiped God.

CHRISTIANA: Now, what was said to us at the gate comes to my mind; namely, that we should have pardon by word and deed. By word, I understand, means by promise—we believe the promise that we shall no longer be held guilty, because another has been held guilty for our sins. But to be pardoned by deed, I do no understand.

GREATHEART: Pardon by deed is pardon by the deeds of another performed for you. Another has lived the life and performed the deeds required of you, and has suffered the penalty of all your misdeeds, that you, here and now, might be set free. So the pardon that you and Mercy and these boys have obtained was obtained by Him who let you in at the gate, and He obtained it in two ways: He performed all your righteousness for you, and then He shed His blood to wash you from all your sins.

CHRISTIANA: But if He gives His righteousness to us, what will He have for Himself?

GREATHEART: It is like the ocean giving up its water every day, and yet it has more than enough for all the land. Christ has more righteousness than He and the world will ever need. Therefore, it is free to all who come by faith.

But, in order for a sinner to receive pardon for sin, a price must be paid to God, and a covering must be provided for the sinner. In order that a convict may go free, his fine must be paid, and then he must have clothing and something to go on after he is released. So we, though guilty before God, are pardoned because Jesus paid our fine, and we have sufficient righteousness to commend us to God and men, because through faith we have become identified with Christ and we have his righteousness. For this cause, the righteous God will not condemn you when He comes to judge the world.

CHRISTIANA: That is wonderful. Now I see how we are pardoned by word and deed. Good Mercy, let us strive to keep this always in mind. And you, dear children, be sure you remember this. I see now what caused Christian's burden to fall from his shoulders, and why he became so happy.

GREATHEART: Yes, it was belief in this that cut the cords binding his burden to his back. They could not be severed by any other means; and it was to give him proof of the virtue of this that he was compelled to carry his burden until he came to the cross.

CHRISTIANA: I see, and this makes me rejoice within. Though my heart was light when I was admitted in at the gate, yet I am ten times more joyous now. And I am persuaded by what I have felt—though I know that I have felt but little as yet—that if the most burdened person in the world were here and could see and believe as I now do, his heart would leap for joy.

GREATHEART: There is not only relief from the burden of sin, and comfort of heart by the sight and reception of this, but a strong and tender affection is imparted to us by the cross and by Him who wrought this out for us by His life and death.

CHRISTIANA: True, but it makes my heart bleed to think that He should bleed for me. O Thou loving One! O Thou blessed One! You deserve to have me—body, mind, and soul—and all that I have and ever hope to be, for You have paid for me ten thousand times more than I am worth. No wonder this made the tears stand in my husband's eyes and made him tread so nimbly on! I know he wanted me with him. But, vile wretch that I was, I let him go alone. Oh, Mercy, that your father and mother were here! Yes, and Mrs. Timorous, and I wish with all my heart that Madam Wanton were here. Surely their hearts would be changed! Surely neither fear nor lust could here prevail on any to go home again and to refuse to become a pilgrim.

GREATHEART: You speak in the warmth of your affections. Do you think it will always be so with you? And don't forget that this revelation you have received is not communicated to everyone, not even to everyone who saw your Saviour bleed. There were those who stood by and saw the blood run from His heart to the ground, who were so far removed from this love that instead of weeping they laughed. So what you have, my daughters, in life and opportunity, is given to you by a special divine grace.

Why Three Sleepers Were Hanged

Now I saw in my dream that they came to the place where Christian had seen Simple, and Sloth, and Presumption sleeping by the side of the road when he went by. And Greatheart showed them the place also where they were hanged.

MERCY: What were those men, and for what were they hanged?

GREATHEART: They were three bad characters who had no intention of going on pilgrimage but sought every opportunity to thwart the purpose and progress of pilgrims and to turn them from their course.

MERCY: But could they find any to listen to them, and accept their propaganda?

GREATHEART: Yes, they turned many out of the way. There was Slowpace, Shortwind, Noheart, Lingerlust, Mr. Sleepy, and a young woman named Dull, that I remember, whom they caused to stumble and forsake the good way. They put out an evil report of the Celestial Country—that it had been overadvertised—and led many to believe that our Lord was a hard taskmaster. They also criticized His faithful servants, saying that they were meddlesome, irksome busybodies. Furthermore the bread of life they called husk; the comforts of the Christian experience, fancies; and Christian service, labor to no profit.

CHRISTIANA: Well, if they were that kind, they shall not be mourned by me. They got what they deserved, and it is well that they were hanged near the highway in order to warn others. And it would have been helpful to travelers if the works of Simple, Sloth and Presumption and the names of their converts had been engraved in brass or stone and set up here where they did their deeds, as a caution to others.

GREATHEART: That has been done, as you may see if you walk over a little closer to the wall.

Stepping nearer the wall, Christiana read of the deeds and the methods of these evildoers and the names of those they had led astray.

Bringing Pilgrims Up Hill Difficulty

They went on till they came to Hill Difficulty, where Greatheart told them what happened there when Christian went by. He led them to the spring, but the water had been muddied to spite pilgrims. They had to fill a vessel and let the water settle and clear before they could drink. Then he showed them the

Greatheart conducts Christiana, her sons, and Mercy up the Hill Difficulty.

two byways, one to the right and the other to the left of the road, which were followed by Formality and Hypocrisy, who consequently were lost. "As you see," he said, "those ways have been closed by ditches, posts, and chains across their entrance; yet some will venture into them rather than climb this hill."

CHRISTIANA: The way of the transgressor is hard. Even the entrance to these byways looks dangerous to me. It's a wonder such characters do not break their necks.

GREATHEART: It's true, but some people will venture. When any of the King's faithful servants happens to see them entering those roads, and warns them in the name of the King, saying, "You are on the wrong road; that way is very dangerous," they retort: "As for your words in the name of the King, we will not regard them, but we will certainly do as we please. You mind your own business." A little farther on those roads are closed by hedges; yet curious, presumptuous souls slip through the hedges.

CHRISTIANA: They do not think, and they are too lazy to toil up this hill. In them is fulfilled the proverb, "The way of the slothful man is as an hedge of thorns."[1]

As the pilgrims were climbing the hill, Christiana, panting, remarked: "This is certainly a breathtaking hill. No wonder those who love their ease more than they love their souls seek some other way!"

"I think I will have to sit down for a minute," said Mercy.

Then the small boy began to cry.

Leading Pilgrims to Prince's Arbor

"No, no," said Greatheart, "don't sit down here; this is no place to rest. The Prince's arbor is a little farther up." Then, taking the little boy's hand, he led him up to the arbor. There they rested, for they all were very warm and tired.

[1]Prov. 15:19.

MERCY: How sweet is rest to the weary, and how good is the Prince of pilgrims to provide such a place! I have heard about this good arbor. Now let us guard against sleeping, for I have heard how tempting sleep is in this place, and that it cost Christian very dear when he was here.

GREATHEART: My good boys, how are you faring? What do you think of a pilgrimage now?

JAMES: I was almost out of heart when you took my hand, and I thank you for lending me a hand at a time of real need. I remember now what my mother has told me. She said, "The way to Heaven is like climbing a ladder, while the way to Hell is down the hill." But I had rather climb a ladder to Heaven, than go downhill to death.

MERCY: But going downhill is easy.

JAMES: Yet I imagine that the day may come when going downhill will be hardest of all.

"That is good, my boy," said the guide, "you have given her the right answer."

Mercy smiled, but the little boy blushed.

CHRISTIANA: Come, let us eat a bite now while we rest our legs. I have here a few pomegranates, a piece of honeycomb, and a little grape juice, which Mr. Interpreter placed in my hands just as we came away from his door.

MERCY: I thought he gave you something when he called you to one side.

CHRISTIANA: Yes, Mercy, he did, and I will gladly share with you all that I have, as I said when you so willingly left your home and loved ones to come with me and be my companion.

Then she gave to them, and they ate heartily. But Mr. Greatheart declined, saying, "No, thank you. You are going on a long journey and will need much strength. Presently I will be returning home, where there is plenty. Really I ate a big meal before I left, and I do not feel the need of more now."

After they had eaten and chatted a while, the guide said, "If you are now rested and ready, let us be going." So they got up and started up the hill, the boys going on before. But Christiana forgot her bottle of grape juice and sent her little boy back to get it.

MERCY: This must be a losing place. Here Christian lost his roll, and now Christiana forgets and leaves her bottle. Sir, what is the cause of this?

GREATHEART: The cause is fatigue, I suppose. Some sleep when they should keep awake, and some forget when they should remember. There is a particular weakness in each person. Pilgrims should watch and remember what they have received, even in their greatest enjoyment. When they fail to do this, often their rejoicing ends in tears, and their sunshine in a cloud, as happened here with Christian.

When they came to the place where Mistrust and Timorous met Christian and tried to persuade him to go back because of the lions, they saw a stage had been erected, and along the edge of its floor were emblazoned the words, "THIS STAGE WAS BUILT AS A PLACE ON WHICH TO PUNISH THOSE WHO THROUGH FEAR OR MISTRUST REFUSE TO GO FARTHER AND TRY TO PERSUADE OTHERS TO TURN BACK."

Leading Pilgrims Past Lions

But they went on until they came within sight of the lions. Here the boys, who had been in the lead, cringed behind the others. Their guide smiled. "What has happened, boys?" he asked. "You like to go before when no danger appears, but as soon as you see the lions, you get behind us."

Now, as they approached, Mr. Greatheart drew his sword to defend the women and children and make a safe way for them to pass. Just then a frightful figure, a huge man of the race of giants, appeared with a club, to help the lions oppose the pilgrims. He was called Old Grim, or Bloodyman, because of his slaying of pilgrims. He said to the guide, "What is your purpose in coming here?"

GREATHEART: These women and children are pilgrims, and this is the way they must go; and they shall go this way in spite of you and the lions.

GRIM: This is not their way, neither shall they go this way, for I am here to prevent them.

Because of the lions and the giant, this path had not been traveled much, and it was almost overgrown with weeds. Observing it, Christiana reminded them of this Scripture: "In the days of Jael, the highways were unoccupied, and the travelers walked through byways, until Deborah arose a mother in Israel."[2]

Then Grim swore by the lions that they should not pass, and ordered them to turn aside, saying, "You shall not have passage here."

Attacking a Giant

Greatheart attacked the giant and forced him to fall back. Then Grim cried, "Will you slay me on my own ground?"

GREATHEART: This is the King's highway, and you and your lions are intruders. You do not belong here. But these women and children shall keep to this road and go through in spite of of you and your animals.

With that he gave the giant such a terrific blow that he brought him to his knees bleeding, with one arm severed. The giant roared so hideously that he frightened the pilgrims, but they were glad to see him lie sprawling upon the ground. Of course, the lions were chained and could do no harm. So when old Grim was dead, Greatheart said, "Follow me and no harm will come to you from the lions." Though the women trembled, and the boys turned pale, they all went by without injury.

[2]Judges 5:6-7.

CHAPTER
15
at the porter's lodge

NOW THEY WERE NEARING the Porter's lodge. Night was falling, and they were walking faster, because it was not safe to be on the road in that country after night. When they came to the gate of the lodge, the guide knocked. The Porter shouted from an upper window, "Who's there?" When the guide answered, "It is I," the Porter recognized his voice, for the guide had often accompanied pilgrims to the Lodge.

When the Porter had come down and opened the gate and saw the guide standing there—the women and children were behind him and the Porter did not see them at first—he said, "Hello, Mr. Greatheart, what is your business so late tonight?"

GREATHEART: I have brought these pilgrims, who—by my Lord's instruction—are to spend the night here. I would have been here earlier if I had not been opposed by the giant who stood directly in our path and fought me with his club in support of the lions. But after a long and difficult battle, I finally cut him down.

PORTER: Well, will you go in and stay till morning?

GREATHEART: No, thank you. I assure you I would like to, but I must return tonight.

CHRISTIANA: Oh, Mr. Greatheart, I do not know what we shall do! You have been so faithful and good to us, you have fought valiantly for us, and you have been so true in counseling us that I shall never forget your favors.

MERCY: Mr. Greatheart, I wish we could have your company to our journey's end! How can such frail women as we continue in a way so tedious and dangerous as this way without a good strong friend and guide?

JAMES: Please, Mr. Greatheart, go with us, and help us. We are so weak, and you are so strong, and the way is so strange and long.

GREATHEART: I am at my Lord's command. If He shall assign me the task of going with you all the way, I shall be glad to return and serve you. But you failed to ask Him for that when you were with Him, even after He told me to come this far with you. At that time you should have begged Him to let me go all the way, and He would have granted your request. However, at present, I must withdraw. So, good Christiana, Mercy, and my brave boys, good-night.

When the Porter, Mr. Watchful, asked Christiana about her country and her kindred she said, "I am from the City of Destruction. I am a widow; my husband was Christian, the pilgrim."

"Well, well!" said the Porter. "Was he your husband?"

"Yes," she said, "and these are his children, and this," pointing to Mercy, "is my friend and neighbor."

Then the Porter rang a bell, and a maid came whose name was Humble. "Go, tell them in the house," he said, "that Christian's wife Christiana, her children, and her friend are here on their way to the City of Zion."

She hastened to break the news, and it created a commotion of gladness. They hurried to the door. One shouted, "Hello there, Christiana." "We are glad to see you," said another. "Welcome to the lodge," said another. Then Prudence, the matron, said, "Come in, all of you, you are certainly welcome here."

They all went into the large reception room, where the pilgrims were greeted by the head of the house. After they had talked awhile, Christiana suggested, "Since it's getting a bit late, and we are weary from our journey, it might be best for us to retire soon."

They were tired, not only from the day's journey but from witnessing the terrible battle between Greatheart and the giant, which had tried their nerves.

"Yes," said Prudence, "but let us first serve you something to eat. We heard you were coming, and we prepared and roasted a lamb. We expected you earlier." When they had eaten, and had their devotions, which they closed with a song, they were ready to say good-night and go to their rooms.

CHRISTIANA: If we may be so bold as to choose our room, let us have the same room my husband occupied when he was here.

Her request was granted, and the women slept in Christian's room. After they were in bed, Christiana and Mercy talked awhile before going to sleep.

CHRISTIANA: Little did I think when my husband took up his pilgrimage that I would be following in his footsteps.

MERCY: And I suppose you never once thought you would be stopping at the same place where he had lodged, and lying in his bed, as you are doing now.

CHRISTIANA: And much less did I ever think of seeing his face one day in glory, and worshiping the Lord, the King, with him in the beauty of holiness, as I now believe I shall.

MERCY: Listen! Do you hear that sweet music?

CHRISTIANA: I believe they are singing with joy because we have come.

MERCY: Wonderful! Music in the night, music in the house, music in the heart, and music also in Heaven, for joy that we have come (Luke 15:10).

Mercy's Dream

Then they went to sleep. Next morning, when Christiana was sure that Mercy was awake, she said to her, "Why were you laughing in the night? Were you dreaming?"

MERCY: I dreamed that I sat all alone in a solitary place, groaning over the hardness of my heart. Soon many people gathered around me to hear what I was saying. I thought they stood there listening, and I went on mourning. Some of them laughed, some of them shook their heads and said I was a fool, and some shook me, and shoved me around.

Then I looked up and saw one with wings, coming toward me. I thought he came to me and said, "Mercy, what ails you?" And when he heard my complaint, he said, "Peace be to you!" and wiped away my tears with his handkerchief, and clothed me in purple and gold. He put a golden chain about my neck, earrings on my ears, and a glittering crown upon my head. Then he took me by the hand and said, "Mercy, come with me." So we went up and up till we came to a pearly gate. After he knocked the gate was opened, and we went in. I followed him up to a throne upon which One sat in splendor, Who said to me, "Welcome, daughter!" The place was very bright and glistening; and I thought I saw your husband there. Then I awoke. But did I laugh?

CHRISTIANA: Laugh? I should say you did, and well you might, if that was your dream. For I must say that was a wonderful dream. The first part of it has already come true; so you can expect the other to come true, too. The Lord was showing you in a dream the purpose of His calling you into His service. "God speaks once, yea, twice, yet man perceiveth it not; in a dream, in a vision of the night, when deep sleep falleth upon men, in slumberings upon the bed."[1] When in bed we need not lie awake to talk to God. He can visit us while we sleep and

[1]Job 33:14-15.

cause us to hear His voice; and He can speak to our hearts, either by words, or by proverbs, or by signs and symbols while we sleep, as well as if we were awake.

MERCY: Say, if they invite us to stay here awhile, let's willingly accept the offer. I would like to get better acquainted with these maids. I think they have such lovable countenances.

CHRISTIANA: Well, we will see what they do.

When they were up and ready, they went down. The maids were waiting for them. They asked each other of their rest and comforts.

"I did fine," said Mercy. "It was the best night's rest I have ever had in my life."

PIETY: We would like to have you folk stay with us for several days.

PRUDENCE: If you will be persuaded to stay awhile, you shall have what the house affords.

"Yes," agreed Charity, "and that with a very good will."

Questioning Christiana's Boys

So they readily consented, and stayed there a whole month. And as Prudence wanted to see how Christiana had brought up her children, she asked permission of her to question them. Christiana gladly gave her permission.

Then she began with the youngest, James.

PRUDENCE: Well, James, can you tell me who made you?

JAMES: Yes, God—the Father, Son, and Holy Spirit.

PRUDENCE: Good! And can you tell me who saves you?

JAMES: God—the Father, Son, and Holy Spirit.

PRUDENCE: Fine! But how does God the Father save?

JAMES: By His divine grace.

PRUDENCE: How does God the Son save you?

JAMES: By His life and death, His blood and righteousness.

PRUDENCE: And how does God the Holy Spirit save you?

JAMES: By illumination, renovation, and preservation.

Then said Prudence to Christiana, "You are to be commended for the way you are bringing up your children. I suppose I need not ask the others these questions, since the youngest can answer them so well."

Then she turned to Joseph, the next in age, and asked, "Joseph, will you let me question you?"

JOSEPH: Yes, gladly.

PRUDENCE: What is man?

JOSEPH: A creature with reason, so made by God, as James has said.

PRUDENCE: What is inferred by the word "saved"?

JOSEPH: That man by sin brought himself into a state of condemnation, corruption, captivity, misery, and death.

PRUDENCE: What is understood by his being saved by the Trinity?

JOSEPH: That sin is such a great and mighty tyrant that it took all of the Godhead—Father, Son, and Holy Spirit—to pull sinful man out of its clutches, and that God is such a great and mighty person of love that He was willing to exercise all His wisdom, power, and skill to save men from this awful state.

PRUDENCE: What is God's design in saving men?

JOSEPH: The glorifying of His name, the revealing of His grace, mercy, and justice, and giving to men everlasting life and happiness.

PRUDENCE: Who are the saved?

JOSEPH: Those who have accepted Christ as their very own Saviour and have been made conscious of forgiveness of sin, who have been born of the Holy Spirit, and are continually committing themselves to the way and will of God.

PRUDENCE: Good! Joseph, your mother has taught you well, and you have retained what she has told you.

Then said Prudence to Samuel, "Would you object if I examine you, Samuel?"

SAMUEL: No, indeed.

PRUDENCE: What is Heaven?

SAMUEL: The place and state of perfect happiness, because God dwells there.

PRUDENCE: What is Hell?

SAMUEL: A place and state of torment, caused by sin, the devil, and death.

PRUDENCE: Why do you want to go to Heaven?

SAMUEL: To see Christ Jesus my Lord and serve Him forever, to live and serve with the saved, to see God and glorify His name.

PRUDENCE: A very wise boy, and one who has learned his lesson.

Then she turned to the oldest boy, who was virtually a young man: "Matthew, may I also catechize you?"

MATTHEW: Yes, I am willing.

PRUDENCE: Was there ever anything that existed before God?

MATTHEW: No, for God is eternal, and God created all things in the beginning. "For in six days God made heaven and earth, the sea, and all that in them is."

PRUDENCE: What do you think of the Bible?

MATTHEW: It is the holy Word of God.

PRUDENCE: Is there anything in the Bible you do not understand?

MATTHEW: Yes, a great deal.

PRUDENCE: What do you do when you come to those places in the Bible that you do not understand?

MATTHEW: I think God is wiser than I. But I pray that God will help me to understand what He wants me to know—that which will be for my good and His glory.

PRUDENCE: What do you believe about the resurrection of the dead?

MATTHEW: I believe that these same bodies we now live in shall be revived and given immortality. But this is one of the revelations of the Bible I do not understand, yet I believe it, because God has promised it, and I know He is able to perform that which He has promised.

Then Prudence said to the boys, "You have learned a lot. However, you must listen to your mother, for she can teach you much more. You must also pay close attention to what older pilgrims say, for they often speak from wide experience and for the enlightenment of younger pilgrims. But especially spend much time and serious thought with the Scriptures. And you are at liberty to ask me questions. I will be glad to teach you what I can while you are here, if you ask questions that tend to godly edifying."

Mercy's Suitor

Now when the pilgrims had been at the lodge about a week, Mercy had a visitor, Mr. Brisk, a young man of some means and culture. He seemed to be sincerely religious, yet very much attached to the things of the world. He came to see Mercy several times, and suggested that they become engaged. Now, Mercy was a charming girl, and very attractive, though of the busy type. She was always making things for herself or others, and Mr. Brisk thought she would make a good housewife. Now Mercy confided in the maids and inquired of them concerning him, for they knew him better than she. They told her that he was a nice-appearing young man, with ambition and ability, who was formally religious, but they said they feared he was a stranger to spiritual life and power.[2]

[2]II Tim. 3:5.

MERCY: Then I will not encourage him, for I do not intend to let any one hinder my spiritual life, or my Christian service.

PRUDENCE: Well, you need not have any sudden break with him, fraught with tension and emotion. Your continuing to do for the poor will soon cool his ardor.

So the next time Mr. Brisk came, he found her very busy, making things for the poor.

"Always at it, I see," he remarked.

"Yes," said she, "either for myself or for others."

"And how much do you earn a day?" he asked.

"I do these things that I may be rich in good works, laying up in store for myself a good foundation against the time to come, that I may lay hold on eternal life."[3]

"What do you do with all these things you are making?"

"Clothe the naked," she said.

Then his countenance fell, and he was silent. He called no more, and when his friends asked him why, he said that Mercy was a very pretty girl, but handicapped by poor conditions.

When he did not come again, Prudence said to Mercy, "Did I not tell you that he would give you up when he found that you were true to your religion? Now, you need not be surprised if he starts an evil report on you, notwithstanding his seeming love for you and his interest in formal religion. You never would have been happy with him. You are of such different temperaments.

MERCY: I might have had a husband before now (though I have never mentioned this to anyone before), if my boyfriends had not objected to my standards. None of them ever found fault with my person; it was my ideals they did not like. Therefore, we could not agree.

PRUDENCE: In this day and time, eternal things make very little impression. With too many, Christianity is but little more than a custom, or a name.

[3]I Tim. 6:17-19.

MERCY: Well, if no one will have me because of my religious convictions, I will die an old maid. My devotion to Christ and His service will take the place of a husband, and I will be happier than living with a man who is not a Christian and is always opposing my way of life. I had a sister named Bountiful, who married one of these conceited, self-willed egotists, and she and he never got along. He violently opposed her becoming a Christian, and finally drove her away from home. Afterwards her health broke, and she died.

PRUDENCE: And yet he was a professing Christian, I suppose?

MERCY: Yes, a professor, not a possessor of true Christianity. Of such the world is full, and I don't care how well educated or how wealthy they may be, I want none of them at all.

Questioning Prudence

Now Matthew came in, desiring to ask Prudence some questions.

MATTHEW: Why is good medicine often bitter?

PRUDENCE: Such is life. The best things of life often lie beyond the disagreeable. The Word of God is bitter to sinners, but when received, it brings salvation.

MATTHEW: What can we learn from seeing flames and sparks go upward, and sunbeams coming downward?

PRUDENCE: Prayers must ascend to the throne, and light and life must descend from the Sun of righteousness. The Saviour of the world reaches down with His grace and love to men.

MATTHEW: What do the clouds mean to teach us by drawing their water from the sea, and showering it upon the land?

PRUDENCE: That ministers of the Word must get their messages from God, and shower them freely upon the people. When Jesus sent forth His apostles, He said, "Freely ye have received, freely give."[4]

[4]Matt. 10:8.

MATTHEW: Why do we have the rainbow, caused by the sun shining through the rain, under the cloud?

PRUDENCE: To remind us that the covenant of God's grace through Calvary can bring us sunshine under clouds of sorrow, after the storm; and that God never forgets His promises.

MATTHEW: Why do refreshing springs come through the earth, and sometimes on the highest hills?

PRUDENCE: To show us that the water of life comes to us through the broken body of Christ, and sometimes flows from high and influential men.

MATTHEW: Why are the wick and tallow of the candle consumed to maintain light, and what does the fire on the wick indicate?

PRUDENCE: That unless the grace of God is in the heart, there will be no true light in the life; and that the body and heart of a Christian must be expended to maintain the light of true love.

MATTHEW: Why does the pelican pierce her own breast with her bill?

PRUDENCE: To nourish her young with her blood. This shows that Christ so loved His young, His people, that He gave His own blood to save them.

MATTHEW: What should the crowing of a rooster mean to us?

PRUDENCE: It should remind us of Peter's unfaithfulness when he denied Christ, and of his sincere repentance. It should also announce to us the coming of a new day: the day of judgment, or the dawning of eternal morning.

When their month's stay at the lodge was drawing to a close, they indicated to their hosts that they must soon be going.

"Mother," said Joseph, "you should not forget to ask Mr. Interpreter to send Mr. Greatheart to be our guide the rest of the way."

"Good boy," said she, "I almost forgot." So she drew up a petition and asked Mr. Watchful, the Porter, to send it immediately to her good friend, the Interpreter, who, when he had read it, sent this message back in haste: "I will send him right away."

Now the keeper of the lodge called the whole house together to worship and give thanks to the King for sending such good guests their way. Then he said, "It is our custom to show pilgrims those things which will be helpful to them on their journey."

Object Lessons

Now they led the pilgrims to a closet and showed them an apple of the forbidden fruit of which Mother Eve ate and gave to her husband to eat, which caused both to be turned out of Paradise. They asked Christiana what she thought it was. She said, "It is either food or poison, I wouldn't know which." When they explained to her what it was, she marveled that the whole human race was contaminated and condemned by yielding to Satan in such a small act.

Then they led them to a hall and showed them a painting of Jacob's ladder.[5] There were the angels descending and ascending upon it. "This ladder," said Prudence, "represents the way to Heaven which Christ opened to all mankind."

When they were about to turn from the scene, James said, "Don't go yet. Please stay a moment, for this is a wonderful picture." So they stood taking it in.

"Marvel not at this," said Prudence. "Hereafter you shall see heaven open and the angels of God ascending and descending upon the Son of man."[6]

After this they conducted them to a room where hung a

[5]Gen. 28:12.
[6]John 1:51.

golden anchor. The guide told Christiana to take it down. "You may have it," he said, "for it is essential that you lay hold of that within the veil,[7] and stand steadfast in turbulent weather."

Then they showed them a scene of Abraham offering his son Isaac upon the altar, high upon the mountain. Gazing upon the scene Christiana, holding up her hands; exclaimed, "Oh, what a man for love to his Maker and for denying himself was Abraham!"

Just then a knock came at the door. The Porter opened, and there stood Mr. Greatheart. The sight of him made their hearts leap for joy.

Handing Christiana and Mercy each a package, he said, "My overseer, the Interpreter, sent each of you a bottle of sweet wine, a jar of parched corn, and some delicious apples to eat on the way; and he sent the boys some figs and raisins."

Then they took their departure, Mr. Greatheart leading the way. Prudence and Piety walked with them to the foot of the hill.

At the gate, Christiana asked the Porter if anyone had passed recently.

"No," he said, "one went by some time ago who told me that there had been a major robbery here on the road a while back. But he said the thieves were caught, and would soon be tried for their crime."

This gave Christiana and Mercy a shudder. But Matthew said, "Mother, Mr. Greatheart is with us, why be afraid?"

Then Christiana thanked the Porter for his kindness, and placed a large gold coin in his hand as a token of her appreciation for all his favors. He bowed graciously and said, "May the blessings of the Lord go with you; and may you boys flee youthful lusts,[8] and follow after godliness with charity. Be

[7]Heb. 6:19.
[8]II Tim. 2:22.

strong and wise that you may please the Lord and bring gladness to your mother and to all who love the right way."

When they got to the brow of the hill, Piety suddenly remembered something she intended to do. "Alas," she said, "I forgot what I intended to give to Christiana." And she ran back to get it. They waited.

While she was gone, Christiana heard beautiful, strange notes coming from a grove some distance back from the road. She fancied she could hear these words:

> Through all my life Thy favor is
> So truly showed to me
> That in Thy house forevermore
> My dwelling place shall be:

Listening closely, she heard another voice, farther away, which seemed to answer the first, saying,

> For why? the Lord our God is good,
> His mercy is forever sure;
> His truth has always firmly stood,
> And shall forever more endure.

Christiana asked what kind of birds made those strange, sweet notes.

"They are our neighborhood birds," said Prudence. "They seldom sing their song except in the spring, when the flowers bloom and the sun shines warmly. Then you may hear them all day long. I often go out into the woods to hear their song. We have had them tame in our house. They are very good company, especially when one is inclined to be melancholy. They also make the woods and groves more alluring with their sweet music.

By this time Piety had returned, and she said to Christiana, "Look, I have brought you a sketch of all you have seen and heard at our house, which you may review for edification and comfort, or when you wish to recall something of importance."

CHAPTER

16

with greatheart on the way

Through the Valley of Humility

NOW THEY BEGAN TO GO down the hill toward the Valley of Humility. It was a steep hill, and the road was slippery. But they were very careful, and they reached the valley in safety. Once in the valley, Piety said to Christiana, "In this valley is where your husband encountered the monstrous fiend Apollyon and fought him to a finish. I know you have heard of it. But be of good courage. You have nothing to fear; as long as you have Mr. Greatheart with you, you need not be afraid of man or demon."

When Prudence and Piety had committed the pilgrims to their guide, they turned back, and the pilgrims went on into the valley, Mr. Greatheart leading the way.

GREATHEART: We need not dread this valley. There is really nothing to hurt us, unless we cause it ourselves. It is true that Christian suffered here at the hands of Apollyon, but he slipped several times coming down the hill, which evoked Apollyon's attack. Those who slip coming down must expect conflicts here, for they always happen. And the reports of these clashes have given this valley a bad name, for the people hearing of these evil conflicts imagine that this place is haunted with vile fiends or evil spirits. Whereas, in reality these difficulties are results induced by the conduct of pilgrims. This valley, of itself, is a peaceful, fruitful country. But pilgrims, not knowing how to adjust themselves to humiliation, yield to wrong feelings. Then Satan, taking advantage of their moods, sends his imps from Hades (farther down the country, in the Valley of Hinnom), and they attack these immature disciples.

Just then James said, "Mother, look, yonder stands a pillar with some writing on it; let's go and see what it is."

They went over and found this written: "LET CHRISTIAN'S SLIPS BEFORE HE CAME, AND THE BATTLE HE HAD TO FIGHT, BE A WARNING TO ALL WHO COME AFTER."

Through the Valley of Peace

"Yes," said Greatheart, "but Christian won a great victory. There have been battles here, yes, and many sorrows, but see how beautiful the landscape is. This valley consists mainly of green meadows adorned with lilies, where weeping willows grow along winding streams. Here also are fruitful fields, herds of cattle, and flocks of sheep. Many humble people have their homes here, and they live in contentment. Many working men have obtained good holdings here. It is those who have accustomed themselves to living at higher altitudes who have the most trouble here. 'For God resisteth the proud, but giveth grace to the humble.' "[1]

As they were going along talking, they heard singing. Turning, they saw a barefoot boy sitting on a rock, watching a flock of sheep. They caught the words of his song:

He that is down, needs fear no fall;
He that is low, no pride:
He that is humble, ever shall
Have God to be his guide.

[1]James 4:6; I Peter 5:5.

GREATHEART: Did you hear what he said? I dare say that this plain country boy lives a happier life than many who live in luxury. This Valley to many is a land of contentment. Our Lord once lived here, and in this valley He taught His great lessons on peace. Here one is free from the noise and strife of the world. The whole world today is filled with racket, grating sounds, and nerve-racking confusion. Only the Valley of Humility is quiet and solitary, providing the atmosphere for meditation and fellowship with the Creator. Though Christian had the misfortune of meeting with Apollyon here, some have been richly blessed in this valley, and some have found the pearl of great price.

SAMUEL: Mr. Greatheart, where did my father and Apollyon have their fight?

MR. GREATHEART: Yonder on that narrow place in the road, just beyond Forgetful Green. That is the most tempting place in the valley. Other servants of the King have been sorely tested there. It is a place where pilgrims are prone to forget the favors they have received or how unworthy they are of them. Then they have their trying conflicts.

MERCY: I think I fare quite as well here as in any place we have been. The place seems to suit my spirit. I love to be where there are no grinding wheels or rumbling traffic; and here one can think on the meaning of life, and ask oneself questions like these: What am I? Where did I come from? Why am I here? What have I accomplished? Where am I going?

GREATHEART: Yes, 'tis true. I have gone through this valley many times, and I have never fared better than when here. I have been conductor to many pilgrims who have testified the same. It may be that our Lord and Master leads us through this valley to condition us for His choicest blessings. He said through His prophet, "I will look to him that is poor and of a contrite spirit, and that trembleth at my word."[2] And our Saviour said, in the beginning of His earthly ministry, "Blessed are the poor in spirit, for theirs is the kingdom of heaven."[3]

Now they came to the spot where Christian fought with Apollyon, and there stood a monument on which was engraved this poem:

> Hard by here was a battle fought,
> Most strange, and yet most true;
> Christian and Apollyon sought
> Each other to subdue.
>
> The man so bravely played the man,
> He made the fiend to fly;
> Of which a monument I stand,
> The same to testify.

Through the Valley of Death

When they had passed by this battleground, they came to the border of the lower valley—the Valley of the Shadow of Death. This valley was much longer than the other; and it was a region most strangely inhabited by evil spirits, as many have testified. But these women and children got through better than many others because they had Mr. Greatheart for a guide, and they had daylight all the way.

However, they thought they heard in the valley groanings of dead men, and mournings of persons in extreme torment. These horrible sounds made the boys tremble, and the women turned pale, but their guide gave them courage with assuring words of comfort.

A little farther on they thought they felt the ground shake, as if they were over some hollow place; they heard also a kind of hissing, as of serpents, though nothing appeared. Then one of the boys said, "Are we not yet to the end of this awful valley?"

[2]Isa. 66:2.
[3]Matt. 5:3.

But the guide exhorted them to be of good courage and watch their step lest they be caught in some snare.

Now James, the small boy, became ill; the cause must have been fear. His mother gave him a little wine, and a couple of pills, prescribed by a physician while they were at the Palace Beautiful, and he began to mend.

So they went on till they came to the middle of the valley, then Christiana thought she saw something on the road ahead. "A thing of such shape," she said, "as I have never seen before."

"Mother, what is it?" Joseph asked.

"Son, I do not know; 'tis a horrible thing."

"But Mother, what does it look like?"

"I cannot describe it. It is unlike anything I have ever seen. Now it is coming closer. It is very near."

"Well, well," said Mr. Greatheart, "let them who are most afraid keep close to me." So the imp of darkness came on, and Greatheart moved out to meet it, but just then it disappeared, and no one saw it again. Then they remembered what had been repeated before: "Resist the devil, and he will flee from you."[4]

Being a little relieved, they went on. But they had not gone far when Mercy, looking back, thought she saw something in the shape of a lion, sneaking up behind them. They all turned to see. It let out a roar and came faster. The whole valley echoed with its coarse, hollow voice, which sent shivers up the spines of the pilgrims and caused their hearts to ache. Then Mr. Greatheart put the pilgrims before him. The lion increased his speed, and Mr. Greatheart prepared to give him battle. But when the lion saw that the guide would resist him to the death, he crouched, growled, and slinked away into the bush.

Now the guide went before them until they came to a pit extending across the road, and before they could prepare a way

[4]James 4:7.

to cross, a thick mist enveloped them, completely obscuring the way. "Alas," they murmured, "what shall we do?"

"Fear not," said Greatheart, "stand still and see the end of this also."

They waited, for their way was completely blocked. Then they thought they heard more noises and rushing of enemies. Fire and smoke from the pit were easily discerned.

CHRISTIANA: Now I see what my poor husband went through. I have heard much of this place, yet I had no idea it was like this. Poor man! He went through here all alone in the night, and these fiends were busy about him, as if they would tear him in pieces. Many have spoken of it, but no one can imagine what the Valley of the Shadow of Death is like until one comes into it himself.

GREATHEART: This is like being in the depth of the sea and going down to the bottom of the mountains. It is as if the bars of the earth had closed about you forever. But let them who walk in darkness and have no light trust in the name of the Lord and rely upon their God.[5] As for me, I have gone through the valley often, and I have been in more danger than I am in now, but still I'm alive. Yet I do not boast, for I am not my own keeper. However, I believe we shall have complete deliverance. Let us ask light of Him who can turn darkness into day and banish all the demons in Hell.

So they cried to God, and the mist cleared away. Now they saw that the pit was only a deep depression in the road, and they easily crossed it.

Soon they began to smell offensive odors. Then Mercy remarked to Christiana: "It is not so pleasant here as it was at the gatehouse, or the Interpreter's, or at the palace where we last stayed."

"Oh," said Samuel, "it is not so bad to pass through this.

[5]Isa. 50:10.

What if one had to abide here always? And, for all I know, one reason we must pass through this to the house prepared for us is to let us see what we have been saved from, that we may enjoy our home the more."

MR. GREATHEART: Very well said, Samuel.

"Why, when I get out of here," continued the boy, "I will value light and the good way more than ever in my life."

"We will be out by and by," said the guide.

JOSEPH: Can't we see to the end of this valley yet?

GUIDE: Watch your step, boys, we will soon be among the snares.

When they came to the snares, they saw a man's body all mangled and torn, lying in a ditch.

GUIDE: That was Mr. Heedless. He has lain there a long time. There was a Mr. Takeheed with him, who escaped. You cannot imagine how many people lose their lives in this part of the valley. Some are so foolishly venturous as to set out thoughtlessly on a pilgrimage to the far country without a directory or a guide. Good Christian! It is a wonder he ever got past this place. He certainly was beloved of God, and he had a sturdy heart. Otherwise, he never would have made it.

Battle with Giant Maul

Now they came to the end of the valley, where Christian had seen the cave home of Pope and Pagan. Out of the cave came giant Maul, who used to pervert young pilgrims with his sophistry. He called Greatheart by name, and said, "How many times have you been forbidden to do these things?"

"What things?" asked Greatheart.

"What things! You know what things. But I will put an end to your trade."

"But wait," said Mr. Greatheart, "before we fight; let us understand what it's all about."

The women and children stood speechless.

"Well," said the giant, "you rob the country in the worst kind of thievery."

"That is your general accusation, but come to particulars, man."

"You are engaged in the nefarious business of kidnapping. You gather up women and children and carry them off to a strange country, weakening my master's kingdom," Maul retorted.

Greatheart replied: "I am a servant of the God of Heaven; my business is to persuade sinners to repent. I am directed to do my utmost to turn men, women, and children from darkness to light, from the power of Satan to God. And if you call this kidnapping and that is your charge, I am ready for you."

Then the giant, bearing a club, came toward the guide, and the guide went to meet him, drawing his sword. They met and went at it in full force. The giant struck Greatheart on the head with his club and brought him to his knees. The women and children screamed. Mr. Greatheart rose to his feet and thrust his sword into the giant's arm, wounding him severely. They fought for an hour—until both were completely exhausted. Each withdrew to his side of the road to rest. Now the guide, in his heart, began to pray. The women and children cried the whole time.

The combatants rose and went at it again. Now Mr. Greatheart brought the giant down with a terrific blow to the abdomen. But he would not attack him while he was down. He waited for him to get up. One of the giant's blows would have broken Greatheart's skull if the blow had not glanced off. Now Greatheart determined to do away with him. He threw up his arm and caught the next blow with his left hand, and stabbed the giant under the fifth rib. The giant began to faint and could no longer hold his club. Then Mr. Greatheart severed his head from his shoulders. The pilgrims rejoiced, and they all (including Greatheart) praised God for victory. They erected a pillar, fastening the giant's head on top, and wrote words underneath to commemorate the event.

Then they ascended the little hill, made as an elevation to enable travelers to see the road ahead. Here is where Christian first sighted Faithful. They sat down to rest. They rejoiced over their deliverance from the Valley of the Shadow of Death and from the hands of Giant Maul and they refreshed themselves with food and drink as they talked of the ordeal through which they had passed.

CHRISTIANA: Mr. Greatheart, were you not hurt in the battle?

GREATHEART: No, except a little on my flesh: and that will be for my good.[6] Already it is proof of my love for my Master and His followers and shall be a means, by grace, to increase my reward at last.

CHRISTIANA: But were you not afraid when you saw him come out with that club?

GREATHEART: Somewhat, but it is my training to mistrust my own feelings and rely wholly on Him who has all power.

CHRISTIANA: But what did you think when he brought you to your knees with his first blow?

GREATHEART: Why, I thought of Christ who was even brought down to death, yet conquered at last.

MATTHEW: I don't know what you all think, but I think God has been wonderfully good to us, both in bringing us out of this valley and in delivering us from the power of this enemy. Now, I see no reason why we should ever distrust Him again, since He has given us such proof of His love, wisdom, power, and grace.

[6]II Cor. 4:17; Rom. 8:28.

Awakening of Old Mr. Honesty

Then they got up and went on their way. Soon they came to a large oak tree, and saw under it an old pilgrim fast asleep. They knew he was a pilgrim by his clothes and his staff. Mr. Greatheart awoke him. At first he was frightened, and asked, "Who are you? What do you want? What is your business?"

GREATHEART: Calm yourself, my good man, we are all your friends. (The old man's name was Honesty.) My name is Greatheart; I am the guide of these pilgrims who are going to the Celestial Country.

HONESTY: I beg your pardon. I was afraid you might be of the gang who sometime back robbed Little-Faith of his money; but now I know you are honest people.

GREATHEART: Why, what could you have done if we had been robbers?

HONESTY: Done? Why, I would have fought like a tiger, as long as I had any breath. And had I done so, I am sure you never could have conquered me, for a pilgrim can never be defeated unless he yields himself.

GREATHEART: Well said, my brother, now I know you are a good soldier.

HONESTY: And by this I know you are informed as to what a true pilgrim is, for all others think that we are the easiest to overcome of any.

GREATHEART: Well, now that we have met, may I ask your name?

HONESTY: My name is Honesty. I came from the town of Stupidity. It is located about ten miles beyond the City of Destruction. I wish my nature harmonized more perfectly with my name.

GREATHEART: I have heard of you, and I have often wondered that any pilgrims at all should come from that town, for it is worse than the town of Destruction.

HONESTY: Yes, we are on the far side of the mountain from the sun and, therefore, colder and less responsive to light. Many of our citizens are like a man frozen in a mountain of ice. But even there, when the Sun of Righteousness shines upon you, as He did on me, you thaw out and move out for God.

GREATHEART: I believe it, Mr. Honesty, for I know it is true.

Then the old gentleman saluted each of them with a kiss of charity and asked each person his name. He said to Christiana, "I have heard of your husband. He was a brave, good man." To Matthew, the oldest boy, he said, "Be like Matthew of old, who left the seat of custom, to follow the Lord." He admonished Samuel to be like Samuel the prophet, a man of faith and prayer. He exhorted Joseph, "Be like Joseph in the house of Potiphar, chaste and one who flees from temptation."[7] And to James, the little boy, he said, "Be like James the Just, the brother of our Lord."

Then they told Honesty of Mercy, how she had left all—her home and kindred—to come with Christiana in search of a better life. He said to her, "Mercy is your name, by mercy you shall be sustained and be carried through all the difficulties of the way till you come to the Fountain of Mercy in the Celestial Country beyond."

Conversation about Mr. Fearing

As they walked along together, the guide asked Honesty if he knew a Mr. Fearing from his town.

"Yes, very well," he said. "He was a man who seemed to have the good life within him; yet he was one of the most difficult pilgrims I ever knew."

GREATHEART: I am sure you knew him, for you have given an accurate description of him.

[7]Gen. 39:7-12.

HONESTY: Knew him! I was closely associated with him for more than five years. He was in my house when he first began to think on what will become of us after death.

GREATHEART: Well, I was his guide from my master's house to the end of the way.

HONESTY: Then you knew him to be a troublesome fellow?

GREATHEART: Indeed I did. But I was able by God's grace to bear with him. Men of my calling are often entrusted with the leadership of such fellows.

HONESTY: Well, then, let us hear a little about him and how he did under your guidance.

GREATHEART: Why, he was a conscientious soul but possessed by fear. He was afraid he would fall short of the goal he desired to reach. Everything that had the least appearance of opposition in it frightened him. I heard that he lay moaning at the Slough of Despond for more than a month. Though he saw many of his acquaintances pass over, some of whom offered him a hand, yet he would not venture in, neither would he go back. He said he would go to the Celestial City or die in the attempt. Still he became dejected at every obstacle and stumbled over every straw that anyone put in his way.

How he ever got through the Slough I do not know, but finally one sunny morning he ventured in and, being afraid he would sink, he soon got through. Yet he would hardly believe it was true. I think he carried a slough of despond in his mind. When he came to the wicket gate, he was afraid to knock. There he lingered for a long time. When the gate was opened to let pilgrims in, he would draw back to give place to others, saying that he was not worthy. There he stood trembling, yet longing to go in.

At last, he took the hammer that hung on the gate and gave a little knock. When the gate was opened he shrank back. The Gateman stepped out and asked him if he wanted to come in.

He dropped to his knees to worship. The Gateman took him by the hand and said, "Peace be to you! Come in, for you are welcome," then led him inside. Still he was afraid that he had deceived the Gateman, and that he was imposing on his goodness. He was ashamed of his appearance, and of his lack of knowledge and experience.

When he left the gatehouse, he carried a note addressed to my master, the Interpreter, requesting the Interpreter to receive him and grant him all the comforts and accommodations of his house, yet he lay outside in the cold, night after night, debating as to what he should do. I happened to see him through the window, gazing at the building. I went out and asked him if he would come in. His eyes filled with tears, and he said nothing for a moment. Then he asked, "Do you think I am fit to be in your house?" I saw what he wanted, so went and told the Master. He sent me out to bring him in, but it took a lot of persuading to get him inside. While at the Interpreter's house, he gained some courage, yet he never conquered his fears. I went with him all the way to the gate of the Celestial City.

At the House Beautiful, when I introduced him to the maids, he was very shy. He desired to be alone. However, he told me afterwards that he liked the place, and he said the same about the Interpreter's house. He went down into the Valley of Humiliation as well as anyone I ever accompanied. He cared not how low he went, if only he could find comfort and peace. It seemed that there was a kind of harmony between him and that valley, for I never saw him behave better in all his journey than when in the Valley of Humility.

But when he came to the Valley of the Shadow of Death, I thought he would die of fright. Yet he was so true, he would not turn back. But he would cry out, "Oh, the hobgoblins! The hobgoblins will get me!" It sounded as if he were inviting or encouraging the spooks to come and get him. The Lord must have checked the evil spirits of that valley for Fearing's sake, for I never saw it quieter than when he was going through.

But when he came to Vanity Fair, he was a different person. His anger flared against all their follies. His indignation seemed to cause him to forget his fears. He appeared bold enough to fight all the men in the place. His words were so hot against their vanities, I was afraid he would cause both of us to be executed or banished.

Also on the enchanted ground, he was a surprise—he was very wakeful. But when he came to the cold river, where there was no bridge, he was extremely pessimistic. He said, "Now, this is the end of all my dreams. I shall sink in this river forever, and never see the face I came so many miles to see."

Yet it was remarkable how low the river was at that time and how safely Mr. Fearing got over. When he was going up to the gate, I began to take leave of him, and to wish him a good reception above. He said, "I shall have it, I know I shall." Then we parted, and I saw him no more.

HONESTY: Then it seems that he proved true after all.

GREATHEART: Oh, yes, I never had any doubts about him. He was a man of integrity and fine Christian qualities, only he was such an idealist that the realities of life kept him very low in spirit most of the time. He was a burden to himself, and troublesome to others. He was more sensitive to sin than others, and he was also very careful not to offend or wound others. To avoid offending others, he would often deny himself things which by rights were his,[8] and he counted others better than himself.[9]

HONESTY: But why should a good man like that always be in the dark?

GREATHEART: There are two reasons for it. One is, God wills it that way. God needs some somber notes on the keyboard

[8]Rom. 14:12.
[9]Phil. 2:3.

of life. Some must dance while others weep. This great harp of human life would be incomplete without bass strings, yet the bass alone does not make good music. Mr. Fearing was one who played the bass most of the time, regardless of how others felt. Yet, for my part, I do not care for any profession that does not begin with heaviness of mind. However, heaviness should not continue after one possesses what he professes. I think one is out of tune and out of balance who sounds the bass notes all the time.

And some pilgrims get out of harmony with the will of God and the symphony of Heaven by habitually yielding to their groundless fears and taking counsel with their gloomy imaginations, refusing to believe in the sufficiency of the grace of God. Thus they become burdens to themselves and to their associates.

HONESTY: I see that Fearing was a zealous Christian who had no fear of lions, or ruffians, or physical suffering. It was sin, guilt, death, and torment that terrified him. His problem was enemies within himself, not the enemies without. The ruffians at Vanity Fair only aroused his righteous indignation—not his fears—and made him as bold as a lion, while the spirits in the shadow of death frightened him. It was really himself he was afraid of.

He doubted that his acceptance of Christ had made him worthy to claim all the promises of God. Therefore he was afraid he would not be accepted by God. He doubtless believed in a brand of religious legalism—that we must obey law to obtain sufficient grace to become worthy of acceptance.

GREATHEART: Yes, but the truth is, we must have sufficient grace before we can obey God's law, and this grace is received through faith in the cross of Christ, and not by works of righteousness.[10] By the Holy Spirit operating through our faith, we

[10]Titus 3:5.

are "created in Christ Jesus unto good works."[11] Good works are the aim and result of grace, and not the cause. Grace is the remedy for fear; and if we pray, believing, we receive sufficient grace.

CHRISTIANA: This discussion about Mr. Fearing has been very helpful to me. I thought no other Christian was like me. But now I see that this good man was something of a kindred spirit. I have some of his fears, only mine are not often expressed.

MERCY: I must confess that something of Mr. Fearing's spirit also dwells in me.

GREATHEART: Well, now I hope you all see how groundless fears may be conquered.

Conversation about Mr. Selfwill

Now Mr. Honesty began to tell them about another character he had known, a Mr. Selfwill: "This man," he said, "was traveling as a pilgrim, though I do not think he had any knowledge of what a pilgrim is."

GREATHEART: Why, did he talk to you about it?

HONESTY: Yes, a great deal.

GREATHEART: What principles did he hold?

HONESTY: He thought a man might practice the vices as well as the virtues of Bible characters. He said that David, a man after God's own heart, had intimate relations with another man's wife; that Solomon had more than one wife; that Abraham took Hagar, his wife's housemaid, to be his wife; that Jacob came into possession of his father's property by deception; that the Israelites borrowed the jewelry of their Egyptian neighbors and took it with them when they left Egypt; that Rahab lied about the spies being in her house; and that the disciples went at their Master's request and took away the owner's mule; therefore, he could do the same. He believed he could do whatever he thought was necessary and right.

[11]Eph. 2:10.

GREATHEART: That is certainly a base and contemptible idea, and a most unreasonable and dangerous conclusion. Some of the things he mentioned were not wrong under the circumstances. It is true that Bible characters sinned. But if anyone will read the whole story he will see that these mistakes were recorded in the Word as warnings, not as examples to be followed by others. And anyone who presumes that he can practice these vices without being punished is a fool indeed. He is so blinded by his own lust that he cannot even see the meaning of the Word when he reads it; or, if he does see it, he closes his eyes to the truth. No sensible person can imagine that because some good pilgrims, blown by the wind, fall into the mire and are restored to a pure life, he therefore can wallow in the mud and still be clean before God and his fellow man. I cannot believe that any person of this opinion has the love of God in him.

HONESTY: Selfwill said that it was better to practice vice of your own free will, unashamed, than to do it against your better judgment, behind the door.

GREATHEART: That is like saying it is better to choose the mud and walk in it than to be pushed into it against your will; it is better to have your garbage can in the front door than in the back alley. Anyone can see the fallacy of that argument.

HONESTY: Yes, but there are many professing Christians who have this man's mind who do not have his mouth for expressing it.

CHAPTER
17

at the homes of gaius and mnason

Welcome to Home of Gaius

THE PILGRIMS WERE GROWING WEARY, and Christiana wished for lodging for herself and her children.

"There is a very good place," said Mr. Honesty, "a little farther on, owned by the well-known disciple, Gaius."

So they all decided to turn in there. When they came to the place, they asked for the owner. He came immediately and received them gladly. They asked him for rooms for the night, and he showed them where they would sleep.

Then said Mr. Greatheart, "Good Gaius, these people have come a long way and they haven't had anything to eat since noon. However, I'm sure they will be satisfied with whatever you have in the house."

GAIUS: Fine! It is late, and I cannot go out and buy at this hour, but we have plenty, and will serve you the best we have.

CHRISTIANA: I am sure that will please us all. We are just common folk and do not require luxuries.

GAIUS: We always give pilgrims the best. You are all welcome here. I am glad I have room for you, and we can keep you as long as you will stay.

Then he went in and asked Tasty, the cook, to prepare supper for eight people. He then invited the guests into the parlor for a get-acquainted chat. "Mr. Greatheart," he said, "give me an introduction to these folk. I know only you and Mr. Honesty."

GREATHEART: This good woman to my left is Christiana, the wife of Christian, the well-known pilgrim of former times. This young lady with her is Miss Mercy, her friend and companion. And these young fellows are Christian's four sons. They are all from the City of Destruction.

GAIUS (*addressing Christiana*): And are you Christian's wife? I knew your husband, and your husband's father, and his father's father. Many staunch Christian characters have come from that family; their ancestors originated at Antioch. I suppose you have heard your husband speak of them. They were very worthy people. Many of them gave their lives for the cause of Christ. Stephen, one of the oldest of the family, was stoned to death for his faith. James, a distant relative in the same generation, was slain with a sword.

There was also Ignatius, who was fed to the lions; Romanus, whose flesh was cut from his bones while he was still alive; and Polycarp, who died heroically in the flames. It would be utterly impossible to name all of that family who suffered injuries and death for their loyalty to Christ. And I am glad to see that your husband has left behind four fine sons to perpetuate his faith and good name in the world.

GREATHEART: So am I, brother Gaius. And these boys are promising young men. They will preserve their father's worthy name and promote his Christian ideals while they live.

GAIUS: That is what I like to see. Consequently, Christian's name and family are apt to continue, and his principles to live.

After supper, the women and young people went to bed, but the men sat and talked till break of day.

Fighting with a Bandit

After breakfast, Mr. Gaius said, "Now, since you are all here, and Mr. Greatheart is an expert with his weapons, if you like, we will walk into the fields to see if we can do any good."

Mr. HONESTY: What do you have in mind, Mr. Gaius?

GAIUS: About a mile from here there is a cave where a notorious robber makes his home. He goes by the name of Patrol, but his real name is Slaygood. He continually torments pilgrims on the King's highway. He is a master of a band of thieves. I know about where his haunt is. It would be a good deed if we could rid this country of him. If you would like a little adventure, go with me and we will search out his hiding place.

They all consented and went, including the four boys. Mr. Greatheart had his sword, helmet, and shield, and the others had spears and clubs. Pressing through thick undergrowth at the far side of the field, they came to the mouth of a cave. Inside was a man Mr. Greatheart recognized, a Mr. Weak, a pilgrim he had seen on the highway. He was being held by the robber Slaygood, who was searching him for money and valuables.

As soon as the robber saw Mr. Greatheart and his band of men, he demanded, "Who are you, and what do you want here?"

Mr. GREATHEART: We want you. Turn that man loose, and come out of your den.

He came out armed with an iron pipe, with which he attacked Mr. Greatheart. Mr. Greatheart fought him off for more than an hour; then they stopped for a moment.

SLAYGOOD: Why are you here on my ground?

GREATHEART: To avenge the blood of the pilgrims you have slain, and repay you for the suffering you have brought on others.

They went at it again with renewed vigor. Slaygood lunged

at Greatheart with such strength as to force him back from the cave. Then, grinning like an imp, he struck at Greatheart's head with his iron pipe. Greatheart caught the pipe in his strong left hand, and with his sword slashed Slaygood's neck. The blood gushed out and he fell, mortally wounded, and they left him in his cave to die.

Freeing of Mr. Weak

They brought Mr. Weak with them to the Gaius Lodge, and asked him how he happened to fall into the robber's hands.

WEAK: You see, I'm not strong. One time in my life, death knocked at my door every day. I thought I would never be well again until I obeyed the voice of the Lord and followed the pilgrims' way. So I left home to obey the call of God and regain my health, that I might be strong enough to render good service to the King and humanity. And I have traveled this far from the town of Uncertainty, where Father and I were born. Different ones helped me at different times along the way. One of the King's servants carried me up Difficult Hill. Indeed, I have received much relief from pilgrims. But no one was willing to go as slowly as I have to travel, though all bade me Godspeed, and gave me encouragement. But when I came to Assault Lane, this robber came out and forced me to walk before him to his cave. I could not run or resist, so I did what he said. I committed myself to my Keeper, trusting that He would not let this bandit kill me; for I knew that He could see that I was not obeying this evil man willingly. Consequently, I believed that I should come out again alive. For I have heard that if any pilgrim, when taken by violent hands, will keep his heart and mind fixed on the Lord, he will not die, nor suffer more than he is able to bear, at the hands of the enemy. I expected to be robbed, and robbed I am. But I did not have much to lose, and I thank God and you His servants for preserving my life.

Other reverses I expect to have; but I am resolved to keep in the good way, to run when I can, to walk when I cannot run, and creep when I cannot walk; yet to keep my face toward Zion. My journey may be long and toilsome, and my mind and body weak; yet my heart is set on that fair City at the end of the way, beyond the river that has no bridge.

GAIUS: Be of good cheer, my brother, for you are welcome at my house. Make yourself at home.

WEAK: This is an unexpected and undeserved favor. It is like the sun shining out of a dark cloud. I am sure that robber Slaygood did not intend this for me, when he stopped me, took me to his hiding place, and rifled my pockets.

GREATHEART: Nor did he intend to lose his life.

Just then, one came running to the door, and shouted: "One Mr. Notright, a pilgrim, was suddenly struck dead by a bolt of lightning about two miles up the road."

"Alas!" exclaimed Weak. "Is he dead? He overtook me today and was with me when the robber took me. But he could run, and he escaped. Now it seems that he escaped to die, and I was taken prisoner to live."

Marriage of Matthew and Mercy

About this time Matthew and Mercy were married; also Gaius gave his daughter Phebe in marriage to James, Matthew's brother.

After this, the pilgrims stayed on with Gaius about ten days longer. When they were ready to leave, Gaius gave them a feast, but never did present a bill. When Mr. Greatheart asked him what the charges were for their stay at his place, Gaius told him that it was not his custom to charge pilgrims for their lodgings, regardless of how long they stayed. "I am happy to have them any time. I board them free for months at a time, and look for my pay to the Good Samaritan, who promised, 'When I come again, I will repay thee.' "[1]

This recalled to Mr. Greatheart's mind this Scripture: "Beloved, it is a fine, faithful work that you are doing when you give service to the Christian brethren, especially when they are strangers to you. Many have testified of your love before the church. And you will do well to forward them on their journey in a way that befits God's service."[2]

When they were leaving Gaius' place, Mr. Weak lingered at the door as if he were hesitating to go.

GREATHEART: Come along with us, brother Weak. I will be your guide and protector, and you will fare as well as the rest.

WEAK: I am sure that is true, but will I not slow you up, and be a killjoy to the party? You are all gay and vigorous. I am weak and have but little joy. Would it not be better that I come along behind you? And that you keep your pace and rejoice in the Lord, since you have His joy in your heart? Then I will not be offended either at your speed or your gaiety. You have no idea how self-conscious and sensitive a weak person can be.

GREATHEART: But, brother, we have been taught to comfort the fainthearted, support the weak, and be patient toward all men.[3] We will wait for you when you are weary, and lend you a helping hand. We will deny ourselves of that which might be lawful for us—whether it be opinion, attitude, conduct, or speech—for your sake.[4]

Mr. Halting Joins Pilgrims

During their conversation, a lame man named Mr. Halting came along, with his crutches in his hands.

"Hey there, Mr. Halting!" piped Mr. Weak, in his tenor

[1]Luke 10:35.
[2]III John 5-6.
[3]I Thess. 5:14.
[4]Rom. 14:1; I Cor. 8:9-13; 9:22.

voice. "How do you happen to be here? I was just complaining that I had no corresponding companion—one handicapped like myself. But you are just the fellow for me. Welcome, Mr. Halting. I hope you and I may be of some help to each other."

HALTING: I shall be glad for your company. If I can be of any help to you, brother Weak, I am at your service. You may have one of my crutches, if you wish.

WEAK: No, no! Though I thank you for your kindness. I am not lame, just lacking in strength. However, your crutch might come in handy as a defense against a dog.

Now this is the way they traveled: Mr. Greatheart and Mr. Honesty went before; Christiana and her four sons and Mercy and Phebe came next; and Mr. Weak and Mr. Halting came on behind.

Arriving at Mnason's Home in Vanity

Night overtook them just as they were entering the town of Vanity. They were wondering where they would stay overnight. At last Mr. Greatheart said, "As you know, I have often conducted pilgrims through this town, and I am acquainted with a few people here. I have a friend, an old saint by the name of Mnason. His house is not far from our route. If you like, we will turn in there." They were all glad to hear this, and readily agreed. It was now dark, but Greatheart knew the way to Mnason's house.

When they arrived at his gate, Mr. Greatheart hollered, "Hello."

The old man inside recognized his voice, and came to the door. "Come in," he shouted. "How are you, brother Greatheart? I am glad to see you."

Inside, Mr. Greatheart introduced each member of his group, and they all sat down. "How far have you come today?" asked Mnason.

"From the house of Gaius," answered Greatheart.

"That is quite a day's journey," said the old man. "I know you are tired. We will fix you places to sleep, and serve you refreshments. Ask for whatever you want, and we will get it for you, if we can."

HONESTY: Our great want awhile ago was a comfortable house and good company. Now we have both, I hope.

MNASON: Well, as for the house, you see what it is, but as for the company, that will appear in the trial.

Then he showed them their respective bedrooms, and a large dining room where they enjoyed refreshments. As they sat at the table, Mr. Honesty asked if there were any disciples in the town.

MNASON: Yes, we have a few—well, a good many altogether, but very few when compared with all the unbelievers.

HONESTY: Could we see some of them tonight? For to pilgrims the meeting with believers is like the appearing of the moon and stars on a stormy night to mariners.

Inviting Neighbors to Visit with Pilgrims

Then the old gentleman called his daughter Grace. "Grace," he said, "go and tell my friends, Mr. Contrite, Mr. Holy, Mr. Lovesaint, Mr. Truthful, and Mr. Penitent that I have at my house this evening some friends who have come from a distance and would like to see them." Grace went, and after a while they all came.

"My neighbors," said Mr. Mnason, "these are pilgrims from another part of the country, who are on their way to Mount Zion. You know Mr. Greatheart here, I am sure; he has been here before. He is the guide of the party, and they are stopping with me because I am Mr. Greatheart's friend. They wanted to meet you and have a little Christian fellowship on the way. This tall, gray-haired gentleman is Mr. Honesty, who has been a pilgrim a good many years. And who do you think this is?" pointing to Christiana. "This is the wife of Christian, that famous pilgrim who with Faithful, his companion, was so cruelly treated in this town."

They were delighted. One said, "Well, I never once thought of seeing Christiana tonight, when Grace came and called us. This is a pleasant surprise."

When they were all seated, Mr. Honesty asked Mr. Contrite about the moral and spiritual condition of the town.

CONTRITE: Well, it is better than it was, yet it is not the best place in the world. Here, everybody is in such a rush to make money or to enjoy some pleasure it is difficult even for Christians to keep their hearts and minds in the best of order. Here, one must be very prayerful and exceedingly cautious, or one will be led or pushed out of the straight and narrow way, and give the Enemy the advantage in the battle for men's minds.

HONESTY: But what is the spirit and attitude of your neighbors?

CONTRITE: They are much quieter, and more moderate and considerate than formerly. You know how violent and cruel they were to Christian and Faithful. They have become much more civil. I think they feel that the blood of Faithful is upon their hands. They have not burned or executed any more Christians since they killed him. Before that happened, there were times when we were afraid to walk the streets. Now, we feel fairly safe anywhere in town. Then the name "Christian" was obnoxious to the masses. Now, in some parts of the city, to be a Christian is counted honorable.

Then Mr. Contrite asked: "How is it with you pilgrims? What is the attitude of the country toward you?"

HONESTY: It happens to us as to all transient humanity. Sometimes we are up and sometimes we are down; we are on the mountaintop, then in the valley. Sometimes our way is joyous and easy—filled with sunshine and gladness—then we go through clouds and darkness, and the way is difficult and long. We seldom fare the same for any length of time. The wind is not always in our favor; though we do sometimes ride the tide. We have our battles and our victories. We meet with friends and foes. We have our trials and triumphs, our troubles and tribulations; yet we can truthfully say that the grace of God is sufficient for every type of person in all situations of life if one will only believe.

MR. HOLY: From my experience and observation, there are two things a pilgrim must have—courage and an unspotted life. If a person does not have courage he will not persevere in his calling, and if he is loose in his living, he will wander from the pilgrim way.

GREATHEART: Yes, and if one is not guided by the Word and the Spirit, one will have neither courage nor purity.

LOVESAINT: I hope this criticism is not needed. But many who enter the Christian life show themselves strangers to a true pilgrimage rather than strangers and pilgrims in the earth.[5]

TRUTHFUL: Yes, and many, instead of being clothed with the spotless righteousness of Christ, are clothed with their own righteousness, which, in the sight of God, is filthy rags.[6] In their great ignorance, they parade their self-righteousness before the world as proof of their superiority while they walk by their own man-made rules.

They sat talking until a late hour; then they told each other good-night and went to their respective places of rest. Next day they had another meeting and a feast at the home of Mr. Lovesaint. Thus the pilgrims became acquainted with many Christians in the City of Vanity. They stayed in the City several months, making Mnason's home their headquarters.

[5]Heb. 11:13.
[6]Isa. 64:6.

A Double Wedding

During their stay at Mnason's house, Samuel and Joseph found suitable companionship with Mnason's daughters, Grace and Martha, to whom they became engaged; Samuel to Grace, and Joseph to Martha.

Before leaving the town, these young people were married at Mnason's home. The wedding was attended by all the friends the pilgrims had met in the city. Christiana wept tears of joy and sorrow. She was glad that now all her sons had found suitable partners for life.

When the time came for the pilgrims to be on their way, they sent for their friends. After many kind words of appreciation and devotion, they all committed each other to the care of the Good Shepherd. The friends gave the pilgrims such things as they would need for their journey, and went with them to the outer edge of the City, where they all shook hands and said good-bye.

CHAPTER
18
christiana at the delectable mountains

Enjoyments on the Way

I SAW NOW that the pilgrims had come to that beautiful green valley and the crystal river, where Christian and Hopeful enjoyed themselves many days. The river was clear, the meadows were green, and the leaves of the trees along the banks of the river were good medicine. Here wayworn pilgrims could lie down and sleep in perfect safety.

And in the meadows were sheepcotes and folds, and cottages built for those women who go on pilgrimage with small children; also there was a strong custodian with tender compassion who cared for all.[1]

When Christiana saw this, she admonished her four sons' wives to commit their children (when God would be pleased to give them children) to the care of this custodian: "This man, if any of them would go astray or be lost, will bring them safely back again. This man will die before one of those committed to his care be lost."

In this agreeable climate Mr. Weak and Mr. Halting gained much needed strength and old Mr. Honesty's vitality improved.

[1]Isa. 40:11.

In fact, they all improved, not only physically but also mentally and spiritually.

But they could not tarry in the Green Valley, so they all kept journeying toward the Delectable Mountains.

Fighting with Giant Despair

On the way they came to the stile that led into Bypath Meadow, the premises of Giant Despair, and they sat down to consider what they should do. Some suggested that they go and demolish Doubting Castle and kill Giant Despair. Others said, "No, we have no right to go out of the King's highway onto another's property. While there might be pilgrims now suffering in Doubting Castle, there is nothing we can do about it." One said, "We can tear down this stile, and erect a sign, warning pilgrims of Bypath Meadow and Giant Despair."

MR. GREATHEART: All this property rightly belongs to the King. This castle and meadow were one time owned by a servant of the King, who entertained pilgrims and strangers on the highway of life. Giant Despair then lived in a cave in the woods. He terrorized the good man of the castle until he moved away, then the giant came and took possession of the man's property. For many years now he has imprisoned and killed pilgrims; and if we have the faith and the courage, there is something we can do about it. I have a commission to resist sin, to fight the good fight of faith, to overcome evil; and with whom should I fight this good fight, if not with Giant Despair? I think we should put an end to his destructive business. Who will go with me?

"I will," said old Honesty. "And so will we," said Matthew, speaking for the four sons of Christiana. These were all young men and strong.

So they left Mr. Weak and Mr. Halting with the women, and went over the stile to Doubting Castle. Mr. Greatheart hammered on the gate with a rock.

The old giant came out to the gate, followed by Gloom, his wife. "Who's there?" he growled. "Who has the audacity to disturb Giant Despair in this manner? What do you want?"

Mr. Greatheart replied, "It is I, Greatheart, a servant of the King. I am one of the King's conductors of pilgrims to the Celestial City. I have with me faithful soldiers of the cross. We want you. Open up! You must give an account."

Giant Despair was not afraid of anybody or anything. He thought within himself, "I have made conquest of angels and conquered the greatest of men, and shall this so-called Greatheart and his handful of weaklings defy me in this way? I will show them their great mistake." So he put on his helmet of steel, iron shoes, and a breastplate of brass, and came out with his huge club, which he called Terror. "Now, what will you migrants have?" he roared.

"Your head," said Greatheart, as he struck at him with his sword. The giant knocked the sword from his hand with his club, but one of the men picked it up and handed it back to Mr. Greatheart. Gloom, the giant's wife, rushed up with a piece of iron pipe to strike Greatheart. But old Mr. Honesty brought her down with one blow. By this time, the men were pelting the giant with stones on all sides. He fought hard and long, swinging his club in every direction. After he was brought down to the ground, Mr. Greatheart used his sword to slash off the giant's head.

Liberation of Despondency and Fearful

Then they went into the castle to see what they could find. They found one Mr. Despondency and his daughter Fearful almost starved to death, standing among dead bodies and human bones. The large backyard was almost covered with graves and skeletons of former pilgrims.

They brought back the scalp of the giant to assure their

friends, waiting at the road, that old Giant Despair was dead. The whole party celebrated the victory with music and dancing, while Despondency and Fearful refreshed themselves with wine and wholesome food which the women brought from the dinner table in Green Valley.

Welcome to the Delectable Mountains

After rejoicing over this victory, the party went forward into the Delectable Mountains. When the shepherds saw the large company of people following Mr. Greatheart (they knew him well), they said, "Mr. Greatheart, you have a lot of pilgrims. Where did you find all these people?"

GREATHEART: Some of them came by my house, others have joined us on the way.

SHEPHERD: They are all welcome with us, for we have ample accommodations for all, the feeble as well as the strong. Our Prince is concerned about that which is done for the least of His followers;[2] therefore, infirmity must not be a hindrance to our hospitality.

So the shepherds led them to the palace door, and said, "Come in, all of you. Let the weak and infirm come first."

Then said Mr. Greatheart: "I see that you are my Lord's true shepherds; for you have not pushed these handicapped aside but have showed them special favors, as you should; and grace shines in your faces."

When they were all seated at a long dining table, the matron said, "We will fix special dishes for those whose physical condition requires a particular diet. Tell us your need, and we will supply it if we can." So they made them a feast of good things easy to digest.

After dinner they all went to their respective resting-places and went to sleep. Despondency dreamed that he saw a humble

[2]Matt. 25:40.

man so full of faith and the goodness of God that he was ordering mountains to move out of his way, and they were tumbling before him as if they were made of straw. Mr. Greatheart told him next day that these were mountains of difficulty that would vanish before him when he exercised sufficient faith and remained steadfast in the will of God.

Sightseeing

Next day, the shepherds took the whole company to places of special interest. First they went to Mount Innocent, where they saw two men in dark shabby clothing throwing dirt on a nice-looking gentleman clothed in pure white. The names of the two men were Envy and Illwill. They despised the cleanliness of their fellowman and threw dirt on him continually, but all of the dirt slipped off, leaving the man perfectly white.

"This," said Knowledge, one of the shepherds, "is Mr. Godly. He is innocent of all the accusations hurled against him. His accusers hate him because his good example shows them up in a bad light. Yet he does not reply, or attempt to brush off the dirt; it falls off of its own weight. And the mudslingers are made worse in the eyes of their fellowmen, while the good man has more friends than before."

Then they went to Mount Charity where they saw a tailor cutting out garments from a roll of cloth which did not grow any smaller. He was making clothing for the poor who stood about him.

"What does this mean?" asked Mercy.

"This," said the shepherd, "is to show that he who gives to the poor lends to the Lord and shall never come to want. You see the cloth is not diminishing regardless of how much he cuts from it. The widow, with but little meal in the barrel, who made a cake for the prophet first, had as much meal after the cake was made as before; and there was no diminishing of the supply though she, her son, and the prophet ate from it many days."[3]

At their next stop, they saw two well-dressed white men washing an Ethiopian to make him white; but the more they washed the blacker he shone. They asked the shepherd what that meant.

"These men," said he, "are overzealous clergymen, washing a sinner to make him fit for their church. But it is the same with any vile person as with this Ethiopian: all means used to give him a good name, or to make him clean, tend only to make him more abominable. So it was with the Pharisees, and so shall it be with all hypocrites. If the Ethiopian would be white, he must be born again. However, he may be whiter inside than the men who are washing him. We cannot judge as to that, because we cannot see the inside of a person. 'Man looketh on the outward appearance, but God looketh on the heart.' "[4]

Now Mercy wanted to see the hole in the hill that Christian had seen, commonly called the Byway to Hell. Then they went to the door in the side of the hill and opened it. They heard voices, and one saying, "Cursed be my father for holding me back from the way of life and peace," and another: "Oh, that I had been torn to pieces before; to save my life, I lost my soul." And another said, "If I could only live my life again; how I would deny myself, rather than come to this place!"

Then it seemed that the very ground under them groaned and quivered. Pale-faced, Mercy turned away, saying, "Blessed are they who are delivered from this place."

Now they went back to the palace where they were entertained with music and refreshments. Then they all went to bed.

It was a beautiful, bright morning when they left the shepherds and the Delectable Mountains.

[3]I Kings 17:12-16.
[4]I Sam. 16:7.

Meeting with Mr. Valiant-for-Truth

Soon the pilgrims came to the place where Little-Faith was robbed. There stood a man with his sword drawn and his face all bloody, who said to them, "I am a pilgrim. My name is Valiant-for-Truth. I was ambushed here by three men, who came out of the bushes there with long knives. One of them said, 'Halt! We have a question to ask you.' I said, 'Well, what is it?' He said, 'Will you go with us, or turn and go back where you came from, or die on the spot?'

"I answered: 'I have been a follower of Jesus Christ for many years, and I cannot now turn back. Where I came from is not where the Lord wants me to be. And you should know that one who has been a follower of Christ for many years would never join a band of thieves. As for the dying on the spot, that remains to be seen. If you undertake to make me choose one of your courses, you do it at your peril. I have considerable strength. I love my life and the pilgrim way, and I will not give them up easily. The Lord put me in this way, and I intend to stay in it to the end.'

"Then, these three—Wildhead, Inconsiderate, and Pragmatic—came upon me with their knives. I drew my sword and fought them all. We fought for more than three hours, and they have left some of their marks of valor upon me, as you see, and they also carried away some of mine. After they saw they could not take my life immediately, they broke and ran. They must have heard you coming, for they ran just before I saw you."

GREATHEART: But you fought great odds—three against one.

VALIANT: Yes, but what does a person care when he knows he has the truth on his side? As one has said, "Though an host should encamp against me, my heart shall not fear."[5] I have

[5]Ps. 27:3.

read in some record that one man has fought an army, and that one Samson slew a thousand men with the jawbone of an ass.[6]

GREATHEART: Why did you not cry out for help?

VALIANT: So I did to my King, who I knew could hear me, and He provided invisible help which was sufficient.

GREATHEART: You have certainly behaved very worthily. What kind of sword do you have?

VALIANT: It is the two-edged sword that cuts both ways.[7] A soldier need not fear if he has this and knows how to use it. Its edge will never blunt, and it will cut flesh and bones, and soul and spirit.

GREATHEART: But you fought a long time; it is a wonder you did not grow weary.

VALIANT: I did, but I waited on the Lord and He renewed my strength, and I fought until the blood dripped from my face and my fingers. I fought with all my strength and courage.

GREATHEART: You certainly did well. You have resisted unto blood, striving against sin.[8] You shall abide with us, and be one of us. We will be your true companions.

Then they took him, washed his wounds, and gave him something to eat; and they all went on together. Mr. Greatheart liked Valiant-for-Truth very much and began to ask him about his past and his hope for the future. He found him true in every respect.

[6]Judges 15:15.
[7]Heb. 4:12.
[8]Heb. 12:4.

CHAPTER
19
on the enchanted ground

Description

BY THIS TIME they were on the enchanted ground, where the air tends to make one drowsy. In places the road was overgrown with briers and thorns, and here and there was an alluring arbor in which if a person sat down he would go to sleep; and once asleep, according to some, he would never wake again in this world. Through this part of the forest they went single file. Mr. Greatheart led the way, and Mr. Valiant-for-Truth brought up the rear. Mr. Weak walked next to Mr. Greatheart, and Mr. Despondency went just in front of Mr. Valiant-for-Truth. Every man walked with his sword drawn.

They had not gone far into the enchanted ground when a mist and darkness enveloped them, so that they could not see one another. For some time they were able to keep in touch with each other only by voice. The frail men and the women had the most difficulty. Yet, encouraging words from their guide kept them plodding on in the way.

The way was also wearisome because of the softness of the earth. And there was not, in all that region, so much as one eating-place. After hours of trudging in the darkness through bushes and weeds, grunting, puffing, and sighing could be heard in the ranks. As one tumbled over a bush, another stuck fast in the mud, and some lost their shoes. One cried out, "I am down!" Another, "Hey! Where are you?" A third plaintive voice said, "I am caught on a bush and I cannot get loose."

Then they came to a beautiful green arbor, furnished with benches and a soft cot. Though this was an invitation to stop and rest, they walked faster, tired though they were, and not one of them even so much as suggested that they stop and rest for a moment. They had been faithfully warned of such places, and this inviting arbor had no effect on these Heaven-bound pilgrims. They would not yield to temptations.

I saw in my dream that they went on in this treacherous region until they came to a place where there were many bypaths and ways leading off from the road, making it very difficult for one to know which way to go, especially in mist and darkness. And if one misses the road in this country, one is apt to be lost in the jungle and never find his way out.

But Mr. Greatheart carried in his pocket at all times a map, showing the right road, the road leading to the Celestial City, and all the roads leading away from it. He also could strike a light whenever needed, which enabled him to read his map in deepest darkness. Yet, if he had not been very careful, they would have taken the wrong road, and might have been swallowed up in deep mud. For, just before them, at the end of the clearest, smoothest path, was a pit—no one knew how deep—filled with very soft mud.

Seeing the Two Sleepers

They came to another arbor by the roadside where two men, Heedless and Self-Confidence, lay fast asleep. These two men, being weary with their journey, had sat down in this comfortable arbor to rest for a moment, and went to sleep. The pilgrims stopped and discussed what they should do—whether to try to wake them, or to go on and leave them in their plight. They decided to try to wake them and to make sure that they themselves did not sit down or even wish that they might be permitted to accept the momentary comforts of the arbor.

They went and spoke to the men, but there was no response. Then the guide shook them and called loudly to them to wake up. One of them groaned and said, "I will pay you when I get my money." The other said, "I will fight as long as I can hold my sword in my hand." At that the young people laughed.

"What is the meaning of this?" asked Christiana.

GREATHEART: They talk in their sleep. If you call them, strike them, beat them, or whatever you do to them, they answer you in this way. Like the drunkard in Proverbs who mumbled, "They have beaten me, and I felt it not: when shall I awake? I will seek it yet again."[1] You know, when men talk in their sleep, there is incoherency in their speech. They say anything. Their words are not governed either by faith or reason. These two men must have been "double minded," as James says,[2] or they never would have considered sitting down here. This is the way heedless ones usually turn out when they go on pilgrimage. This enchanted ground is one of the last places the enemy of pilgrims has. As you see it is placed almost at the end of the way, and this gives the enemy more advantage, because pilgrims are naturally more weary near the end of their journey. Therefore, the enchanted ground is placed near the land of Beulah, and near the end of the race. So let all pilgrims take heed lest it happen to them as it has happened to these, who, as you see, have fallen asleep and no one can wake them.

Then the pilgrims wished for a light on the way. So Mr. Greatheart lit his lantern, and they went the rest of the way through the enchanted forest following the light, though the darkness was very dense.

[1]Prov. 23:29-35.
[2]James 1:8.

Now the travelers were exceedingly weary, and they cried to Him who cares for pilgrims to make their going more comfortable. Soon a wind arose that drove the fog away. Now they could see each other better and more easily keep in the road.

Coming Upon Mr. Standfast

When they were almost to the edge of the enchanted ground, they heard a solemn voice up ahead, as of one who was much concerned. A little farther on, they saw a man upon his knees, with his hands lifted towards Heaven, pleading earnestly with the One above. They drew near, but could not understand what he was saying. They walked softly to keep from disturbing him until he was through. When he concluded his prayer, he got up and started to run towards the Celestial City.

Mr. Greatheart called after him, "Wait, my friend, let us have your company, if you are going to the great City."

The man stopped, and they came up to him. As soon as Mr. Honesty saw him, he said, "I know this man. He comes from my part of the country."

"Then tell us who he is," said Valiant.

"This is Mr. Standfast, an old friend of mine, and a true pilgrim."

Then Standfast said, "Why, hello there, Father Honesty. Are you here?"

"Yes," said he, "I am here as surely as you are there."

"Well, I am certainly glad that I have found you on this road," said Standfast.

"And I am indeed glad to see you, and that I found you on your knees."

"What? Did you see me on my knees?"

"Yes, I did," he answered, "and it made my heart glad."

"But, what did you think?" asked Standfast.

"Think? What should I think? I thought, here is an honest,

sincere Christian on his way to glory, and we should have him in our company."

"Well, if you thought right, how blessed I am," said Standfast. "But if I am not what I should be I alone must answer for that."

"That is true," said Honesty, "but your fearing for yourself confirms my belief that you are right within, and the Prince of pilgrims is pleased with your spirit; for He says, 'Happy is the man who feareth always.' "[3]

VALIANT: Well, brother, tell us what caused you to be upon your knees? Were you praying for deliverance, or for some special blessing?

STANDFAST: Let me tell you what happened to me. As you know, this is the enchanted ground. Well, as I was coming along, I thought of what a dangerous place this is, that many have come even this far on pilgrimage, yet have been stopped and ultimately destroyed. I thought also of how persons die here. They do not die of wounds or any violent disease; the death to which they succumb is not painful. They go away in sleep. They begin that last, lonely journey with pleasure and desire.

"Did you see the two men asleep in the arbor?" interrupted Mr. Honesty.

Mr. Standfast's Deliverance

STANDFAST: Yes, it's too bad. They were too bold, or had too much self-confidence. I did not try to wake them, because I knew it was no use. Their sleep is spiritual and final. But let me go on with my story. As I was walking along, thinking of this mysterious sleep and how easily men are overcome by it, there appeared one in very attractive dress who came and spoke to me and offered me three things: her body, her purse, and her

[3]Prov. 28:14.

bed. Now the truth is I was both tired and sleepy, and I am also as poor as a church mouse. But I repulsed her. She smiled and paid no attention to my rebuffs. Then I began to be angry. But that mattered not at all with her. She said that if I would yield to her, she would make me both rich and happy, and that I would become very famous. "For," said she, "I am the mistress of the world, and men are made famous and happy by me." I asked her what her name was, and she told me that it was Madam Bubble. This caused me to leave her. Still she followed me with very strong enticements. Then I went to my knees, and prayed to the Judge of all the earth to rid me of her presence and her ungodly enticements. Then this woman went her way. She must have heard you approaching. And when you heard me I was thanking God for my great deliverance.

HONESTY: Without doubt her designs were evil. She intended to ruin either your pilgrimage or your life. But wait a minute! Since you have spoken of her traits, it seems to me that I have seen her, or have read some story of her. Madam Bubble! Is she a tall, attractive woman, with a somewhat swarthy complexion?

STANDFAST: Yes. Well, it was growing dark when she came up, but that's the way she appeared to me.

HONESTY: Does she have a mellow voice and does she smile triumphantly at the end of every sentence?

STANDFAST: You are right. That describes her exactly.

HONESTY: Does she not carry a large purse at her side, and are not her hands often in it, fingering her money?

STANDFAST: Right you are. If she were standing before you right now, you could not have given a better description of her.

HONESTY: Then he who drew her picture was a good artist.

GREATHEART: This woman is a servant of Satan. It is by virtue of her witchcraft that this region is enchanted. Whoever lays his head in her lap or upon her shoulder lays it on the block over which the fatal ax hangs; and whoever admires her beauty or her ways is accounted the enemy of God. She it is who maintains and supports the enemies of pilgrims in splendor.

Yes, she is the one who has bought off many a person from a pilgrim's life. She is an exceedingly shrewd, hypnotic person. She and her daughters are always at the heels of some influential pilgrim, commending or preferring the excellences of this present world. She is a bold and brazen mistress, laughing poor Christians to shame while highly complimenting the rich. If she knows of one who is cunning to make money, she speaks well of him from house to house. She loves banqueting and feasting. She has put out the word in many places that she is a goddess, and a lot of people worship her. She has her places of graft and open gambling, and she boasts that no other person can match her profits and gains. She promises to enrich children's children if they will but love and serve her. She is very liberal with her money when she sees that there is a chance to gain by her liberality. She loves to be sought after, spoken well of, and to lie in the bosom of men. She never tires of lauding her goods. She promises crowns and empires to those who will follow her advice. She has brought many under her control, and ten thousand more to Hell.

"Oh," said Mr. Standfast, "what a blessing that I resisted her and was delivered from her power! For where would she have led me?"

GREATHEART: Where indeed? None but God knows. But we know that those who follow her counsel "fall into temptation, and a snare, and into many foolish and hurtful lusts, which drown men in destruction and perdition."[4] It was she who set Absalom against his father, and Jeroboam against his king. It was she who led Judas to sell his Lord, and who persuaded Demas to forsake a godly life. And she prevails on millions to

[4] I Tim. 6:9.

reject the only Saviour. She brings division between ruler and subjects, between parents and children, between neighbors, and husbands and wives, between a person and his better self—between the flesh and the spirit. Therefore, my dear Mr. Standfast, you have done well. Live up to your name, and when you have done all you can against evil, then stand, and watch your enemies go. The victory is yours.

Pilgrims Go On Their Way Singing

Then the pilgrims were happy—yet cautious. But at length, they all joined in and sang:

By peril the pilgrim is often surrounded,
  His enemies want him to fall.
By strongest temptations and sins he is hounded,
  He surely can't conquer them all!

But God will deliver the man who in earnest
  Beseeches His help from his knees.
He'll turn back the tempter, encourage the pilgrim,
  And answer his desperate pleas.

CHAPTER
20
beulah land

Beulah's Joys

NOW THE HEAVENLY TRAVELERS were in the land of Beulah, where the sun shines all the time. Here they took time to rest, and they helped themselves to whatever they wanted. The orchards, vineyards, and all the bounties belonged to the King of the Country to which they were going; so they felt free to make use of anything they saw and needed. Soon they were refreshed in this wonderful climate and needed no more rest or recreation.

Bells were ringing, and melodious trumpets were sounding from morning till evening; and these happy travelers could no longer sleep. Yet they never grew drowsy or felt the least bit weary. They were full of energy and abundant life.

The talk of those who walked the streets was: "More pilgrims have come to town." "And so many went over the river today and were let in at the golden gate." Then a loud voice would announce: "A legion of shining ones has just arrived, by which we know that there are more pilgrims on the way who will soon be here, for angels come to wait for pilgrims and comfort them after all their sorrows."

Then our pilgrims got up and walked the streets, enjoying

the soothing music. And, oh, how their eyes were delighted with celestial visions, and their ears filled with heavenly melodies! Here everything was pleasing. There was nothing offensive to body, mind, or spirit. Only the water of the river, over which they were to go, was a little bitter to the taste, but proved sweeter after it was down. There was much talk of how high the river seemed for some, when they crossed over, and how low for others. They said that in a manner it had been almost dry for some; but for others, it had overflowed its banks.

They found that there was a list of names of all the noble pilgrims of old times, and a record kept of all their famous deeds.

In this place it was the practice of the children to go into the gardens and gather flowers, and present them to the pilgrims with tender affection. And the gardens produced all kinds of spices and perfumes, to fill their rooms with fragrance and to embalm their bodies when they went over the river.

Christiana's Summons to the Celestial City

Now, while they waited here for the good hour, there was a rumor in town that an important message had come from the Celestial City for one Christiana, the wife of Christian, the pilgrim. So inquiry was made for her, and the house was found where she lived, and the message was presented to her in a letter, which read: "Greetings, good lady. I bring you tidings from the King. The Master calls for you, and He will expect you to stand in His presence, clothed in immortality, within ten days."

When the messenger had read this letter to her, he gave her a token that he was a true messenger, come to bid her make haste and prepare to leave. The token was an arrow, sharpened with love, slipped gently into her heart, which by degrees wrought so effectually that at the appointed time she was ready to go.

When Christiana saw that her time had come, and that she was the first of her company to go over the river, she called for Mr. Greatheart, her guide, and gave him the news. He said that he was glad to hear of it, and could have been just as glad if the summons had been for him. Then she asked him for advice on how to prepare for her journey. He gave complete instruction on everything pertaining to her departure, and said, "We who survive will accompany you to the riverside."

Christiana's Farewell

Then she called for her children, and gave them her blessing. She told them that she could still read with comfort the mark that was placed in their foreheads, and that she was glad to see them still on the way, and to have them with her in her last hour; and she especially rejoiced that they had kept their garments so white. Then she bequeathed to the poor what little she had, and admonished her sons and daughters to be ready when the call came for them.

When she had spoken these words to her children and her guide, she called for Mr. Valiant-for-Truth and said, "Sir, you have at all times shown yourself to be true. Be faithful unto death, and my King will give you a crown of life.[1] Will you please watch over my children? And if at any time you see them weaken, will you speak comfortably to them? For my sons and my daughters—my sons' wives—have been very faithful, and the fulfilling of the promise to them will be their reward."

To Mr. Standfast she gave a ring, with these words: "Be ye stedfast, unmoveable, always abounding in the work of the Lord, forasmuch as ye know that your labour is not in vain in the Lord."[2]

Then she called for Mr. Honesty, and said to those standing

[1]Rev. 2:10.
[2]I Cor. 15:58.

by when he came in, "Behold an Israelite indeed, in whom is no guile."[3]

He said to her, "I wish for you a fair day when you leave for Zion. I could pray that you might cross the river on dry ground."

She replied, "Come sunshine or rain, I want to go on my Lord's appointed day. However the weather is in my journey, I shall have time when I get to the end to sit down and rest, and become perfectly dry."

Then Mr. Halting came in to see her, and she said to him, "Your travel thus far has been difficult, but that will make your rest all the sweeter. Watch and be ready, for at an hour when you think not the messenger may come."

After him came in Mr. Despondency and his daughter Fearful, to whom she said, "You ought with thankfulness to forever remember your deliverance from Doubting Castle and the hands of Giant Despair. Because of that great favor you are here today in Heaven's borderland. Be watchful and dismiss all fear. Be sober and hope to the end."

Then she said to Mr. Weak, "You were delivered from the cruel hands of robber Slaygood that you might see the King in peace and live in the light of Heaven forever. I only advise you to turn, before God sends for you, from your aptness to fear and your readiness to doubt His goodness, lest you be ashamed when you stand before Him."

Christiana's Crossing of the River

Now the day drew on that Christiana must be on her way, and the road was full of people to see her embark on the mysterious river. Now there came a vision of the other shore, and the whole congregation could see that all the banks beyond the river were crowded with horses and chariots, and a great concourse that had come down from above to accompany Christiana to

[3]John 1:47.

the city gate. Then she came forth and entered the river, waving farewell to all who had followed her to the riverside. The last words they heard her say were, "Lord, I come to Thee, to be with Thee and bless Thee for all the grace given to me."

Her children and friends, feeling so lonely now that she was gone, though glad within that she was free from the toils of the road and had gone to be with her King and her husband in a home far better than earth could afford, turned away from the river weeping—yet some were smiling through their tears—to go to their respective places, since those who waited for Christiana on the other side had carried her out of their sight.

Other Pilgrims Summoned

In process of time, there came a message to the town again. This time it was for Mr. Halting. The messenger said to him, "I have come to you from Him whom you have loved and followed all these years, even on crutches, to tell you that He expects you at His table to dine with Him the next day after Easter. So prepare for your journey." Then he gave him a token of the truthfulness of his message: "I have broken the golden bowl, and loosed the silver cord."[4] When the messenger was gone Mr. Halting called for Mr. Valiant-for-Truth to make out his will. Since he had nothing to leave to anyone except his crutches and warm wishes, his will simply read: "These crutches I bequeath to my son who shall follow in my steps, with a hundred warm wishes that he may prove to be a better pilgrim than I have been." He thanked Mr. Greatheart, who had given him so much encouragement and help on the way, for his guidance and all his favors, and began to prepare himself for his departure. When he came to the brink of the river he said, "Now I shall have no more need for these crutches, since yonder are horses and chariots on the other side, waiting to take me

[4]Eccles. 12:6.

Christiana crosses the river to the Celestial City.

to the Celestial City, and there I shall have a perfect body." His last words were, "Welcome, life!" So he went away.

After him, Mr. Weak had tidings. The postman sounded his horn at his door. When Mr. Weak invited him in, he said, "I have come to tell you that your Master has asked for you, and in a very short time you must see Him in glory. And take this as a token of the truth of my message: 'Those that look out at the windows [shall] be darkened.' "[5] Then Mr. Weak called his friends and told them. And he said, "Since I have nothing to leave to anyone, there is no purpose in making a will. As for my feeble body and mind, I will certainly leave them behind, for I shall have no use for them in the place where I am going. But they are not worth bestowing upon the poorest pilgrim. So I will ask Mr. Valiant to bury my frail physical frame in an obscure spot down by the river bank, where no one will ever wish to go. But remember, I am not there. For I know that when my earthly house of this tabernacle is dissolved, I have a building of God, a house not made with hands, eternal in the heavens."[6] When his time arrived, he entered the river alone without trembling. His last words were, "Hold out, good faith and patience." And he went over to the other side.

After many days, Mr. Despondency was sent for. A postman brought him this message: "Kind trembling one, this is to summon you to appear before your King by next Lord's day. So you may shout for joy because deliverance from all your worries and cares has come. And that my message is true, take these words as proof: 'The grasshopper shall be a burden, and desire shall fail.' "[7]

When Mr. Despondency's daughter Fearful came in and heard the message, she knew that her time had come also, because she knew that she could not survive the death of her

[5]Eccles. 12:3.
[6]II Cor. 5:1
[7]Eccles. 12:5.

father. So she said that she would go with him. Then Mr. Despondency said to his friends, "You know how troublesome my daughter and I have been. My will and my daughter's is that our despondency and slavish fears be not received by anyone, from the day of our departure forever; for I know that after my death they will offer themselves to others. For to tell you the truth, they are ghosts which we entertained when we first became pilgrims, and we could never afterwards shake them off. I am sure they will walk about seeking lodgment with other pilgrims. But to all who read or hear this message, we say, 'Shut the door against them and never let them in!' " When the time came for them to go, they went to the brink of the river together. The last words of Mr. Despondency were, "Farewell, dreary night! Welcome, precious day!" His daughter went through the river singing, but no one could understand what she said.

It came to pass, after Mr. Despondency and his daughter had gone, that there came a postman to town, who inquired for Mr. Honesty. He found the house where he lived and handed him this note: "You are commanded, after seven days, to present yourself before the Lord in His Father's house. And for a token that this message is true, are these words: 'All the daughters of music shall be brought low.' "[8] Then Mr. Honesty sent for his friends and said to them, "I am going to die, but I shall make no will. As for my honesty, it shall go with me. Let those who come after me be told this." When the day came for him to go, the river overflowed its banks in places. But Mr. Honesty, in his lifetime, had asked one Good Conscience to meet him at the river and help him through the deep waters, which he did. And the last words of Mr. Honesty were, "Grace reigns!" So he left the world.

After this it was rumored that Mr. Valiant-for-Truth was

[8]Eccles. 12:4.

given a summons by the same messenger who came to Mr. Honesty, and this was his token, "The pitcher shall be broken at the fountain."[9] When he understood it, he called for his friends and told them, "I am going to my Father's house over the river. You will see my face no more. I have been on the road a long time, and have come through many difficulties; but now I am not sorry for any troubles I have had nor for my attitude and my resistance to evil. My sword I give to him who will follow in my steps, and my courage and skill to him who earns them. My marks and scars I carry with me for a witness of my suffering in the service of my Lord. And as one who went before me has said, 'I am now ready to be offered, and the time of my departure is at hand. I have fought a good fight, I have finished my course, I have kept the faith: henceforth there is laid up for me a crown of righteousness, which the Lord, the righteous judge, shall give me at that day: and not to me only, but to all them also who love his appearing.' "[10]

When his day came, many accompanied him to the riverside. When he went down into the water, he said, "O death, where is thy sting?" and out in the deep water he cried, "O grave, where is thy victory?" As he was nearing the other side, they heard him say, "Thanks be to God, which giveth us the victory through our Lord Jesus Christ."[11] So he passed over, and all the trumpets sounded for him on the other side.

Finally there came a message for Mr. Standfast (the man found upon his knees in the enchanted ground) which said that he must prepare for a change of life, that his Master was not willing that he should live so far from Him any longer. The message put Mr. Standfast into a deep meditation. "You need not doubt the truth of the message," said the postman, "for here is the token: 'The wheel is broken at the cistern.' "[12]

[9]Eccles. 12:6.
[10]II Tim. 4:6-8.
[11]I Cor. 15:54-57.
[12]Eccles. 12:6.

Then Mr. Standfast sent for Mr. Greatheart and said, "Mr. Greatheart, it was not my good fortune to be in your company very long in the days of my pilgrimage. But you have been very helpful to me since the time I met you, and I want you to know that I appreciate a true, reliable guide. When I came from home I left behind a wife and five small children. Let me entreat you, at your return (for I assume you will return to your Master's house that you may be a conductor to more pilgrims) that you send to my family my very best wishes and tell them what has happened to me in the way, of my safe arrival here, and of the blessed life I have gone to enjoy. Tell them also of Christian and Christiana, his wife, and how she and her children followed in the path of her husband, what a happy ending she had, and where she has gone. I have nothing to give to my family except my love, my prayers, and my tears. Tell them I hope some day they too may experience this salvation."

When Mr. Standfast had thus set things in order, and the time had come for him to depart, he also went down to the river. There was a great calm on the river at that time. So Mr. Standfast went out into the water, stood awhile, and talked to his companions gathered on the shore: "This river," he said, "has been a terror to many. Yes, and the thoughts of it have also frightened me. But now I stand easy. My feet are fixed upon that on which the priests stood, who bore the ark of the covenant when Israel went over Jordan. The waters, indeed, are to the palate bitter, and to the body cold; yet the thought of what I am going to and of the convoy that awaits me on the other side lies like a glowing coal on my heart.

"I see myself now at the end of my journey; my toilsome days are over. I am going to see the head that was crowned with thorns and the face that was spit upon for me. I have been living by hearsay and faith, but now I am going where I shall live by sight, and I shall be with Him in whose company

I delight. I have loved to hear Him spoken of, and wherever I could see His footprints on the sands of time, there I delighted to walk. His name has been to me a precious treasure—sweeter than all perfumes. His voice I rejoice to hear, and His face to me exceeds all beauty in earth and sky. His Word I have used as food for my soul and for an antidote against my faltering. He has kept me back from my iniquities, and He has held me fast. Yes, my steps He has strengthened in His way."

As he finished the last sentence, his countenance changed, his strong frame bowed under him, and he was gone after he said, "Take me, Lord, for I come to Thee." They could see him no more.

The Faithful Welcomed to the Eternal City

But how glorious it was to see the sky beyond the river filled with horses and chariots, trumpeters and pipers, with singers, musicians, and myriads of immortals with waving palms to welcome the faithful home as they filed through the gate of the eternal City.

In the dying music and fading glory of that scene, I awoke from my dream.

Moody Press, a ministry of the Moody Bible Institute, is designed for education, evangelization and edification. If we may assist you in knowing more about Christ and the Christian life, please write us without obligation to:
Moody Press, c/o MLM, Chicago, Illinois 60610.